OF FIRE & BONE

NATALINA REIS

HOT TREE PUBLISHING

M/M Stand-alone Romances

Infinite Blue

Lavender Fields

Sleeping Love

Of Magic & Scales Series

Of Magic and Scales

Of Scales and Fire

Of Fire and Bone

Of Magic & Bells

M/F Stand-alone Romances

Loved You Always

Blind Magic

Fictional-ish

Her Real Man

The Jewel Chronicles

Desert Jewel

Rebel Jewel

Snow Jewel

Of Fire and Bone © 2021 by Natalina Reis

Of Fire and Bone is a work of fiction. All names, characters, events and places found therein are either from the author's imagination or used fictitiously. Any similarity to persons alive or dead, actual events, locations, or organizations is entirely coincidental and not intended by the author.

For information, contact the publisher, Hot Tree Publishing.

www.hottreepublishing.com

Editing: Hot Tree Editing

Cover Designer: BookSmith Design

Ebook ISBN: 978-1-922359-62-9

Paperback ISBN: 978-1-922359-63-6

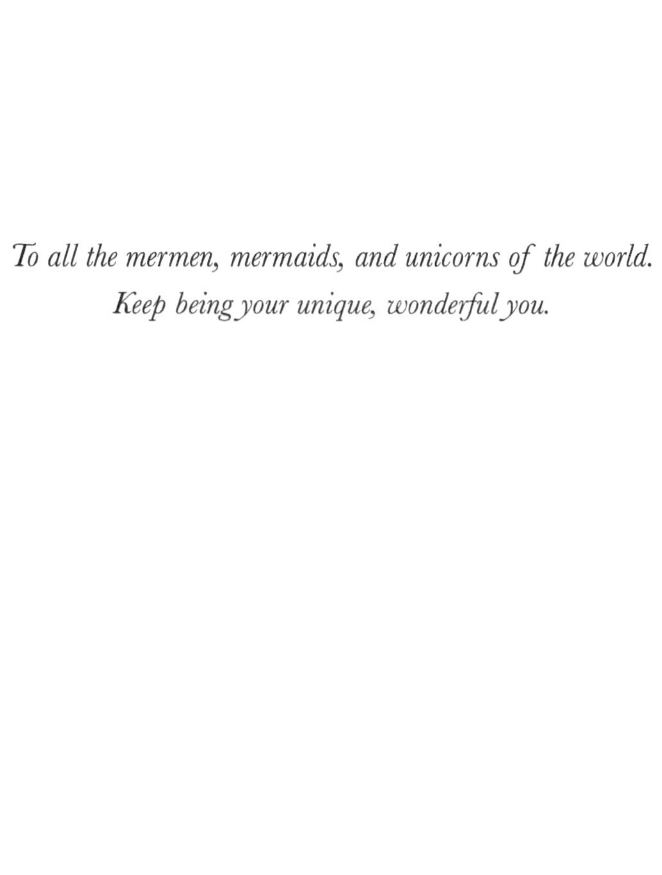

To all the mermen, mermaids, and unicorns of the world.
Keep being your unique, wonderful you.

ONE

CALL OF THE OCEAN

"Will you stop that?" Fouchard's whisper reached my ears in a sudden blow of hot air. "Pay attention."

Attention had never been one of my fortes. I'd sat there for the past twenty minutes, listening to the buzz of people talking, an undercurrent of excitement in everyone's tone. I tried. I really, really tried to be still and feel as excited as everyone else was—including my mate. When we first arrived at the theater, I was in stitches. Hard to believe that after more than two years of living in Portugal this was the first time I was attending a play. I'd gone to clubs pre-Fouchard, and a couple movies, but had never set foot in a theater to enjoy a stage performance of any kind. Which was strange, because I had been very active in DC, even going as far as having season tickets to the Kennedy Center for performances that ranged from simple plays to operas.

Sitting there at that small, intimate theater house made me itchy though. Maybe it was because my Portuguese was still pretty rudimentary. Maybe it was the crowded space, or the fact that I was a different man than the one I had known—and not loved—a few months back.

"Why is it taking so long?" I asked, miffed that my boyfriend had brushed my hand away from his upper thigh. I was restless and when that happened, I could think of only one thing: how I could make my merrow scream out in ecstasy. Okay, so maybe this was not the time or place for that, but you couldn't blame a man for trying. It was a totally altruistic desire, or at least that's what I told myself when my mate practically hissed at me. "I'm bored, Naël."

Fouchard sicced his hooded brown eyes on mine, a warning in his posture. "What are you, Aiden? A child?" He might sound angry, but I knew him well enough by then that I could see the slight twitch of his lips, the precursor of all-out laughter. "It will start soon." Before he even finished the sentence, the lights flickered and the universal *trois coups* hammering from behind the curtains announced the beginning of the play. "See, here we go. Can you stay still for once and enjoy this play?"

I sighed, deeply exaggerating the level of my discontent with the whole thing. "What are we even watching?" I whispered, casually leaning against him.

"Shhhh." All righty then. He wasn't going to indulge me this time.

I slid further down my seat and got ready to at least attempt to pay attention to the performance. Hopefully the actors would speak slowly so I could understand what was happening. I could always take a nap, I guessed. My long legs didn't allow me to slide as far as I would like without entangling my feet with the woman sitting in front of me, so I crossed them instead. My boyfriend surprised me by reaching for my hand and lacing his fingers through mine.

That was more like it.

The lights went off completely, the stage lights illuminating the scene taking place several rows ahead of us. I'd been extremely restless for the past couple of months, ever since finding out that my father, the man who had abandoned me shortly after birth, was one of the monks who kindly sheltered and protected me and my new family. As the summer heat gave way to cooler temperatures and the leaves on some of the trees began turning a beautiful rainbow of earthy colors, my discomfort with the whole situation only grew. I hadn't seen my father, Brother John, since the day the Oracle had revealed that unsettling truth, and my heart had become a strange mixture of anxiety and longing. I wanted to connect, to get to know my father, but at the same time, I found it hard to forgive him, to forget being abandoned by the two people who should have loved me the most.

I'd spent a miserably lonely childhood, hating creatures who had been born into magical families like me but not fitting into the mold of a regular human life either. I had been an outcast my whole life and I just recently understood why.

I must have fallen asleep because I was startled almost out of my seat when applause erupted around us, and Fouchard practically jumped to his feet exclaiming, "Bravo." Still a bit dazed, I stared up at him in awe and surprise. Who would have guessed that giant specimen of a merman was an enthusiastic supporter of the Arts?

I watched him, still slumped on my chair,

taking full advantage of the fact he was thoroughly engaged with whatever was happening on the stage—which I couldn't see because everyone else was giving the actors a standing ovation. I apparently had slept through the whole thing. Oops! How was I going to explain to my boyfriend when he started talking about it? It wasn't as if I didn't enjoy a good play, but the mixture of my overall anxiety about my parentage and my lack of local language proficiency plotted against me.

We left the theater house soon afterward, hand in hand, carried away in the wave of people and chatter. Outside, the night was warm with a touch of coolness typical of this time of the year. We rode the wave until the crowd finally thinned out into almost nothing. The ocean, sparkling ahead over the wall that separated the coastal highway from the residential area, called me, a call so strong I could have sworn there were actual threads pulling on my arms and my legs.

"Let's walk on the beach, Naël," I suggested, tugging on his hand. I often felt the urge to be near the beach, but this overwhelming pull was unusual. Fouchard raised an eyebrow, and I shrugged. "Something is calling…. Maybe I need a recharge after wasting so much energy trying to figure out what the actors were saying."

My boyfriend snorted. "You mean sleeping, right? You were snoring by the end of the first act."

I bumped my hip on his in protest. "I don't snore." I didn't. At least I didn't think I did.

He smiled and leaned over to plant a kiss on my lips. "Okay, not a snore but that adorable sexy sound you make when you are deep asleep." I'd never heard him talk about this. "It's sort of the same sound you make when we're making love." I actually blushed. Shit, who knew what X-rated dreams I had while we were in the theater. Had I made any more embarrassing noises? He cupped my cheek with his other hand and brushed a thumb over my hot skin. "Made me want to take you home and ravish you."

For a moment, I hesitated. Should I listen to the call of the sea or let my man take me home? "Tempting, but I must go to the beach." I couldn't believe it was me uttering those words. I'd definitely changed. I pulled on his hand and we resumed our stroll toward the sparkling waters.

The closer we got, the stronger that magnetic pull was, and soon I was practically dragging my merrow toward it, blinded by the urgency of the call. "Slow down, sweetheart," Fouchard said, digging in his heels and stopping me. "What's the rush? You're freaking me out a little."

I swallowed, glancing at the view of the ocean across the road and then at my boyfriend. "I don't know what this is," I said, anxiety taking residence in my chest. "It's weird but I can't resist it. I feel as if there are hands pulling me to the beach, to the ocean."

Fouchard stood in silence for a moment as if considering my words. "I don't like it, Aiden," he finally said, a frown pulling down the corner of his lips. "After everything that happened to you, to us, this does not bode well. Should we call reinforcements? Taz or Silva?"

I shook my head. I wasn't sure of much, but I could assure him of one thing at least. "It's not evil. It won't harm us," I muttered, my eyes roaming to the sea again. "I don't understand how I know this, but I do. We'll be okay."

He thought about it for a heartbeat, and then he walked beside me, his long legs devouring the space between us and the ocean waters. We had to veer off down the road some distance because there were no crossing spots close by, and that coastal highway was busy with cars that zoomed by like honeybees on a mission. But soon we were on the beach side, tracking down a walking path to take us down to the white sands. I kicked my shoes off as soon as they hit the yielding ground, not bothering to pick them up, and charged to the water's edge instead, Fouchard in tow.

When the cool salty water washed over my bare feet, soaking the edges of my jeans, I sighed as if whatever was growing inside me had finally relaxed its grip. I squeezed my merman's hand but didn't say anything. He took a deep inhale beside me and I followed suit. The briny air was a tender perfume that relaxed me one muscle at a time and it had the same effect on my man. Maybe I had some merfolk DNA after all. Since nobody seemed to really know who or what I was, it was a definite possibility.

"Feeling better?" Fouchard asked me after a moment. The ocean spread in front of us, dark and sparkling under the moonlight, reflecting the stars that studded the sky. I was feeling better but rather confused; what exactly had me running to the water's edge? My boyfriend read my thoughts as usual. "Let's stay here for a while," he said, turning his gorgeous face to me. "Afterward, you'll be all recharged and full of energy to make me cry in pleasure when we get home." He winked, and parts of me immediately responded to his words.

"Men haven't changed much over the centuries." The female voice made us jump and my heart stampeded up my throat. A beautiful woman stood a few feet away from us, barefoot in the wet sand with a complacent smile on her lips. "What a pity. I was so hoping that had improved and that the male of the species could actually hold a thought that didn't include sex or war."

I bristled at her words. Not fair and not true; I had lots of other thoughts, and I never thought of war unless I had to. I might have been a man-whore not that long ago, but I was now a well-rounded human being. But more to the point, who was this woman? She looked vaguely familiar, but I couldn't place my finger on it. "Sorry, do we know you?"

She was beautiful with dark skin, long shiny black hair, and elegant in her blue sari. Wait! Sari? Shit, was she another goddess out to get me? I blatantly positioned myself between her and Fouchard in case she'd try to hurt him.

"Don't worry, Aiden," she said with a wave of her hand. "I have no intentions of hurting either of you. I need to talk to you, that's all."

My shoulders relaxed but I stayed on guard.

What do they say? Once bitten, twice shy? "What do you want?"

She tsked, her dark-as-onyx eyes filled with mischief. "So suspicious. Our fault, I guess." Her cryptic words made me blink. "I came with a warning, child. Unfortunately, your would-be assassins are back in Portugal and gathering forces to try to kill you."

Not the best news, but then again, I knew it. As much as I wished the deadly duet had left for good, that hate didn't just dissipate but rather grew and expanded, fed by the desire to wield more power. "We kind of figured they'd be back, but what's that to you?"

"Neither your father or I want to see you hurt after all that was sacrificed to keep you safe and sound for over thirty years." She knew my father? Who was she? "Be at the ready. They will attack when you least expect it, so expect it at all times." Lovely advice and so conducive to a happy, relaxed life. "I must go now, but I will come back."

"Who are you?" Fouchard asked from behind me, his hand on my shoulder.

The woman smiled again, brought her palms together to her chest, and bowed slightly. "Namaste, children," she said, before turning around and walking into the ocean. A mermaid? I looked up at Fouchard, who shrugged as if to say he had never seen her before. She kept walking against the calm waves, her translucent sari floating around her like a cloud of blue, and a heartbeat later, she had vanished under the waters. Had she been the one calling me here?

"Well, that was interesting," I mused, still staring at the dark spot where she had disappeared. "Why would she come and warn me, and how does she know my father?"

When I raised my eyes to my mate's, his lifted eyebrows caught my attention. "Are you kidding?" he said. "You're really that clueless?"

"What?" I had no idea what he was talking about. "Clueless about what?"

He sighed, dropping his arms along his body in exaggerated frustration. "I can't be sure, but I think she gave us enough clues as to who she is." I raised my brow. "Seriously?" He shook his head. "She was obviously Indian, and she talked about the sacrifices made by her and your father to protect you. Who else could she be?"

A wave of recognition crushed down on me. How could I have missed it? *Fuck my thick brain.*

"Lakshmi!" I whispered in awe. "My mother."

TWO
PREMONITIONS, SPIKED TEA, AND DECISIONS

"No way." I punctuated my words with an emphatic shake of the head. "I am not going to talk to daddy druid." Despite my words, I wanted to; deep inside me, there was this strong desire, a *need* to make my peace with him, to have him in my life. As ridiculous as it was for an almost thirty-seven-year old to need a father in his life, I did. The yearning filled my days and my nights, leaving me breathless and desperate for something I couldn't put a name to.

I shook my head again. *Stop being an idiot, Aiden.*

Fouchard wrapped his big hand around the side of my neck to pull me in and kiss the top of my head. "You're so stubborn, Aiden. I know he did you wrong, but it was for a good reason." I told myself the same thing every day but couldn't accept it fully. "They did it because they loved you and wanted to protect you. You're here alive and well today thanks to their actions, however misguided they seemed at first."

I offered them another obstinate shake of my head. "Not ready. I'm not ready for that." I spied the glance exchanged between my boyfriend and Cristina. "Don't try to change my mind because I won't." I had learned a thing or two from my merrow's sister, Vee, who was headstrong and an expert at digging in her heels. Yes, she was not yet twelve but still wise beyond her years, or so I told myself.

Cristina came around the counter and grabbed my arm with both hands. "Amigo, your mother—a freaking goddess no less—is now in your life again whether you want it or not. Doesn't that tell you the universe is pushing you to forgive and forget?"

"Something wicked this way comes." We all started as our sneaky witchy friend popped before us, her red hair, made brighter by the past summer sun, sloppily gathered into a bun, and a mischievous grin on her lips.

"For all that's holy, witch, can you stop showing up like that?" I exclaimed, lifting a hand to my heart. "And who do you think you are anyway? Ray Bradbury?"

She scrunched up her nose at me. "Whatever. It's true though," she said, pulling out a chair and taking off her sunglasses. "Aren't you curious why both your mom and dad chose to reveal themselves now?"

I crossed my arms like a rebellious child. "I don't care. I can look after myself." Hell, I even had magic powers now. I had almost destroyed one of Lisbon's oldest historical sites with my anger alone —and nearly killed my man in the process, I hated to admit. Okay, I so couldn't take care of myself. Someone needed to teach me how to use these newly acquired powers before I killed someone. But if my attempt at learning Portuguese was anything to go by, I was in for a long haul.

Taz sat down at a table, waving her hands in front of her, undoubtedly setting up some ward around us so the regulars in my coffee shop couldn't hear what was being said. "You have to stop acting like a little spoiled kid and accept the fact that your parents are here and willing to help you. If you can't do that for yourself, what about those you love?" *Low blow, witch, low blow.* "What about Naël and Vee? What about Cristina?" I sneaked a glance at my friend now serving a table by the window and who still wore the scars from an attack aimed at me. Guilt constricted my insides. "Think of them, Aiden. Or do you want them to be casualties of your childish attitude?"

Fouchard took a step closer to Taz, his body a wall of menacing strength. "That's enough, Taz," he said in a dangerously low voice. "That's not fair and you know it. Aiden has good reasons to not want anything to do with his parents." My heart turned into a puddle. My merman stepping up to defend me. No wonder I loved him so much.

I opened my mouth, but Taz beat me to it. "So, Naël, you're saying you don't think he should make nice with his powerful parents and try to get rid of the two idiots from hell once and for all?"

Fouchard's lips twitched and his brow furrowed. We had talked about it many times and he had tried to sway me into forgiving my parents, but I loved that he wouldn't let the witch tell me off. "That's between the two of us, Taz. You're stepping over the line."

I stepped between the two of them before the fire in their eyes became a real thing. "Stop fighting." I threw my mate a warning look and then faced Taz. "You're right, witch, but I am not ready yet. I promise to give it some more serious thought." She humphed and crossed her arms over her generous breasts. "In the meantime, what exactly do you know that you're not telling us?"

She bit her cherry red lips. "Nothing concrete. Visions I've been having." Taz had predicted—not with any particular accuracy or detail—a few events in the last few months, and I had quickly learned to take her visions seriously. "I talked to the high priestess about it, and she said you really should take precautions; having the protection and aid of your parents wouldn't hurt."

Cristina, tray in one hand, stepped into the circle of silence Taz had conjured and stared at us. "What did I miss?"

"Girl, you should have seen the giant merman almost biting my head off defending his lover," Taz said, a smile curling the corners of her lips. "It was a sight to be seen. I was almost afraid." The tension of a moment ago washed away in laughter. "I think we all need a round of that special iced tea you make." The so-called iced tea was more of a spiked lemonade with a bit of chai in it, one of Cristina's creations that had become vastly popular with our customers.

I followed Cristina to the kitchen to get a pitcher of tea and four glasses. I had just opened the refrigerator when Cristina wrapped her arms around me and hugged me. "Don't let guilt bully you into doing what you are not ready for," she whispered against my back. "We love you, and all we want is to make sure you're safe and happy."

I couldn't see her face, but I felt the warmth of her breath seeping through my thin T-shirt and smiled, covering her hand with mine and giving it a reassuring squeeze. "Thank you, *amiga*. I love you too." Those three little words were easier to say out loud than ever before. My new family had brought a totally different color to my life, and I couldn't be more grateful. "Let's go water the beasts."

Cristina laughed, and I followed her into the main room. A few steps in and I stopped. A sunbeam drenched all of my friends with warm light, illuminating them and making the outlines of their bodies sparkle and flare as if on fire. *Message received loud and clear.* I needed to focus on them, on my family. My lonely years were over, and I couldn't be selfish any longer. No more protecting myself from emotions I struggled with. They were first—my beautiful merrow, my lovely brown friend, and even the crazy ginger witch—they should be whom I thought of first, the ones I should strive to protect at all costs.

I approached the table, setting the pitcher down and wiping my sweaty palms on my pants. "I need a volunteer to drive me to the Convento dos Capuchos," I announced, my voice catching a bit. My hands shook as I held them by my sides, a small quake that spread quickly up my arms and into my shoulders. Try as I may, I couldn't control it, so I hung my head before looking up at my friends. "Any takers?"

Fouchard was by my side quicker than lightning, his arms sliding over my trembling shoulders, steadying me, my anchor. "Are you sure?" he asked in a soft voice that belied his size. "You don't have to do it no matter what Taz says."

I nodded, my chattering teeth making it hard to speak. "I'm sure." He drew me closer to him and my muscles relaxed a little. "It's time I face my father."

My boyfriend brushed his lips on mine and then whispered, "Besides, we can find something to distract and relax you while at the Convento." The lilt in his words left little to infer. We had some good times in that beautiful place, and if I hadn't been as anxious about the visit as I was, my toes would have curled in my flip-flops. I smiled. "When do you want to go?"

The rest was a whirlwind. We had taken shelter in the convent a few times before, and I now knew I was part of their community via ties with my druid father, who lived among the monks. After we'd picked up Vee from school and taken her to Cristina's for safekeeping, we went back home to prepare for the visit. It didn't take long to pack a couple of bedrolls and a change of clothes.

We were already outside by the car when I turned around, making my way back in. "Forgot the lube," I yelled out at Fouchard, who grunted half from amusement, half from frustration. It wasn't true. I had a bottle of my favorite lube in my backpack, but I had forgotten to bring a protective amulet Taz had given me some months ago when I had to go face-to-face with the depraved king of the Fae. Not that I thought it would be of much use against the emotional turmoil I expected to feel when talking to Daddy dearest, but it would somehow make me feel safer, more grounded. With it tucked safely in my jeans pocket, I joined my boyfriend in the car, closed the door, and leaned back on the seat as Fouchard started the drive to Sintra.

After driving for a while in complete silence—only broken by the whistling of the wind through the cracked window—Fouchard brushed a hand on my thigh and gently said, "You know I will be there for you whenever you need me, right?" I nodded, my throat still too constricted for words. "If you need me to kick your father's ass I will." The deadpan statement was said with such conviction, I roared with laughter, the weight of my anxieties floating out the window. He gasped. "What? I'm not kidding, I will kick his fucking ass from here to the moon if he so much as whispers a hurtful word toward you."

I glanced at my mate, still shaking with mirth. "Just the way you said it," I explained. His lips stretched into a smile. "I love you, Naël, and I don't doubt for a moment that you would do it."

He snorted. "You better believe it. No one puts Aiden in the corner." His allusion to the movie *Dirty Dancing* made me laugh even more. I was normally the one with all the pop culture references. I was beginning to rub off on him. With his hands firmly on the wheel, my merrow navigated the zigzagging roads of the *serra* while laughter filled the interior of our car.

Soon we were standing by the glamour that kept the convent safe from regulars' eyes after closing. Now that I knew it was there, I could sort of see through it, the fuzzy image of the old convent buildings peeking from behind the shrubs and trees that formed a physical wall between the monks and the outside world. It took only a few moments for the illusion to dissipate and allow us both to walk through it into the path leading to the buildings.

My feet weighed tons, I realized in surprise. It was as if I was swimming against the tide. My mate, always attuned to my moods, slipped his fingers between mine and held my hand tightly. "Whatever happens, remember you have a family now. You're not alone anymore." I knew that, and it did make all the difference, but I still wasn't certain about how to feel about my father and his rather sudden appearance in my life after a lifetime of absence. I guess I'd find out when I faced him.

One of the brothers met us halfway, his humble brown habit blending in with the surroundings. "Greetings, friends," he said, his cowl draped behind his neck and shoulders. "We're so glad you came. The others are waiting for us in the refectory." He pointed toward the building the monks used as their gathering place. "I hope you're hungry. Brother Manuel outdid himself today."

Normally my mouth would be watering at the mere thought of the simple but delicious meals the monks served, the one luxury they allowed themselves, but my stomach was tied up in knots and I didn't think I could eat a thing.

We followed the slim monk, his dark, longish hair swishing in unison with the edge of his habit. The rest of the monks were sitting in silence around the makeshift table facing a true feast. As we walked in, all eyes fell on us, their lips stretching into welcoming smiles. My eyes, despite all my efforts not to, immediately searched the room and latched on my father's. His eyes were as blue as mine, the color of the midnight sky during a full moon—a shade of blue unusual enough that I wondered why I had never noticed the resemblance. There was softness in those eyes, unlike mine where the ice and hardness of anger had settled. He didn't blink as Fouchard and I took our seats at the table across from him, my gaze never leaving his.

"Welcome, friends," one of the monks said. "Let's eat." The silence of a heartbeat ago lifted and was replaced by banter and laughter. The quiet monks were anything but during their meals together.

Fouchard engaged in conversation with the man next to him, but I couldn't take my eyes away from my father, Brother John, as we had known him all these months. He didn't speak either, breaking chunks of the homemade bread and slathering it with butter that he chewed on slowly as if allowing me to have a good stare.

"Are you going to stare at me all night or are we ever going to talk?" Brother John leaned over the table, his voice crossing the short distance loud and clear.

I gulped and was only half aware that the chatter around us had faded into silence, and all eyes had turned toward me. Fouchard covered and squeezed my hand resting on the table. I swallowed again before replying, "Tonight we eat. Tomorrow we'll talk."

There was a momentary wall of silence, broken shortly after as the monks resumed their talking. I lowered my eyes to the untouched food on my plate, and Fouchard whispered in my ear, "Are you all right?"

Strangely enough, I was. It seemed as if the mere decision to talk to my father had lightened my mood. I would listen to the man who had aban-doned me as a baby and give him a chance to explain himself. I would give myself the chance to forgive and accept my absentee father back into my life. I would perhaps finally accept who I really was and let go of the past.

THREE

TO SERVICE AND PROTECT

Autumn was screaming out its arrival. The cell the monks always had ready for us was usually comfortably cooler than the air outside, built higher than the others where the brothers resided, but still half underground. The walls, covered almost completely in cork, both insulated the room from sound and provided us with soft walls against which we had many times made love in the past. But now that the summer was on its way out, the place was positively chilly.

"Shit. We should have brought an extra blanket," I exclaimed, unrolling the sleeping bag over the hard mattress on the floor. "You don't think the monks would have one we could borrow, do you?"

Fouchard twisted his mouth to one side and

snorted. No, of course they wouldn't. These monks —druids really—lived in such abject humility, I had to admire them. Then again, they all possessed powerful magic, so who knew? Maybe they had magical ways of keeping warm. I probably did, too, but considering what had happened the last time my magic ran away from me, I was not about to risk trying it.

"We'll have to come up with a different way of keeping warm," Fouchard said with a wicked wink. "I can be pretty creative." He raised his brows up and down and smiled. Definitely wicked.

I slapped his ass as I passed by him to put the backpacks against the opposite wall. "I like the way you think," I said, dropping the bags on the stone floor.

"When you date a former man-whore you have to find new and more creative ways of binding him to you or he might wander off."

His words, said in jest, hit me like a hammer. Was that what he really thought of me? That I was so shallow, I would just be unfaithful if he didn't satisfy my sexual needs anymore? Then, another thought assailed me; was this giant, tough man still unsure of how much I loved him?

"I would never leave you," I said, my mouth dry

and eyes burning. "Even if you couldn't perform. I love you, Naël. I may have been sex-crazed before, but my love for you is much stronger than my need to get laid."

Fouchard's smile died on his lips, and after a moment of hesitation, he drew me into his arms in a fierce hug. "Jesus, Aiden, I didn't mean it like that. It was a joke." He kissed my temple and tightened his hold further. "I'm sorry if I sounded as if I was doubting you. I don't. I trust you completely." I nuzzled his neck, relishing his ocean scent. "But just so you know, I will never *not* perform for you."

I chuckled quietly, raising my face toward his. He kissed my mouth, his taste instantly taking me to a place between worlds where only we mattered and existed. The kiss deepened, and the next thing I knew, I had stripped my merrow of all his clothes and pushed him gently onto the bed, face down. He chortled, a combination of excitement and anxiety mixed in the sound. He turned his head so his right cheek lay on the bedroll and watched me as I shed my own clothes, my eyes never leaving his, hungry and wild with desire.

"Not sure what you are planning, sweetheart, but it's making me hard." He smiled, turning his body slightly on his right side, a hand supporting his head.

A choking sound escaped my mouth before I could say, "Good, that's the whole point." I was not terribly eloquent when turned on, obviously.

Butt naked, I kneeled beside him and pushed him flat on the mattress again, my hand cupping the back of his neck for a heartbeat. I let my eyes run his body's length, slowly and purposefully, my insides igniting hotter with every inch I caressed with my glance. I wanted to forget what I was about to do, forget about the deadly duo, the premonitions and magical bullshit my life seemed to be irreversibly entwined in. I wanted to be me, the former man-whore who had fallen head over heels in love with the giant who lay bare in front of me. I wanted to taste and feel the intimacy that came with trusting someone so deeply. Being vulnerable was easy, exciting, tantalizingly sexy, and sweet. I trusted Fouchard and he trusted me.

With a sigh, I dragged my hand over his back, starting at the base of his neck and slowly making my way down his spine. I drew lazy circles over his shoulder blades, then went down to do the same over his lower back, smiling satisfied when that loosened a moan from him. Fouchard shifted a bit, wiggling his naughty bits against the softness of the sleeping bag beneath him. I brushed my fingers even lower, sketching smaller circles over his butt cheeks, stopping to cup his hard mounds and squeezing until I heard him grunt softly.

I continued my track down his body, caressing the back of his thighs, sliding my fingers suggestively in between his legs and rubbing the sensitive skin and muscle there before proceeding to the back of his knees, his calves, and his feet. Fouchard was not ticklish, so I rubbed the soles of his feet with my fingers and my knuckles, bending down to kiss them afterward.

"So your nefarious plan is to tease me until I either explode or beg for release." It was not a question. I chuckled, my lips trailing up to his ankle and calf. He groaned, his face half turned to look at me. "I like it. I like it a lot."

I never thought it would be possible to be this close to anyone, physically and otherwise, but I walked around with a heart full of joy and love, none of my previous loneliness rearing its ugly head. Fouchard filled a space in my life I hadn't even noticed was empty until I met him.

My lips continued their way along his legs, fluttering kisses on his soft skin and hard muscle until they found the muscled rise of his butt. He had a perfect ass. I must have stared at it for too long because he turned his face to me, his eyebrows risen. "Have you given up?"

I let out a sound I couldn't identify, a mix of a grunt and a laugh. I nibbled on his skin, kissing the spot I had bitten afterward. My mate shivered at my touch and I swelled further. I made my way up his back, reversing the earlier path of my lips until I met with the back of his strong neck, soft to the touch and sweet on my tongue. He sighed. Deeply. I could make him mine right then. He was ready and so was I, but I wanted to make this night last forever. Misguided avoidance of what lay in wait the next morning? Perhaps, but what a divine distraction Fouchard was. When I made love to him, the world ran away with all my worries, all my fears. All that was left was me and him in a world we had built for the two of us, a place no one or anything was allowed.

"I'm not done yet," I whispered more to myself than him. He groaned, in frustration or delight, I wasn't certain, but I'd bet on the latter. I scooted down and, holding both his hips, I propped his lower body up so I had access beneath him. He looked back at me, a question in his eyes, but I winked and smiled and said nothing while he braced himself on his forearms. I parted his legs to make room for me to slide between them, scooting underneath him on my back. He gasped, no doubt realizing what I was about to do. His gasp turned into a moan of pleasure as I latched my lips around his arousal, his hips arching toward me to allow me full access. He was as hard as he was soft in my mouth. I ran my tongue over him, gently scraping his velvety skin with my teeth. A deep intake of air was all the confirmation I needed of my performance. On the eve of my possibly life-changing conversation with my absentee father, I wanted to make my man soar with pleasure.

Thankfully my trusted bottle of lube was within reach. I held on to his hip with one hand while threading the other between his spread legs to push a lubricated finger inside him. He yelled out, and I knew I'd managed to surprise him. With my mouth still around him, I smiled before teasing him further with my finger. His hard muscles had tensed up into hard rock. He was almost over the edge. Much in his usual style, he pulled away from me with a moan and scooted down until our groins touched, hardness against hardness, muscles throbbing with the need for release.

"We're doing this together," he whispered, his lips over mine. Like a retreating wave upon the sand, Fouchard slid to the side, our hips touching. I felt it before I saw his big warm hand wrap around me, sliding up and down my length, stealing a stream of moans from me. I mirrored his moves, and we both touched and coaxed each other all the way into bliss.

Later we lay side by side, my leg draped over his, all thoughts of cold gone. Fouchard sought out my hand and laced our fingers together. I was still breathless from the sensory explosion of moments ago, assailed by one of those times when I wondered how I had gotten so lucky to find someone like my mate. I tightened my grip on his hand as if afraid he may spirit himself away.

"Are you going to be okay?" He wasn't inquiring about my postcoital feelings; the damn meeting with my father still loomed on the horizon like a bird of prey waiting to swoop down on me. "If you want, I can go with you, be there by your side."

I wanted him to, but I needed to face this on my own. "I'll be all right. Just knowing you're on the premises eases my anxiety." I turned halfway to place a brief kiss on his lips. "Thank you, Naël."

My boyfriend chuckled quietly. "What are

mermen for? We serve and protect." He winked.

I burst out laughing. "You idiot. That's the police," I told him. "Yours is more like, to service and protect."

He turned toward me, grabbing my leg to drape it more firmly over his hip. "Should I service you again, sweetheart?" he purred, a wicked smile on his lips.

"You know I am always ready and willing," I said, throwing a meaningful glance at my favorite appendage.

Fouchard threw his head back and laughed. "Gotta love those demigod genes." He kissed my nose. "As much as I'd love to go another round, we probably should rest. You want to have a clear head when you go see Brother John tomorrow." I really would rather be drunk out of my mind, but I guessed he had a point.

I had almost drifted off to sleep when I felt the warmth of a blanket covering my naked body and the touch of soft lips on my cheek. I didn't stir. My merman's tender care filled me with joy. It was the little things sometimes that told me how much he loved me, how much he cared. I snuggled closer against him, relishing his body heat and wishing for many years to come in his loving arms.

FOUR
OF FATHERS AND DRUIDS

I NEVER WENT TO A PROM, MY HIGH SCHOOL DAYS being a haze of loneliness and terrible sexual experiences. But I imagined it felt a bit like this as I fidgeted, a bundle of nerves, waiting for my father to join me in one of the guest cells. I thought we would be meeting in the library where the Oracle made his home but was escorted instead to the empty part of the building where the rare guests slept. I had been there for what felt like an eternity already but was probably no more than five minutes. I wanted to get this over, behind me.

"You get that from your mother." Brother John's familiar voice made me spin around in surprise. There he was, my father, wearing his usual brown habit, not a thing on him that would mark him as the powerful druid he was. "She tends to fidget a lot."

Immediately my defenses went up, prickly and unyielding. "I wouldn't know," I said, bitterness burning in my tongue. "She never bothered to visit." Or let me know she was alive. I still found it hard to believe that woman on the beach was her.

My father pointed at the simple wooden benches against the wall and we sat across from each other. I glared at him, feeling like a spoiled brat who had not gotten his way. Except I had a good reason to be upset.

"I'm sorry." I wasn't expecting those words from him. At least not right away. His piercing blue eyes, so like mine, were pleading. "There isn't much else I can say. I'm sorry for what you had to go through, for the years of loneliness, the pain of not knowing who you were. We made a tough choice."

My breath caught in my throat. "Tough for me." I spat the words with as much anger as I could muster. "You and dear Mom didn't have to worry about anything. You didn't have to feed me, or tuck me in at night, stay up with me when I was sick, stand up for me when I was unfairly accused of all sorts of things in school. Yeah, it was tough for me, not for you."

The monk placed his hands on his knees and sighed. "I know. We watched you grow." What? He had been watching me? "We couldn't get very close for fear you'd be identified and become the prey of every power-hungry god out there, but we watched from a distance." I threw him a dubious glance. "We watched the first time you went to school, and that brat, Jack, made fun of your pants because they were too short." *Holy shit. He knew.* How could he have known that? I had never told that humiliating incident to anyone. "We were watching when your high school PE teacher called you a fag in front of the whole class and told you to go home and grow some real balls."

I heard a keening, and it took me a few seconds to realize it was coming from me. I had been crushed that day, not because of what the teacher had called me—that was not an uncommon occurrence, and I had grown a thick skin—but because of the looks of pity it engendered from my classmates. It had been bad enough to be pitied for being the poor kid who wore clothes that didn't fit him and often had no money for lunch but to fan the flame with sexual issues at a time when I just wanted to be invisible had been overwhelming.

"We threw all caution to the wind when that

troll stuck your head in the toilet and had a little *chat* with him afterward." That would explain why, despite his threats, the creature had never come back to make good on his promise of an eternity of beatings. My parents had come to the rescue. Once. "It was a big risk, but we couldn't stand the idea of our son being stalked and beaten because of a lover's spat." His eyes shone with a note of mischief. "Even though you really could have been a bit wiser about your sexual flings, son."

The thorns poked through my skin again. *How dare he call me son?* "How would I know how to make wise choices? How to deal with the fact I was not only gay but had this weird gift to see monsters? Do you have any idea how scary it was for me at first? A small child well aware the monster in his closet was actually real?" I had hardly taken a breath between words and panted, my lungs begging for a reprieve.

"You have the right to be angry, furious at us," my father continued, wringing his hands on his lap, his eyes never leaving mine. "I would understand if you hated us, your mother and me. But we were there all the time, watching from the sidelines, suffering when you suffered, hurting for not being able to protect you, proud that despite all the difficulties, you were smart and capable and grew defenses against the many kicks life threw at your shins. We never stopped loving you."

Something inside me broke, and tears flooded my eyes, burning and stinging, desperate to be released. But I couldn't cry. Not yet. Not while my anger still burned hot, not while I still felt the scars of a life of loneliness, of being picked on and abandoned over and over again.

No, I needed time.

"I know this must be very difficult for you, son," the monk said, his knuckles turning white as he clutched the brown, rough fabric of his habit. "I hope you can forgive us eventually. In the meantime, we are hoping you can at least trust us enough to help you. Baburaj and his mother haven't given up on you. They are simply regrouping to come at you from a different angle and with more power. We can help you." He paused, licked his lips, and added in a softer voice, "Let us help you, son. No strings attached."

I swallowed whatever was blocking my throat and took a deep breath. He was right about that; the deadly duo would be back to kill me and take whoever was around at the time down with me. I couldn't risk having someone I loved getting hurt again because of my anger, because of my reckless-ness. Fouchard, Vee, Cristina, and even Taz should be paramount in my actions and thoughts in what related to this issue. I certainly didn't have a death wish, but I could deal with the danger on my own, though not when it involved my loved ones.

Reining in my anger for just a moment, I nodded. "Okay, I will accept your help. Only for the sake of my family." He winced at the words. He knew I didn't include him or my mother in that circle of love and trust. They were not my family. A slice of pettiness made me smile at his discomfort: let him feel the sting of being unloved and unwanted. "What's the next step?" Being all busi-ness would protect me from further emotional turmoil.

At least that's what I was hoping for.

"Your mother is searching for Baburaj," my father said, his voice hoarse with some emotion I couldn't identify. "There have been signs that he and his mother may be back in Portugal. Once we find their location, we can set something up." He sighed, his wide shoulders slumping forward as if in surrender. "Being proactive and going on the attack before they have the chance to attack you is the best chance we have of succeeding."

I wiped my burning eyes with the palm of my hand. "Using the element of surprise," I whispered.

Brother John nodded. "The oldest strategy in the history of the world. Catch them when they least expect it." He straightened his back, some of his usual confidence restored. "And son, be on your guard at all times. I know that Silva is keeping an eye on things too, but you must be extra vigilant."

How fatherly of him. Bile rose to my mouth. "Don't you worry, *Daddy*, I've been in tighter spots before." A wave of sick satisfaction ran through me when he flinched as if slapped. "Oh wait, you know that; you've been watching me getting in all kinds of trouble and not doing anything to help. Funny you'd worry so much now."

I stood up and walked out of the room before he could recover from my blow. This deep, burning anger surprised even myself. I was not normally one for grudges. Okay, maybe I'd held a lifetime grudge against all magicals, but that was because I was in denial of who and what I was. It had always been easier to think of myself as a regular with some freakish gifts than a magical being like the creatures I had worked so hard to avoid most of my life. But I had never held a grudge against one single individual. I didn't like it a bit.

My boyfriend was waiting for me outside, pacing underneath a large chestnut tree. As soon as he saw me, he stopped and studied me, arching his eyebrows in question. I didn't say anything; instead, I strode toward him, threw myself in his arms, and opened up the gates to the flood of tears I had been holding back all that time. Always perceptive, my merman didn't say a word and allowed me to cry my eyes out into his shirt, his warm hand caressing my neck and his lips skimming the top of my head. I needed that silence, that warmth he was always so willing to share with me; I needed to absorb some of his strength and love.

After many heartbeats, my tears finally dried. Fouchard pulled away, wiped the tears from my face with his thumb, and kissed me. In silence, we walked away hand in hand to our cell to pick up our gear. We were going back home now that I'd met my father and begrudgingly accepted his help. I was certain we'd be back sooner or later, but for now, I wanted distance from this place, plain and simple.

We were already halfway home when I finally found my voice. The lump constricting my vocal cords had dissipated at last, and my breathing, erratic and shallow until then, had finally settled into a normal rhythm. "Thank you, Naël." It was a whisper, but he heard it, his face turning to me momentarily. "It wasn't easy, and I'm not sure I'd be able to do it if you weren't with me."

Fouchard placed a warm hand on my upper thigh. "Of course you would," he said. "Your skills as an entrepreneur leave a lot to be desired, but you are much stronger than you look."

That ruffled my feathers a bit, but I noticed that wicked smile on his lips and relaxed. "I have awesome skills in other areas, though." I laughed, feeling the remains of stress evaporating from my chest.

He chuckled. "You certainly do, sweetheart, you certainly do." He threw me a sideways glance. "Maybe you can give me another demonstration later." A frisson of pleasure ran up my spine, making me shiver. "That one last night was superb, but I didn't have the chance to show you *my* skills." Another shiver and every one of the tiny hairs on the back of my neck stood up. "Maybe another trip to our secret cave is in order."

My mate was amazing. With just a few words and a lot of innuendo, he made me forget all about my conversation with the father I didn't know I had. At least for now.

My phone rang. "What's up, Cristina?"

"How did it go?" She must have just opened the store because I could hear the buzzing of voices and the scraping of chairs on the floor. "Are you okay?"

"I'm fine," I said, not willing to elaborate. "You'll be happy to know that my druid father offered to help us with our Bob problem."

"Fuck the miniature god," she exclaimed. "All I care is if you are comfortable with your father hanging around. If you aren't, we can manage without him." Strong words from a regular with not an ounce of magic in her blood. That was why I loved my friend so much. Even after almost dying and being scarred for life because of my dealings with the deadly duo, she still had my back.

"I'll be fine." I realized I meant it; I would be fine. I was an adult—for the most part anyway—and I could work with someone whose very presence brought back so many bad memories of a childhood I would rather forget. "We will need the help. He's a mighty druid and he has the support of his brothers. It will all work out."

Cristina snorted. "I hope so. I don't want you hurt again." She knew how it felt to be left by parents and brought up in the system. "Are you guys on your way back?"

"Yes, why?"

She cleared her throat. "I just need to know how long I have to hide the evidence from Naël."

Uh-oh, what had she done now? "What evidence? What are you talking about, *menina*?"

"Nothing you should worry about," she said, her voice higher than usual. "Vee had a bad encounter with some hair dye last night."

I was not sure whether to laugh or worry. Fouchard was going to flip when he found out his little sister had dyed her hair. I hoped it was just that and didn't involve something worse like a tattoo. "What color are we talking about?"

Cristina mumbled something into the phone, cleared her throat again, and repeated, "A seaweed green. It's not a pretty sight."

Shit. All hell was about to break loose. At least it would be something different to focus on. I stole a glance toward my merman and smiled. "Okay, Cristina. Raise all the shields and prepare for war," I whispered into the phone. "He will take no prisoners."

FIVE

THE FAE SURPRISE

S‍ILVA FLIPPED HIS LONGISH RAVEN-BLACK HAIR OVER his shoulder, and I almost puked. Damn warlock thought he was a chick magnet—which he was, but still. Even though he had been there for us more than once, he still rubbed me the wrong way most of the time, the fact that he was sleeping with my best friend notwithstanding. Cristina's full red lips were extended into a sunny smile, her eyes dazed with something I recognized as love. *Wait!* No, it couldn't be. They had only known each other for a little more than a couple of months. How could she be in love with him already? *Idiot.* I had fallen in love with my merman in even less time, so who was I to judge?

"Cristina, you still work here, right?" I called,

irritation getting the best of me. "There are customers waiting to be served outside."

My friend, brown skin darker from the summer sun, glanced at me and frowned. "I don't see you doing anything important." I was indeed loitering by the counter, trying to kill the cop with my pointed stare. It wasn't working.

"I'm the boss, and I decided this is my afternoon break," I said, crossing my arms like a pouting child. "Stop ogling the warlock and go do your job."

Cristina flipped me the finger, and Silva glared at me. *Ouch.* I thought I actually felt the sting of his displeasure. Maybe warlocks could use their eyes as weapons. I pretended not to see it and got busy making idle circles on the counter with my index finger. I had been restless and cranky since I'd talked to my father a little over a week ago. Not even Fouchard with his magic touch had been able to totally soothe my orneriness. I hadn't heard from Daddy dear since then, but I was guessing he was doing whatever it was he did to find where the deadly duo was. I refused to think about my mother. The fact I had a fucking goddess for a mom had not quite sunk in yet. It all sounded like some story one of my foster parents had told me as a child, maybe a dream I had or something I had read.

"Why don't you go to the beach, Aiden?" Cristina said, stealthily sidling beside me. "Go recharge. Maybe you can ease all that crankiness you've been carrying around with you for days." She walked around and behind the counter to brew a *bica*. "You're lucky I love you, amigo. You haven't been the easiest person to work with lately." The machine whistled and spat a hot cloud of steam into the small espresso cup, quickly followed by the divine black brew. "I don't know how Naël can put up with you."

Me neither.

My amazing boyfriend had been so patient with me I was considering starting a petition to declare him a saint. But even saints had their limits, didn't they? I was fully expecting him to tell me off real soon. Cristina was onto something though; the warmth of the sun and the sand might perform miracles on my mood. As reluctant as I was to leave Cristina in the hands of Mr. Wicked Handsome, I relented and left the store shortly after with my towel draped over my shoulder.

Pedro, my faithful cabana boy, waved as soon as he laid eyes on me. "Come, *Senhor* Mercer, I have a chair for you," he yelled out, his accent coloring the words. I didn't want a chair. I wanted to feel the sand beneath me. He knew my signals, and after a shake of my head, he pointed somewhere else and said, "No problem. I will remove the chair." And so he did.

At the last minute, I decided against the towel and went for the complete experience. Lying directly on the sand, my hands and feet buried in it, I immediately felt a surge of energy run through me. I sighed in relief. Being anxious and frustrated was depleting my energy storage quicker than anything else. I closed my eyes and settled to fully enjoy the feeling of the gritty substance beneath me and the warmth of the sun above. It didn't get any better than this.

"I have some bad news." Taz's voice made my heart jump up to my throat as usual. I sat up to find her daintily sitting on a tie-dyed towel beside me, a yellow polka-dot bikini—I was so not kidding— and large sunglasses perched on her freckled nose. She had removed her wide-brimmed hat and set it down between us.

"Jesus, Taz." There was no point in telling her never to do that again because, after as many times as I had told her in the past, she still seemed to take particular pleasure in scaring the crap out of me every time. "What bad news?"

She licked her cherry red lips, staring at the blue ocean. "There is someone you must talk to." I threw her an inquisitive glance, and she looked at me from the corner of her eyes. "You're not going to like it, but remember I am only a messenger."

I wiped my face with the palm of my hand and groaned. "Spit it out already, witch."

"Your friend, Alabyron, sent a message that he has information pertaining to the mini-god and his mother," Taz said, worrying the edge of her hat. I'd never seen her nervous. It didn't bode well. Since I didn't say anything, she continued, "Well, he won't talk to anyone but your man."

My stomach flipped. No way in hell was I letting that depraved Fae have his way with Fouchard. Not on my watch. I shook my head so hard I made myself dizzy. "Uh-uh, no fucking way."

Taz twisted the brim of her hat tighter around her fingers. "But Aiden, he has important information—"

I didn't let her finish. Jumping to my feet and feeling as if I was about to explode, I growled like a disgruntled bear. "No, it's not going to happen," I repeated. "Alabyron wants to get in my boyfriend's pants. No way. I'm the only one allowed to do that."

Slowly, the witch made her way to her feet. "I know how you feel, Aiden, but this is for a good cause."

My face burned and there was so much tension building up inside my chest, I thought I would start whistling like a teapot at any time. "Are you telling me that I should just tell Naël to go fuck the king just so we can get information from him? Have you lost your mind?"

Taz lowered her voice and her eyes. "Maybe we should ask Fouchard first."

Was she for real? Why would I even consider asking my boyfriend to go rekindle his sexual relationship with the fucking king of the Folk? We all knew what Alabyron wanted in exchange for the information, and if I had anything to say about it, he was not going to get it. I couldn't even talk. Instead, I groaned and shook my head again.

"Listen, Aiden. I understand how you feel about him, but the fact remains that he claims he has solid information about Bob's whereabouts, information we need to plan ahead." No matter how sensible she sounded, there was nothing short of a *Buffy the Vampire Slayer* end-of-the-world scenario that would convince me to ask Fouchard to go see him. "Why don't we just talk to your hot merman about it and come up with a reasonable solution?"

I knew my mate. "He will do it if he thinks it will help keep me safe," I said, my Adam's apple bobbing up and down in my throat. "He will swallow his pride and disgust and will fuck the Fae king or whatever else he wants my man to do for him. I will not put him in the predicament of having to choose. I won't."

Yes, jealousy played a major role in my decision and the way I felt, but there was more to it; I really didn't want Fouchard in that position, to ask him to debase himself to get information to help me. Memories of that night when I visited Alabyron's domain with Fouchard flooded my mind and made my jaws clench. Images of the king groping my merman as they stood entangled in an intimate embrace still haunted my dreams. Okay, so maybe jealousy was indeed a major part of my reaction.

"So what, Aiden? You are going to wait for your druid dad to dig up some information that may come too late. Is that it?" I nodded. That solution sounded so much better than the other option. "All right, Aiden. It's your skin, after all."

I raised my eyes to hers, the bright green glittering in the sunshine as she peeked over the rim of her glasses. "Promise me you won't mention this to Naël," I begged, desperation in every word. "Promise me."

Taz nodded, surrendering to my unmovable determination. "I promise. Under protest, but I promise." That was good enough for me. After months of mistrusting the witch, I had finally come to the conclusion she was trustworthy. She was on my side, whatever that meant in the crazy world of magic. I knew I could trust her to stick by me when it counted.

She left shortly after that, leaving me alone to sunbathe, but I couldn't relax anymore. My thoughts were reeling nonstop, images zooming past one after another, making me dizzy and unsure of my own decisions, my own feelings. Was I doing the right thing by hiding this from Fouchard? Did I even have any choice in the matter? Fuck! Love was not easy.

By the time I got home—yes, I was most definitely thinking of my merman's house as my home too—I was suffering from a terrible headache and a seriously foul mood. Vee, who was in the living room watching TV with the mermaid doll I had given her a few months back, twisted her lips into a frown as soon as she laid eyes on me. I slumped into the seat beside her, grabbing and hugging a cushion as a protective shield, with a loud groan.

"Uh-oh, what happened?" the young mermaid asked, twisting her body to face me. "Do you need a hug?"

"I need more than a hug, Vee," I told her, another disgruntled groan escaping my mouth. "I have to make a decision, and I think I'm screwed no matter which way I go." Hell, I was confiding in an eleven-year-old. I had totally lost my mind. I glanced at her with a half-hearted smile and added, "But a hug would be nice."

She threw her skinny arms around my shoulders and gave me a surprisingly strong hug. "It will be okay, Aiden. You and Naël will figure it out together." For a preteen, she sure was preceptive and wise. There it was in a nutshell; I needed to talk to my boyfriend about it instead of agonizing over it. I trusted Fouchard with my life; he would make the right choice.

I pulled away from her hug and smiled, a bit more sincerely this time. "You're right, Vee. We'll figure it out." I looked around the room. "Where is he?"

She shrugged and gave the doll an even tighter

hug. "You know him. He said something about having to talk to Neptune and took off after making me promise I wouldn't move off of this couch until you got home." She made a face. "Ugh, my brother is so controlling. When will he realize I'm old enough to take care of myself?" *Oh no, you aren't.* Considering what had happened that spring, I was surprised he'd left her alone for even a moment. It must have been rather urgent. "I will be twelve next week. That's practically adulthood for a mermaid." I suppressed a chuckle with my hand and pretended to cough. "You should check that cough, Aiden. Old people get pneumonia easily."

I gaped at her. "I'm only in my thirties, Vee," I protested. "Hardly old."

She laughed at my protest. *Little imp!* "You sure act like you are." I stopped myself from humphing like a pissed-off bull and offered her a smile that probably looked more like a grimace. "Are you hungry? There are pastries in the kitchen." I *was* hungry. With the unsettling news of the past hours, I had forgotten to eat. I slid off the couch to headed to the kitchen. "Make sure you don't eat the ones with cream filling. Your old man's stomach might not be able to handle it."

For a brief moment, I contemplated turning

back and throttling her, but I don't think Fouchard would appreciate that. That and the fact that I had come to love the infuriating mermaid as a sister. Like the mature adult that I was not, I walked out of the room with just a slight stomping of my feet and a low rumble under my breath. She had, however, distracted me from my own thoughts long enough for my heart to feel lighter, if only for a moment.

I hoped to god that Fouchard could come up with a solution to this problem. One that didn't involve Alabyron getting into his pants again.

SIX

TO MATE OR NOT TO MATE

"WELL, THAT WAS INTERESTING." THE COMMENT was made with a crooked smile. Fouchard stood in the kitchen, his strong arms crossed over his bare chest and his brown skin glistening with diamond-like droplets of ocean water. He had climbed the stairs from his basement beach, still dripping wet, covered only by an old pair of gray lounging pants that hung low on his narrow hips.

My eyes roamed over that sweet body of his with hunger, and I caught myself salivating at the thought of all that in bed later. I shook my head, trying to focus on the matter at hand. "What was?" I leaned on the kitchen island, my hands laced together as I fought with myself not to touch him; his sister was mere feet away from us, still absorbed by whatever show she was watching, and I didn't trust myself to be able to stop myself once I felt his skin under my fingers.

"The conversation with Neptune," he replied, stretching over the marble counter to grab a peach from the fruit bowl. He chuckled and took a bite from the fuzzy fruit, not bothering to wash it. "You're going to laugh." Something told me I wouldn't. In fact, my stomach clenched. I had grown so close to my mate that sometimes it felt as if I could read his mind—no, that wasn't it, because it was not clear, more of a feeling than anything else. "He wanted to negotiate my marriage."

I almost choked on my own spit. "What? Your marriage?" What the hell was he talking about? Didn't Neptune know about the two of us? "I don't understand." My mouth had gone dry and my eyes threatened to pop out of their sockets.

"Merrows are traditionalists." *Yeah, tell me about it!* Due to their insular character, a serial killer had almost murdered Vee because she was not a pure-blood mermaid. "Neptune is worried I have no children and thought he would advise me on who I could possibly snag as a wife and be the mother of my kids."

I tried to protest, but all I managed to do were

sputtering sounds. Fouchard stared at me and smiled. I swallowed before being able to spit a few words out. "What? You and a mermaid? What is he thinking?"

Much to my consternation, my boyfriend laughed. "It's tradition for a merrow of my age to produce heirs to perpetuate the species," he said with infuriating logic and composure. Was he kidding me? Was he really considering it? "He's just doing his duty as my sovereign, especially since my parents are no longer living."

My hunger for him of a few moments before was replaced by pure hurt. I chided myself for feeling like that. After all, he was not telling me he would do it; he was simply relating what Neptune had told him. But from deep inside me, my old insecurities crept up to invade and take siege of all my senses; I wasn't enough for him, I'd known all along. He deserved better than me, a man-whore who was content with a life of mostly leisure. The litany of self-flagellating thoughts kept coming, fast and furious until I could barely breathe, much less talk.

His smile flattened as he peered at me. "Are you okay, Aiden? You look a bit pale." He took a step forward and made a move for my arm, but I moved away. A frown covered his face in shadows. "What's wrong? You know I have no intention of marrying any mermaid, right? I love you and only you."

"I can't give you heirs." Mortified by my own words, I stared at my feet. "I don't want to be the one preventing you from perpetuating the species like you said."

He took another step forward, and before I could move away from him again, he had me gripped in a hug. "What are you going on about, fool?" I swallowed, divided between the need to put some space between us and wanting to lean in onto his hard chest. "You're my mate. Why would I want any spawns with someone I didn't love? I have Vee. She is more of a daughter than a sister with our age difference. I don't need heirs. She is it."

I exhaled the poison collecting in my lungs and allowed myself to yield to him, his arms tightening around me and pulling me closer. "I don't know what's wrong with me lately, Naël," I confessed. "This whole deal with my parentage and magic talents I had no idea I had is driving me fucking bonkers. I'm sorry I snapped at you."

His warm lips brushed against my right temple. "But why even consider I would marry someone else? I thought we were way past that, that you were sure of my love for you."

I flattened one hand on his back, letting his body heat provide the comfort I so desperately needed. I wanted to answer his question, but the truth was I didn't have a clue. Did it have something to do with what Taz had told me? I made a decision right then. "Taz said Alabyron wants to see you." His body went rigid against mine. After a few heartbeats, he pulled away from me, his eyes searching mine. "He claims to have information about the whereabouts of the deadly duo." I gulped, a giant knot suddenly preventing me from breathing properly. "I don't want you to go to him, Naël." My voice had gone quiet, a mere whisper.

Fouchard blinked and licked his lips as if hesitating. "Does Taz think he is telling the truth?" I nodded, incapable of speaking. "Then I must go, sweetheart. We need to know where those idiots are."

I slid my hands to his upper arms, gripping them so hard it would probably leave a bruise. "You can't." I wanted to scream, but instead, my voice came out strangled. "He wants *you*. You, Naël. Why do you think that is?" My merrow hid his eyes. He knew exactly what the king of the Fae wanted from him: another bargain where my boyfriend's body would be a nonnegotiable condition. "I won't let you do that for me."

"We don't know if that's what he wants," he said without any conviction.

I let out a cackle. "Of course that's what he wants. The man is depraved and he got a taste of you." I shook him a little as if attempting to snap him out of the lie he was telling himself. "I know from experience that you are not a one-time taste. You're intoxicating, addictive, and he wants some more."

"You think I'm intoxicating?" His attempt at humor didn't work. I stood my ground, my eyes glued to his. "Let me think on it, Aiden. We'll think of something, you and me together. We're two intel-ligent—okay, you a bit less than me—males in a relationship." I couldn't help it and smiled at his usual lack of tact, something he did to amuse me when things were tense. "We'll figure it out."

I believed him, and the weight lodged in my chest gave in enough to allow me to breathe. I nodded and dropped my forehead to his chest and left it there for a moment or two, breathing slowly until my heart stopped racing inside my chest. After a while, he pulled me up to look at him. The sight of his gorgeous face made me smile. Okay, maybe we could weather this too. We had taken on serial killers, mad gods, and merfolk poachers; we could deal with a lascivious Fae royal and come out on the other side victorious.

"Let's go to bed," Fouchard said, dropping a kiss on my forehead. "I've been dreaming about this moment all day." I grinned, my naughty bits getting excited in anticipation. "I may have spaced out for a while when Neptune was trying to convince me to let him find me a wife."

The smile died on my lips. "Are you sure you didn't accidentally agree to some marriage pact?" My heart began thumping again.

My boyfriend chuckled. "I'm pretty sure, considering he was seriously pissed at me by the time I bid my goodbyes." Fouchard pulled me closer to him. "Will you stop worrying about this? I love you. You, not anyone else. Did I tell you merrows are monogamous?" No, he hadn't. How could he have forgotten such an important detail about his species? I shook my head emphatically. "My bad. Yes, we're more like geese than fish; we mate for life."

There was a question hanging on the tip of my tongue, but I didn't dare ask. Were we officially mated or just dating? How did the merfolk mating protocol go? Instead, I smiled like the idiot I was and resigned myself to the idea I would have to live in ignorance for a while longer.

I admit the aura of insecurity over our relationship put a major dampener on our lovemaking. For the first time ever, I was so distracted by my own doubt-riddled thoughts I couldn't put my heart and soul into it. Good thing I wasn't a man-whore anymore. This would definitely ruin my reputation as a fantastic lover—I almost didn't reach a climax, a sure sign of my troubled mind.

"What is wrong, sweetheart?" Fouchard was breathless after exerting himself to the max to please me—with very poor results, it turned out. "You weren't into this at all tonight."

Remorse made me cringe. "Sorry, I should have been more attentive, but I'm just a bit distracted about this whole thing with Alabyron." It was not the full truth, but it would do for now. I had no intention of forcing my hand about our mating or lack thereof. "I'll make it up to you tomorrow." I hoped.

My merrow didn't probe any further, intuitive as

he always was. He knew I would tell him when I was ready. He drifted off to sleep soon after, but I couldn't find the peace of slumber and lay wide awake most of the night, using the high ceiling as my focus point. Needless to say, morning came to find me as cranky as I had been in a long time. Not even my merman's pancakes were able to snap me out of my funk.

Fouchard dropped me off at Bicas R Us before driving Vee to school. Her birthday was coming in early November, and he was busy planning her party. The little force of nature that was Vee was determined to have a fabulous "party to end all parties" to celebrate her twelfth birthday since this was the first time she would be inviting both her land and aqua friends. Her big brother was doing his best to accommodate her wishes, still feeling guilty for her abduction all those months ago.

Cristina was already in full work-mode, in the small kitchen preparing sandwiches for the few faithful patrons who would be coming through our door very soon. Now that the weather was cooler, the crowds had dwindled somewhat, and the waves of customers were not as overwhelming. There were still plenty of tourists around though, and even though work had definitely slowed down, paying customers still filled most of the tables inside and out on the patio most of the days.

"You look like shit," Cristina said, twitching her nose as if something reeked.

I helped myself to an *italiana*, which was what the locals called a double espresso. "Thank you, Cristina. I appreciate your honesty." She snorted at my sarcasm. "I didn't sleep much, okay?"

"If it was because of all the crazy monkey sex you were having with your hot merman, then I guess it was worth it." She peered closer, studying me. "But if not, then what the hell were you doing all night to make you look like that?"

"Alabyron has information about Bob and his mommy." Yes, I was going to deflect the conversation from my mating status for as long as I could. I was afraid of finding out we were not officially mates, as it were.

Cristina's eyes went round as saucers. "The freaky king of the Fae?" I shook my head. "I know you don't like him, but why would that keep you up?"

"He wants my man to meet him, not me." The words left a sour flavor in my mouth. "In other words, he wants Naël."

"Like sexually?" I had never told her about the

incident at the Quinta da Regaleira when Fouchard went with me to ask the king for a favor. I nodded, the large lump in my throat refusing to go down. "Holy fuck. What are you guys going to do?"

Good question, my friend, excellent question.

It sucked that I had no answer.

SEVEN

LESS TALK, MORE ACTION

"I'll now have to poke my eyes out, Cristina. Why did you do that?" I'd inadvertently walked in on my best friend having sex with her boyfriend earlier that day. Thankfully they were still half dressed, but regardless, I'd never be able to wipe that image from my mind.

Cristina braced her hands on her hips and gave me one of her don't-you-dare looks. "You should have knocked," she said. Duh, I knew that now.

"I never had to do it before, menina," I complained. I had her house key and had always walked in without ringing the bell. "How was I supposed to know you and the warlock were going at it?"

She pursed her lips. "Well, he is my boyfriend,

and we were behind locked doors." Logic didn't work with me, and she should have known that. I rubbed my eyes with the back of my hands. She was not moved. "Don't even try to blame me or Tó for this." She tapped her foot on the tile floor. She pointed her long nail behind me. "Those customers are about to give up on us." We should have opened the store almost twenty minutes ago, but I couldn't get over the shock of what I'd witnessed. Without waiting for my response, she walked around me and opened the door, making sure to apologize to the people waiting in line.

I drained my espresso cup in one single gulp and turned around only to almost crash into Taz. "Shit, witch. What do you want now?" Her bright red lips stretched into a smile, the skin around her eyes crinkling like chocolaty Christmas cookies. "Don't give me that flirty smile. You know very well it doesn't work on me."

"You can't blame a girl for trying." Yes, I so totally could. "But I wouldn't steal you from your lovely merman. He's too sweet to deserve that." We agreed on something at least. She sat down on a nearby chair, crossed her long legs, and removed her trademark wide-brim hat. "Have you decided?"

I knew exactly what she was talking about, but I

was not going to give her the satisfaction of knowing I had been agonizing about it. "What are you talking about? Stop speaking in riddles, woman."

She pouted and swung one leg, her high-heeled red shoe almost falling from her foot. "You know what I'm talking about, Aiden. Stop messing around. We need to figure out how to get that information out of Alabyron soon."

A loud, long sigh escaped my lips. "What is your high priestess saying about that? Does she have a suggestion?"

Taz shook her head, the long red locks fleeing from her messy bun. "Other than let your man go talk to him, nothing." *That's not going to happen. I can promise you.* "What about you? Did you talk to Naël?"

As if on cue, my lovely merman walked in the store, his delicious lips curved into a smile. "Two of my favorite people together," he said with a wink. To think that just a few months ago he couldn't open his mouth without saying something nasty to me made me smile. "I have good news. Or possible good news at least."

I kissed him as soon as he got close enough. Mmm, he tasted of sunshine and brine, an instant boost to my energy level. "What is it? Please tell me you have a solution to this mess."

His smug smile told me he did. "I reached out to Neptune, and he called a couple of his contacts in the police force. I need to run it by Silva, but it looks as if we now have something to pressure our depraved friend into complying. Without strings attached." That last part was said with emphasis and a meaningful glance toward me. My heart did a flip. Should I dare to feel hopeful? "You're going to love this."

Fouchard and I pulled a chair to sit with Taz, but my butt never reached the seat. Cristina threw me such a poisonous look from across the room. I swear I actually felt it. "Boss." It didn't bode well when she called me that. "We need your help." And she was using the royal we. Holy shit, I was in trouble.

I whispered some excuse to my merman and scampered to her, a forced, nervous smile on my face. "What do you need?" We were face-to-face in a corner of my store, a foot or so away from the next occupied table. She actually hissed at me. I raised my hands between us. "Whoa, menina. What have I done to you?"

"Look around you. What do you see?" I

obliged. After surveying the room, I looked back at her, confused. "Have you noticed how many customers are in this room right now?" I nodded. "Now, look outside on the patio. Can you see how there isn't a single free table?" I nodded again. She grabbed onto the front of my T-shirt and pulled me down toward her so suddenly I stumbled. "I am not a machine," she hissed, her face so close to mine I could feel her breath. "Do your job."

"But—" She didn't let me finish. Letting go of my shirt, she placed her hands on her hips and tapped her foot with fire in her eyes. I raised my hands again. "Okay, okay, don't kill me. Naël just arrived with news." A quick glance told me she couldn't care less at that moment. "I'll tend the tables first. Sheesh, you'd think you're the boss."

I didn't remember ever serving tables that fast, but I had a sneaking suspicion my magical powers had something to do with it. As soon as I delivered the last pastry-and-coffee-laden tray, I swerved back and raced Cristina to the table where my boyfriend and the witch were sitting. Fouchard was laughing. "You're like a blur out there," he told me, closing a hand on my wrist. "I hope the regulars didn't notice." At that point, I didn't even care. I wanted to know what the possible solution to the kinky Fae conundrum was.

Cristina, more than a little annoyed with me, dropped to the chair next to Taz. "Not fair. I'm the only one here without any magic."

Taz tried to hide a muffled chuckle behind her hand. "I don't know, Cristina. The way you made this lazy dude work just a moment ago was pure magic."

I scowled at her. "Come on, tell me what you found out, Naël. Stop torturing me or you may be sleeping alone tonight." There was very little chance of that ever happening, but he didn't have to know that. In this relationship, I was the needy one, I thought. Despite his willingness to be totally vulnerable with me, he did hold the upper hand when it came to me. I loved and needed him so much. All he had to do is wiggle an eyebrow, and I would be all over him, no questions asked.

"All right, lover, I'll tell you," he said, leaning over to kiss my cheek. "Rumor has it that our warped Fae has been breaking more than a few council rules throughout the years. The council has some strict laws in order to allow all species to live in harmony in a world that does not belong to magicals any longer. There are very severe consequences when you break them."

I didn't get it. Maybe my brain had been fried the last time I used more magic than anyone should ever do, despite the fact I did it to save Cristina's life. "So what? We're not the cops."

My best friend slapped the back of my head. Not too gently. I grunted and rubbed the soft spot. "Parvo. You now have a bargaining chip that doesn't require your boyfriend to prostitute himself to get the info."

My eyes met Fouchard's, and the excitement I saw in them confirmed Cristina's claim. The urge to jump my boyfriend's bones right then and there was strong, but I had indeed grown quite a bit these past few months—or at least, I hoped I had. Instead, I smiled like an idiot and reached out for his hands. I couldn't say anything. I was afraid that if I tried to speak, I would only utter humiliating squeaking sounds. We'd been saved by the bell, so to speak.

"So when are you going to see Alabyron?" Taz asked. She bit her lower lip and blinked her green eyes a few times.

I froze and stared at her, confused. "What do you mean? Someone else will do it, right?"

Taz shook her head. "No, dummy, it has to be Naël. He won't even allow anyone else to go close to him." *No, no, no way.* "There is no danger now. The hot merman here will have enough ammunition to shoot him down before he makes his move."

I raised my eyes to Fouchard's again, hoping he'd contradict her. But he didn't. "It will be okay, Aiden," he said, pulling on my hands. "He doesn't pose a danger anymore."

"He's the king of the depraved and criminally insane." My eyes were nearly popping out of their sockets. "I'm going with you."

Fouchard sighed. "Sweetheart, if he sees you, he will clam up, and we won't get anything useful out of him." I hated when he made sense. "This way, we give him a little of what he asked, make him think he has the upper hand, and then strike. A surprise attack is the best strategy here." He sounded like the ex-marine he was, all strategic maneuvers and misplaced heroism. I pouted. "He won't know what hit him."

I was not ready to give in yet. "What exactly did he do anyway?" And what risks was he running? Enough to warrant his agreement to furnish information without the nooky?

"He has been pocketing a great portion of the

tithe his subjects pay him instead of sending it to the council treasury." Fouchard couldn't help smiling. "In order not to get caught, he has also been forging the results of the yearly censuses. The council has no idea of how large the magical population is around Sintra where he rules."

I frowned, not understanding it completely. "What is the penalty for that? Prison, a hefty fine? Somehow I don't think that would faze him too much."

Taz was the one who answered, "No, it would hit right in the cojones—or in his case where it hurts him the most, his power. He would be divested of all authority and would have to live the rest of his life working for the council as an underling."

A wave of relief washed over me. The Fae king would never go for that. Fouchard was not kidding; we really had him this time. While normally I wouldn't rejoice in someone else's troubles, I made a gleeful exception this time; I couldn't be happier that fucker was about to get his ass kicked. I smiled so big my face hurt.

My boyfriend pulled me closer against his side and kissed my forehead. "See, sweetheart? No danger here."

He was so wrong. Just because we had the upper hand this time didn't mean I felt even remotely comfortable knowing Fouchard was going to meet with Alabyron by himself. "You must take a back-up," I insisted, attempting a stern look that probably looked like a frown. "If not me, someone we trust." I threw Taz a particularly pointed look. "Maybe you, witch. You seem pretty chummy with the king."

Taz guffawed as if I had said something extremely funny. "You gotta be kidding, Aiden. Me, chummy with Alabyron? Not in this lifetime."

"But you were there that first time, and you seemed pretty familiar with the whole place." Taz twisted the brim edge of her enormous hat. "I figured you knew him well."

"I don't know him any more than anyone else in the magical world," she said. "I was there that day as an envoy of the high priestess. As such, he had to give me access to his den of inequity, no questions asked."

I liked her label for the king's domain at the Quinta. It was fitting. I still got the shivers every time I thought of that first time I met him and the invisible strings he tied around me to make him irresistible. I had almost given in, but my immunity to certain voodoos had spared me. Nevertheless, I felt dirty for days afterward.

"Can't you ask Dona Moreno to send you in an official capacity with Naël?" Cristina asked, throwing a worried look at the busy store. Customers would begin grumbling soon if we didn't tend to their needs.

Taz bit her lower lip and looked momentarily confused, her usual expression when she was considering her options. "I'll talk to her but can't promise anything."

"Get on it then, witch," I said, quickly losing my patience—the thin slice I had left. "We need less talk and a lot more action."

Cristina grumbled and pointed at the unattended tables. "You're one to talk, amigo. If we don't take some action to serve our customers, we may have a riot on our hands."

Reluctantly I left my friends and, closely followed by Cristina, went to see to my neglected customers. In a way, I was grateful for the distraction; I didn't want to think about what Fouchard was about to do.

MERMAN KISSES

"WE HAVE THE GREEN LIGHT." SILVA WALKED INTO the coffee shop like an unexpected wind gust, blowing cold air into my delicate state of mind. I shivered, knowing too well what he meant. He had checked the information about Alabyron, and Fouchard was being asked to go see him. "I don't know where your people dug up the information, Fouchard, but it's solid gold. He'll be totally screwed if it becomes public knowledge."

Fouchard smiled at me as if that were the best news ever. I groaned as if in pain. As much as I acknowledged the necessity to get the much-needed information about the idiot god who was after me and my loved ones, my heart couldn't accept the way we were getting it. To offer my boyfriend as a sacrificial lamb was not my idea of a good strategy. Not that Alabyron would be able to blackmail him into trading sex for the data—we had an ace up our sleeve—but images of that last meeting, when Fouchard and I were not dating yet, still haunted my dreams.

"We have to celebrate," my boyfriend said with a chuckle. "Bring the expensive wine."

Cristina laughed. "This is a coffee shop, not a winery, merman. But I will break out the expensive coffee." She turned around and walked behind the counter to brew the promised coffee.

"I don't know why we're celebrating," I moaned. "Isn't it a little premature? Alabyron is cunning and has mad magic skills. Who knows? He may surprise us and have something in store for us."

Taz, who had sneaked behind me as usual and just about made me jump out of my skin, said, "Oh, he does indeed have something in store, but that magic trunk of his won't help him this time." Everyone laughed except me. I, the original joker, was finding zero humor in the whole situation. Maybe the king of the Fae wouldn't be able to demand any sexual favors anymore, but that didn't mean he was harmless. "Stop worrying about it,

Aiden, and drink that coffee. Too good to go to waste."

I felt a hand slide over my shoulders and settle behind my neck. My boyfriend leaned forward just enough to place a kiss in that small hollow between my shoulder and my neck. I shivered, and my muscles relaxed, some of my anxiety dissipating as the warmth of his lips traveled through my body to wake up my favorite body part. I leaned back against his hard body and closed my eyes for a moment, losing myself in the sensation.

How had I survived almost thirty-seven years without my merman?

"Can you at least have the decency to keep it in your pants until you're alone?" Cristina said. I opened my eyes and glared at her, but she was smiling. My best friend could be such a pain sometimes. "When are you going to do it?"

"Make love? Not until we get rid of all of you." I knew exactly what she meant, but I needed that easy levity our relationship thrived on. We'd had so many scary and heartbreaking moments in the past few months, I just wanted to rejoice in the knowledge my best friend was still alive and well and that everything else seemed to be okay for the moment. Cristina crossed her arms in front of her and stuck her lower lip out, much in Vee's typical style. "All right, I know. How does tomorrow night sound?" It sounded terrible to me, but I had to let go, I guessed.

We all agreed and drank some more of the amazing coffee Cristina had wrangled from a mysterious friend who, she claimed, had connections with a coffee plantation in Africa. It was better not to ask too many questions. After they all left, Fouchard and I closed the store and drove to his house in Cascais. The *palacete*, a beautiful example of Portuguese architecture, appeared around a curve on the coastal highway, its soft pink walls and wrought iron balconies glistening like jewels under the light of the moon.

Home.

The word still sounded strange to me after a lifetime of having no place to call that. Not really. I had had roofs over my head most of my life, but inside of their walls, there was no love. Until I met Cristina, I had never loved or been loved in any shape or form. Until Naël, I had never been truly loved and wanted by anyone. I felt privileged but lived in fear of losing what I was pretty certain I couldn't live without any longer—didn't *want* to live without.

Vee was spending the night at a friend's house. Fouchard, to his credit, had been loosening his control over his sister, even if his totally justified fear of losing her was very much alive in his heart. He just didn't want to limit the young girl because of something that was someone else's fault.

As soon as we were behind closed doors, my boyfriend held my hand and pulled me hard against him. "How does an underwater outing sound?" I might be tired, but every muscle in my body perked up at the idea. One muscle in particular got very excited. We hadn't been to our love cave in a while, but the memories of the last time were still so vivid, my body reacted in recognition. I caught myself nodding like a crazy bobblehead. Fouchard smiled, his lips curving upward on one side. "I guess that's a yes."

We didn't waste any time and dashed downstairs to the basement beach, shedding our clothes along the way. Who needed clothes? We'd be wearing each other in no time. One of my toes got stuck on my flip-flop, and I almost fell face first on the sand but managed to find my balance just in time. "Fuck." I threw the shoe across the beach and continued sprinting toward the water's edge. Fouchard was ahead of me, his powerful body already changing into his aqua form, the vibrant blue of his tail beginning to spread along his sexy butt and legs. Right before his legs were completely enclosed by the tail, my merman dove into the water, surfacing a few seconds later to wave me in.

"I'm not a fish, Naël, and I don't have a tail, so be patient." I laughed and groaned at the same time, impatience taking over. I wanted to be in that water, glued to my merrow, but my very human body was making it difficult as I kept tripping over my own feet. I finally reached the water and waddled ungracefully in my boyfriend's direction. The water was cool but pleasant, another sign of fall, so I dove in as soon as the water was deep enough.

I broke the surface right in front of Fouchard, our skins almost glued together. "You may not have a tail, but you have a great ass." He reached around me and emphasized his words with a stimulating squeeze. "Perfect." He leaned over and captured my lips with his, our tongues sliding against each other's. I moaned inside his mouth and swelled against his velvety upper tail. "Whoa, boy, we have to get there first." Without any warning, he held my hand and pulled me under with him. He stopped just long enough to blow his magic into my lungs so

I could temporarily breathe underwater and then flipped his strong, beautiful tail in quick, powerful strokes to pull me toward our secret cave.

When we finally surfaced inside the cave, my lungs were beginning to burn as the magic air inside them dissipated. I took a long deep breath before turning to my lover. He was watching me, his eyes half closed and lips ajar, and I couldn't hold it any longer; I crossed my arms behind his neck and went in for a kiss, wanting to savor those wine-colored lips.

One major advantage of being me—and what I was nobody seemed to know—was not being affected by things other males were, like cold, for example. I was easy to arouse and had impressive staying power. Yes, humility was not my forte, but of all my newly discovered gifts, this one was by far my favorite, and I was willing to bet Fouchard felt the same way. The cold water didn't bother my merrow either since he was an aquatic being. Together, we were pretty much like the postal service; neither snow nor rain nor heat nor gloom of night stayed us from the swift completion of our lovemaking.

Fouchard braced his hands on my waist and lifted me up onto the rocky ledge, and then hopped on it himself, pushing me until my back was flush with the mossy wall. He scooted on the rock, waving his magnificent tail from side to side until he was beside me. I turned halfway and brushed a hand on his wet chest, from the base of his neck down to his waist and the edge of his tail, and lingered there, fingers skimming the soft velvet of his skin.

"Have I told you lately how much your tail turns me on?" It was a rhetorical question. As if to prove he knew it, Fouchard laid his hand on my lap, moving his fingers in a gentle but sexy caress. "It's yours if you want it," I said with a wink. He didn't need me to invite him twice. In one smooth move, my merman had dropped his head down and wrapped his lips around me. "Holy Mother of God, Naël." He was doing something with his tongue and his teeth that was quite possibly the best thing anyone had ever done to me. I wanted more. With a wiggle, I slid further to give him better access to my naughty bits. My merman didn't disappoint; responding to my voiceless request, he doubled the efforts to make me fly. And fuck, was he effective!

With the passing of the months, we had become better and better at reading each other's minds. Sometimes it spooked me a bit. He knew that no matter how close to the edge I was, I wanted him to be there too. Another strange thing that came out of my love for him—no pun intended; I was no longer the selfish bastard who was only interested in one thing, and that was how number one was feeling. Before I met Fouchard, much like Julius Cesar—but slightly out of order—I would see, conquer, and come, but now I had done a one-eighty; I wanted *him* to do the conquering and the coming first. He made that very hard sometimes—again, no pun intended.

"One more lick, and I'll be known as the new Krakatoa, Naël," I groaned, the back of my head solid against the wall. "I want to touch you, love."

He backed away after a heartbeat, but not before sliding his tongue and warm lips over the length of me, making me yell in surprise and pleasure. "What? You're not enjoying my loving?" His usual sarcastic tone was back. If I hadn't been so busy trying to control my body, I would have laughed.

I took a couple of deep breaths and groaned before answering, "Shit, Naël. You just about undid me there. I love your tail, but can you get your land form back so I can love you like you deserve?"

Without as much as a blink, his beautiful iridescent blue tail faded, and his strong, dark legs and the part of him I was yearning to touch appeared in its stead. I smiled, and I was pretty certain I looked like a ravenous mad wolf, my eyes fixed on his lower body. Eager to reciprocate his tender loving care of the last few minutes, I bent over his lap and suckled him, too intoxicated by his taste to worry about my own state of arousal. That's something I never expected to say. Nothing gave me more pleasure than making him soar.

We stayed in our cave for a few hours, making love, talking, dozing off in blissful exhaustion, bodies entwined, and souls merged into one. A thought occurred to me as my eyes drooped close. "Why have people been calling us mates?" I asked, my hand resting on his rock-hard abs and my ear against his heart. "I mean, we're not in Australia or anything."

Fouchard stirred and lifted his head from the rock to peek at me. "You don't know?" He sounded surprised, which in turn surprised me. What exactly was I supposed to know? Then again, I was the master of being the last one to know anything worth knowing. I arched my eyebrows, and he smiled, a languid ever-so-sexy movement of his full lips. "Idiot. People are calling us mates because that's what we are." I still didn't understand it. "Sometimes I forget you lived in the fringes of the magical world. Magicals often have a fated mate, someone the universe, the gods, Mary and Jesus— whoever you want to blame for this—has picked for you to mate for life." That was new. "If you're lucky, you will cross paths with this other half of you. Many of us never meet our mates. We, sweetheart, were two of the lucky ones."

"What do you mean, Naël?"

He slid a hand from my cheeks to my neck in a gentle caress. "You are so thick sometimes, Aiden." Good thing I knew he loved me. "I'm your mate, dummy. Whether you like it or not, you're stuck with me for the rest of your life."

Comprehension slowly dawned on me. Deep down inside, I thought I knew it. This need, this overwhelming love, could only mean one thing; we were meant to be together no matter what. If you told me that before I met Fouchard, I would have thought I'd end up feeling trapped, but now I didn't mind at all. I loved knowing we were connected that way and that those ties would be there forever, as long as we lived.

"I like it," I said, a dazed smile spreading across my lips. "Think about it; we can have this kind of sex for the rest of our lives." I was only half kidding, but my merrow burst out laughing. "I'm serious," I protested.

"Oh, sweetheart, I know you are." He brushed his thumb on my cheek. "That's why it's funny. You're my sweet, sexy, clueless, and oversexed detective." And he planted a wet merman kiss on my lips.

NINE

DANGEROUS LIAISONS

Two days later, I stood by the door at Fouchard's house, Vee tucked under my arm, and watched my lover drive away in an Uber straight into danger. I couldn't be sure of what kind of danger, but I was certain there would be some—either of a sexual predatory type or the more basic type; after all, Alabyron claimed he knew where the deadly duo was, so who was to say he wasn't in cahoots with them?

"You're not worried about my brother again, are you?" Vee turned her freckled face toward me, furrowing her brow. "He will be okay. Have you noticed his muscles lately?" Had I ever! Unfortunately, Alabyron wouldn't miss it either.

"I know he'll be fine, but I can't help but worry

about him." I still had nightmares about the time he was kidnapped by poachers. I gave her shoulders a squeeze. "Let's go inside. I'll take you to school as soon as you're ready."

Vee ran upstairs to grab her things, and I stood in the middle of the kitchen, staring at the walls. The house felt so empty now that my merrow was not in it. It had only been a few minutes, but it felt like an eternity already. My insides were all twisted and knotted, and it would take more than the trust that our "advantage" over the king of the Fae would work to unravel it.

I took Vee to school and then drove to Bicas R Us to start the day. I would pretend everything was just like it always was, even if it killed me—and it probably would. I parked the car by my house and walked the short distance to the coffee shop. As soon as I turned on the lights, my phone rang.

Fouchard!

"Are you keeping your cool?" he asked as soon as I muttered a hello. He knew me too well. "It won't do anybody any good if you are working yourself into a tizzy. I left you with my sister so you need to be the adult and make sure she's not anxious."

I snorted. "I kept it together until I dropped her

off in school, but I can't stop worrying about what may happen, Naël." The knot in my throat made it hard to talk. "Please promise me you are going to be super careful and not go all marine on me. I love that you're so manly, but muscles and attitude don't hold water when it comes to magic." He knew that better than me, but I felt I needed to remind him just in case his testosterone had taken control of his brain cells. He grunted, annoyed. "Promise."

"All right, I promise," he said, letting out a loud exhale. "I won't do anything that will put me in any danger. We have the upper hand this time, Aiden. I'll be fine."

Right, and I was Casanova. "There is no such thing as an upper hand with Alabyron and the likes. Remember that."

We talked for a few more minutes, and then I hung up. Cristina was just walking in when I made a weird noise of frustration. She stared at me, eyes widening. "What the hell, Aiden. You need to take a chill pill."

I dropped to the nearest chair and hmphed. "Why doesn't anyone believe me when I say I have a very bad feeling about this?" I've had premonitions before that came true in one shape or another, and Taz had been warning us with her own. Doing the math didn't add up to anything good.

"I believe you." Taz popped right in front of me out of nowhere, her arms crossed over her generous boobs and a frown on her face. Something had to be up if she had forgotten her wide-brim hat and sunglasses. Even more worrying, she was wearing flats. "Something is definitely off, but I can't pin it down. You might be right about this meeting with the Fae degenerate. Something smells fishy, and it's not your merman."

Cristina turned on the coffee machine and some of the lights in the pastry displays, which, in my worry, I'd neglected to do. "Don't feed the fire, Taz," she said from behind the counter. "The man is already an insane ball of nervous tinder; you fan that fire, and he will go up in flames."

I did indeed feel as if something was burning inside me—it could be acid reflux or some of my still unknown magic flared by all the worry churning in my heart.

"Well, I am going to make an unannounced visit to the Quinta and just hang around a while." I could have kissed her. She could be just as wonderful as she was annoying. "I will let you know if something weird is going on. I can't join them in the tower, but I can skulk around. It's a public place, after all."

"Wait! I hadn't thought about that," I exclaimed, jumping to my feet, my heart taking off running. "The Quinta will be open to regulars, so they can't meet in the usual place in the tower. He'll take him into his chambers instead where no one else is allowed." The idea covered my skin in goose bumps. Naël would be at his mercy. "Fuck. Why didn't we think of that? We could have insisted on a night meeting instead."

Taz laid a hand on my arm. "Calm down. Naël is not affected by his magic. He'll be fine." I couldn't disagree more. I was immune to most magic, yet I'd almost jumped the king's bones that first visit. Fae magic didn't play by the rules of the magical community. "I will be there, watching."

I nodded, grateful for her willingness to help but not in any way relieved. This was going to be a very long day. She vanished the way she had appeared, and I decided I should get busy so I didn't have time to think too much.

Unfortunately, the customer traffic was very light all morning as if mocking me, daring me to worry myself into a state of madness. The hours trickled by without any word from my lover. Taz called a couple of times to assure me nothing suspicious was going on, but nothing short of having Fouchard in my arms would appease me.

When noon came and went without any news from my merman, I began fretting in earnest, and by the time daylight started fading in the horizon, I was in full panic mode. Where was Fouchard? Taz was still wandering the Quinta, but such a long time without any word from him was more than worrisome. I knew something was up.

With my forearms across the top, I bent over the counter and dropped my forehead between my arms. The coldness of the countertop made me shiver—or maybe it was the fear swelling in my heart. "Something is wrong. Something is very wrong," I moaned, the beating of my heart vibrating in my throat.

Cristina brushed a hand on my back. "Stop worrying, Aiden. Naël will be just fine." I groaned again like a disgruntled bear. "Come on, he wouldn't want you to worry this much. He'll call any minute now." I had called several times in the past couple of hours, but the call went straight to voicemail. This was not in itself an indicator of danger since cell service at the Quinta was spotty at best, but the fact that it was almost time to close the store and there were zero signs of life from my merrow was a big, unmistakable red flag.

"Aiden is right." It was Vee, sitting at a corner table, pretending to do her homework. I had picked her up a few hours before and tried to hide the fact I was in a panic from her for as long as I could. I couldn't anymore. Both Cristina and I glanced at her. "Something is wrong. My brother wouldn't leave us all hanging for this long. Something happened." Her tiny voice sounded strangled, and her eyes were suspiciously shiny. Shit. I'd promised Fouchard to keep his sister calm and look what I'd done. I should never be allowed around children. If I had my own, I would be a terrible father, I was sure.

I made a decision. "Cristina, can you take Vee to your apartment? I'm going to go to the Quinta and look for Naël." A brief smile surfaced on Vee's lips. "I will call as soon as I have any news."

Cristina took a step forward and held my wrist. "You shouldn't go alone. Wait, and I will ask Silva to go with you."

"Taz is already there," I said, grabbing my coat from the hook on the wall. "Tell him to meet us there if he can. I don't want to waste any more time."

Cristina nodded, and Vee slid off her chair and ran to hug me. "Be careful, Aiden, and bring my brother back safe, okay?" Fear constricted my vocal cords, so I only nodded and ran my fingers through her hair.

I couldn't remember how I got to the Quinta. It occurred to me that I could have just wished myself there, but we would need a car to drive back when I found my merman, so I did it the regular way. I must have driven on instinct because I didn't remember a single detail of the drive. Taz was waiting for me just beyond the main gates where I wished myself into. Whatever assurances she had given me all day, her eyes reflected the same fear I felt; something terrible had happened.

We left, running uphill toward the inverted tower where the king was normally found. By the time we got there, we were both out of breath and sweating despite the coolness of the autumn night. I knocked and yelled out Alabyron's name until my throat was raw, but he didn't answer.

"I'm going to kill you, son of a bitch. If you touch as much as a hair on my boyfriend's head, I will slice you from head to toe with my nails." Could I even do that? Not sure, but I needed some scary threats more for my comfort than to actually scare off the king of the Fae. "Open this fucking door, now."

A small creature resembling an animal rather than a two-legged Fae came around the corner, hands hidden in his pockets. "His Majesty is not home," he said in a squeaky voice. "He had some business to take care of with the Council. He'll be away for a few days."

I stared at him in disbelief, his yellowish-brown fur covering small eyes that glowed in the dark. "Where's Fouchard? What has Alabyron done to him?"

The creature lowered his eyes and took a step back. "I don't know anything about Fouchard. He left many hours ago." Lies. I could smell them in his stinky breath even from a couple feet away. "He's probably on his way home right now."

I didn't know I could move that fast. In a blink of an eye, I had crossed the space between us and had my hand clenched around the creature's neck so tight, I was sure he couldn't breathe. "Liar. Tell me the truth or I will snap your neck." I had never killed anyone, no matter how angry I was. Even as a detective in DC and having encountered so many criminals, I had never wished to kill anyone. I wanted to do this poor excuse for a living being in. I wanted to tighten my fingers until the bones on his short neck collapsed under the pressure, one at a time. "Tell me the truth or you're dead."

Taz grabbed my arm from behind. "Let him loose, Aiden. He can't talk if he's dead." Wise words from the usually unwise witch. I let out a breath and loosened my hold just enough for the Fae to inhale some much-needed air. "Now, little furry creature, where is Fouchard? This man holding you by the throat will snap you in half if he doesn't hear the truth out of your lips."

The creature coughed and tried unsuccessfully to free himself from me. I wasn't letting him go any time soon. "I don't know." I tightened my grip again, and he choked on his own words. "All right, I'll tell you, I'll tell you." Hate oozed out from my eyes as I threatened him with another squeeze. "He's in the oubliette."

"What? Where's that?" I asked, shaking him. "Where is that? Take us there now."

The Fae looked at me with his beady eyes and gulped. "I can do that, but by now, the merman is dead. He's been under the water for over eight hours."

My heart fell. "He's a merman. Water doesn't

kill him." Despite the protest, deep inside I knew that wasn't the case. "Take us there."

Taz slapped the creature over the head. "Take us there, you poor excuse for a teddy bear, and you better pray he's still alive. For your own sake."

Oh god, please don't let him die. Don't take the one good thing in my life from me. Take me instead.

TEN

FURRY CREATURES AND WATERY GRAVES

The terrified creature scuttled in front of us, constantly throwing worried glances our way. It was a dark night, the moon completely hidden behind dark clouds, and the air heavy with the promise of rain. If panic hadn't filled my chest, strangling me out of breath, I would have felt revitalized, renewed by the overwhelming sense of nature around me. We didn't speak, but the night was full with the noise of our rugged breathing, our hurried steps, our heartbeats. At least we were going downhill, and our bodies were carried by momentum as much as our feet.

I could hear Taz behind me muttering curses under her breath. I had never seen her this angry. It was heartwarming to know her anger sprouted from real concern for my boyfriend, but I would have to think about that later.

The little Fae stopped abruptly, and I just about tripped over him. "The oubliette is here, in the grotto." He pointed at the Grutas do Labirinto—the labyrinth grotto—completely engulfed in darkness. "Inside there is a gallery not accessible to visitors that is much deeper than the others. Your merman is there." He pointed at one of the openings to the grotto.

"You better not be tricking me, asshole." The creature cringed, his whole body tensing up. "Taz, you stay here and watch this creep while I go look for Naël." Taz nodded and grabbed the Fae by the shoulders. "If you can, call Silva. He was supposed to follow me here. Tell him where we are."

"How are you going to see inside those caves? It's too dark, Aiden." She was right, but I had my magic. I had been able to illuminate several dark places before, one even underwater, so that should be no problem.

The one thing I didn't understand was why keep a merman underwater, the one place he would have no problem surviving in. "I know he'll be okay. He's underwater, his own habitat," I said, trying to comfort myself.

The fucking Fae snorted. "You don't know much about merfolk, do you?" I lifted a hand as if to smack him, and he brought his furry hands up to protect his face. "Merfolk can survive in saltwater. Like most marine creatures, they can't survive in fresh water for long. The salt in their bodies will absorb too much water, and then they'll literally explode."

An invisible dagger went right through my heart. What was he saying? Was he telling the truth? I looked at Taz, an unspoken question in my eyes. Taz nodded. "He's speaking the truth. Merfolk can be under fresh water for just a few hours."

Fuck, fuck, fuck.

I didn't have any time to waste. Eight hours had passed since Fouchard had been put underwater in the grotto, according to the furry creature. Since he was not swimming to the surface, they must have anchored him somehow. I waddled into the freezing water in the direction of the dark caverns. I heard Taz wishing me luck, but it all sounded muffled and far away. My mind zoomed in on one thing and one thing only—to get to my boyfriend as quickly as possible and rescue him before he perished in that freezing mossy tomb. With every step, my brain tried to prepare me for the worst, but my heart refused to accept it. Fouchard was strong; he'd find a way to stay alive. He had to; otherwise, how was I supposed to go on living?

After some frantic heartbeats, the floor collapsed under me, and I sank like a rock. Caught by surprise, I swallowed enough water to make me choke. I managed to break the surface and spit out most of the disgusting water before diving in again. This was it, the deep gallery the Fae was talking about. My boyfriend was somewhere at the bottom. I willed lights to materialize inside the water, allowing me to see a few feet in front of me, but the water was so murky even the light couldn't totally penetrate it.

I swam around, looking for him for as long as my lungs would allow it. I had to swim back to the surface a couple of times before I saw it: a large form swaying at the bottom. It was Fouchard, I was certain. The hint of blue told me all I needed to know; the shape was my boyfriend, and he was still alive. His tail would have gone gray had he been dead already. I resurfaced one more time, inhaled as much air as I could, and dove, swimming as fast as I could to the bottom where my man was fighting for his life.

Anger fought for room inside my burning chest.

My tough ex-marine boyfriend was upside down and trussed up like a turkey on Thanksgiving, hands and tail wrapped tightly together with underwater vine. His beautiful brown eyes were closed, bloated, and his dark skin a sickly tone of beige. He didn't have much time. Some of the blue in the velvety scales of his tail had already begun fading. Ignoring the burning in my lungs, I searched for what was anchoring him to the bottom.

It's so damn dark. What do I do?

My thoughts created a few more lights, strategically placed around Fouchard's head, just a few inches off the bottom. I saw it then; the vines imprisoning him were still rooted to the underwater soil and holding him securely down. I wished I had brought a knife, something sharp to cut those vines, but I had not. The burning had turned into ferocious pain. Any other time I would have been scrambling up to the surface, but I couldn't leave him there one more minute. My mind conjured memories from when I had fought with Bob in the Roman galleries a few months back. In anger, I had then produced fireballs capable of obliterating anything in their wake.

I am angry right now. Shit, I'm raging mad. I can conjure them again.

I tried to focus, but the pain in my chest was not making it easy. *For Naël, Aiden. For your love.* I closed my eyes for a second, and when I opened them again, it was there, a bright flame sprouting from my outstretched hand. I could feel its heat, but it didn't burn me. Wasting no time, I aimed the fireball at the roots of the plant, which exploded in a massive ball of dirt, rocks, and water. We were both carried by its force, the power of the explosion forcing the water and soil to pull us up, up until my head broke the surface and I was able to inhale life-giving air. As soon as the stale but welcomed air reached my lungs, I began looking around me, frantically seeking my sweet merrow. He was floating a couple feet away from me, face in the water, his body still wrapped in the vine. I swam to him and slid one arm under his to begin pulling him toward shallow waters. His unconscious body was heavy and hard to maneuver even with the help of buoyancy, but I eventually reached a place in the water where I could stand and walk instead of swimming.

The second I brought Fouchard's inert body out from the caves and into the open air, Taz yelled out my name. I waved at her to say it was indeed me and was shocked when she showed up right next to us, waist-deep in the water.

"Oh my god, Aiden. Is he okay?" Without waiting for an answer, the witch slid her hands under my boyfriend's armpits and pulled him toward the bank. I grabbed his tail but quickly realized we had to switch positions. Taz didn't have the upper body strength to carry such a heavy man. She didn't complain and quickly swapped places with me. Painfully slowly, we made our way to dry land.

Once we had rolled my merman into the dirt path by the artificial lake, I immediately checked for signs of life. "He's breathing." But not well enough to assuage my fears. "Can you go to the car and bring a blanket?" Taz didn't hesitate and disappeared before my eyes. I turned my attention back to my merrow. "Sweetheart, you're going to be okay," I told him, hoping that he could hear me somehow. I tilted his head back slightly and began mouth to mouth. The first few breaths filled my mouth with rotten water that nearly made me retch, but afterward, his lungs seemed to be clear. "Now, don't go getting too excited with my kisses, sweetheart." He didn't react to my attempt at humor. Instead of laughter, I let out a sob, but I wasn't about to give up on him. "Come on, Naël, you have to come back to me, damn it!" I breathed more air into his lungs, but he still didn't wake up. His skin was cold and his lips an alarming tone of blue. "Fuck. Why isn't this working?"

Taz appeared beside me, a blanket in her hands. "Still not responding?" I shook my head, too choked up for words. The witch kneeled on the other side of my boyfriend and covered his bare chest with the small blanket. "He's breathing on his own, Aiden. He needs heat, not air. The cold water of the pond is inside his body, in his cells, freezing him from the inside."

I looked at her for a moment, not completely understanding what she was saying. Freezing from the inside? How is that possible? And more importantly, what could I do to prevent it? I'm not sure how I did it, but I conjured another fireball and set a small bush near us on fire. Taz started, surprised at first, but then, realizing what I was doing, she stood up and went to drop more kindling into the fire. The heat reached us almost instantly, but Fouchard needed to be closer, so I pulled him a few feet closer. I dropped to the ground and stretched along his body, draping my arms and legs over my man, hoping my body heat would help keep him warm. I tucked the blanket around us and shivered as the ice of his body touched mine. Taz was right; he was freezing.

Taz had a sizable fire going before she came to us. "What do I do?" she asked.

"His tail, hold on to his tail," I said. "Wrap yourself around it to warm it up."

She didn't question it and did as I told her. We both held on to Fouchard's body like barnacles holding on to the hull of a sunken ship. I wasn't sure how long we stayed like that, but after a while, my boyfriend's skin warmed up just enough to bring hope back to my heart. I heard a sob and realized it was Taz, still holding on to his tail as for dear life. I would never be able to thank her properly.

"His tail—" Taz started, and I let go of him for a moment to see what she was talking about. Fouchard was slowly turning into his land form, his long brown legs replacing the iridescent blue of his tail. I was not sure if that was good or bad news, but soon there were no vestiges of a merman tail, and the sexy form of my mate was in its place. Taz looked at me, panic in her eyes.

I placed a hand right over his heart and was grateful to feel a strong, steady beat beneath it. His lips were almost their normal dark burgundy, and his brown face had smoothed out, his chiseled jawbones and cheeks full of life again. I let out a sigh. "He's coming back," I whispered, not able to take my eyes out from my hand rising and falling with the rhythm of his breath. I heard a whistling noise and realized Taz had been holding her breath for the past few minutes. I looked at her still holding on to Fouchard's legs as if afraid he would slip away. I smiled. "I hope you don't get too attached to him, Taz," I said, jutting out my chin in the direction of her hands. "He's still mine."

Taz looked down at her own hands and, realizing she was holding the legs of a very naked man, let go of him as if she had been burned. "Fuck. Don't you ever tell anyone I did this," she said, half chuckling. "I will put a curse on you if you do."

"Sorry, I will most definitely tell Naël," I told her, amused by her reaction. There was such relief washing over me, I felt like laughing out loud. "You really didn't want to let him go, did you?" She looked outraged, her face turning bright red under the lights I had conjured, but then burst out laughing. I joined her gladly. Fouchard was still unconscious, but he would be okay. I could feel life running through him where my fingers touched his skin.

"Why wasn't I invited to this party?" We had

been so busy releasing the tension that held us captive for the last hours that we hadn't seen the warlock come around the bend. Silva stood not five feet away, his legs spread apart and arms crossed over his chest. He took in the scene and dropped to his knees by us. "Shit. Is he okay?"

"Now he is," Taz said, "but it was touch and go just a few minutes ago."

I was still laughing when her words hit me with the force of a tornado. The laughter died, caught in my throat by a sob. My man, my life, had almost died in front of my eyes. I threw myself over Fouchard, lowering my head to his shoulder, arms across his chest, and cried against his warming skin.

Alabyron, I will get you for this. I will hunt you down and skin you alive.

This time it wasn't an empty threat.

ELEVEN

THE VOICES IN MY HEAD

Silva was still in the room doing his voodoo on my boyfriend. "Not voodoo, you idiot," he had said to me, ruthlessly ignoring my pain. "I'm going to use magic to try and drain the excess water from Naël's cells. Voodoo is bad, Aiden. What I'm doing is good." Semantics! Whatever he was doing, it'd better work, or I might lose it. God knew I was close enough, out of my mind with worry for my merman who was still unconscious and unresponsive in our bed.

The warlock kicked me out of my own bedroom, claiming I was making him jittery and irritated and thus less capable of focusing on his magic. I took exception to that, but since he was helping Fouchard,

I couldn't in good conscience begrudge him. I sat on the floor, just outside the bedroom, my back against the wall and my fingers interlaced over my knees. My brain was a jumble of unconnected and mostly irrational thoughts. The only clear thing in my mind was the urge to kill the king of the Fae. I wanted to make him pay for what he had done to my merrow.

"I'm going to cut you in tiny little pieces and feed you to the fish in that pond of yours, Alabyron." I had meant to whisper the threat, but it came out more like a scream of hate.

"Why would you do that, Aiden?" I hadn't noticed Taz leaning against the wall a few feet away from me. The witch looked tired, her disheveled red hair framing a face paler than usual. "You kill him, and you're the one who will have to answer to the Council."

I raised my eyes to her. "He is a perverted murderer," I spat out. "Why would the Council intervene?"

"Because their job is to keep the peace and order among our people," she said, crossing the short distance between us and sliding to the floor by my side. "Not an easy job when you have so many different species of magicals. If they condoned revenge, they would have massive chaos on their hands."

I snorted. "Magicals kill each other all the time over the most stupid of reasons."

"Have you ever stopped to ask yourself what happened to them afterward?" No, I can't say I had. My lifelong avoidance of those who, like me, belonged to a group of magical beings had prevented me from being too curious about what happened in their world. "They stand before the Council, and most end up in prison." I was not going to ask where that prison was. "I'd hate for you to end up there as well, Aiden."

I inhaled and exhaled deeply before replying, "You think I can just sit and let Alabyron get away with trying to kill my boyfriend?"

The witch shook her head, her eyes rimmed in red and smudged mascara. "What I'm saying is we don't know yet what happened. In the confusion, we let that furry beast escape, not that I think he knew anything very useful, but he was the best witness we had."

"I don't get you sometimes, witch,' I said, anger swelling inside my chest again. "Why would you be defending that depraved motherfucker?"

Taz ran a palm over her face and groaned.

"Stop being so dumb, Aiden. I'm not defending him. I'm being rational. Something I'm afraid you are not even close to being right now. Someone must keep a head screwed on the right way."

I clenched my jaw tightly until it hurt. I knew I was snapping at the wrong person. Taz had been there with me all along. She had jumped in that water to rescue Fouchard; she had cried and threw herself over my boyfriend's tail to warm him back to life. She was a friend, and the last thing she would do was defend the bastard who had done this. I reached out and closed my hand over hers. "Sorry, Taz. I'm…." Destroyed, broken into a million pieces. I needed my man back from that in-between place he seemed to be at right now, and I had no clue how to do it. It was as if the world was falling apart around me, and there was nothing I could do to stop it.

"I know, I know." She offered me a sad smile. "What I'm saying is that he couldn't have done this to Fouchard without some help. Think about it; Naël is a big guy who is immune to Alabyron's magic. How would the Fae be able to subdue him long enough to tie him down to the bottom of that pond? Fouchard would have kicked his ass." I couldn't argue with her solid reasoning. Fouchard definitely would have beaten the shit out of the gorgeous but wimpy king.

An idea popped into my mind. "Do you think Bob had something to do with it?"

Taz nodded. "Remember how you overheard his mother say he should kill your boyfriend first?" I did remember that conversation between the silly god and his evil mom inside the underground Roman galleries in Lisbon. "I'm thinking that Bob somehow managed to coax Alabyron to his side and planted a trap for your merman."

I made a very accurate impression of a pissed-off bull. "More the reason to kill the bastard." Yeah, my brain didn't work logically when I was emotionally messed up. Taz shook her head and tsked me. "Don't give me that, witch. You know I'm right.'

Cristina appeared around the corner with Vee in tow. "I'm taking her to school," she announced, her eyes searching mine for confirmation or assurance. I had none to give so I just tried to smile for Fouchard's sister's sake. "Then I will go open the store. You stay here as long as needed."

Vee, eyes swollen from crying, took a few hesitant steps toward me. She looked like I felt—in need of a hug and a good cry—so I stood up and opened my arms to draw her in. "He'll be okay, Vee. I know he will," I whispered into her hair. "You go to school and do what you do every day. I will text you every hour to let you know what's going on, all right?"

"I want to stay here, Aiden." She whimpered in my arms. "Let me stay home."

I tugged her closer. "Honey, your brother would kill me if he knew I kept you from school. I don't dare piss him off." My attempt at humor fell flat. "I promise I will keep you informed. There is no point in staying here and worrying yourself sick. In school, you'll be distracted." Planting a kiss on the top of her head, I added, "Be a good girl and do what you know Naël would want you to do, okay?"

She sniffed against my T-shirt but pulled away, her lips contorted and wet. "Okay, but you better let me know." She turned around to join Cristina, but at the last minute, she twisted around. "He should have listened to you, Aiden."

My stomach cramped. He should have. The witch's premonition, my own fears, they all pointed at danger. But I knew how he was, stubborn and strong. I should have been more forceful. I should have made sure he didn't go meet the royal ass. It was my fault. People around me, those I cared about, always got hurt one way or another. It was as if I carried some kind of curse that obliterated anything and everything around me.

Don't be stupid, Aiden. Stop blaming yourself for all the woes in the world.

Fouchard's voice rang loud and clear in my head, and love, anger, frustration, and pain all assailed me at the same time, tearing me apart. Grateful that Vee had left already, I slid all the way back to the ground and cried, my head on my knees. Little, warm fingers curved over the nape of my neck, a small mercy that brought me a measure of comfort. Taz didn't say a word. She sat beside me, her hand still cupping the back of my head in companionable empathy.

An hour later, we were still sitting next to each other, my head now resting on the witch's bony shoulder. I knew I'd be mortified later every time I recalled this moment. I had an image to uphold, one that didn't include accepting the kindness of someone I had viewed as an annoyance just a few months ago. But for now, I was grateful for her company, her warmth. Knowing my mate was lying just beyond that door, still fighting for his life, was painful enough; to feel abandoned and alone all over again would have added pain to injury.

The door creaked open suddenly and I jumped to my feet. "Silva, how is he?" My heart pounded in my ears, half with hope and the other half with fear.

Silva looked exhausted. He had been doing whatever it was warlocks did for more than three hours, and if using magic was as taxing for him as it was for me, he must have been in need of a well-deserved recharge.

"He's still unconscious." Not what I wanted to hear. My shoulders slumped. "I was able to pull all the excess water from his system, but his body was weakened by the struggle to stay alive. He needs time to recoup, but I think he'll be all right."

Panic rose inside of me. "What do you mean 'you think'?" I snapped with misplaced anger. "Is he going to be okay or not?"

Silva's hard eyes fixed on me. "Don't make me punch you again." He growled low in his throat. "I did everything I could for him. Now time will do the rest. His brain was under attack for a long time. We must give it time to bounce back."

My cheeks burned. "I'm sorry. I'm grateful for your help, Silva, really. I'm just worried."

Silva squeezed my forearm, an odd friendly gesture I wasn't used to coming from him. "I know," he said softly. Then he growled again. "That's the only reason I haven't punched the daylights out of you yet. Don't try my patience, Aiden."

Taz suggested we eat something, but I had to be by my man. I watched the two of them go downstairs to the kitchen, opened the door to our room, and walked in. The room was still dark, the curtains drawn tight so as not to attract attention. The warlock's magic was flashy. Literally. Flashes of light sprung from his fingers every time he used a spell. Of course, the windows faced the ocean so the only possible witnesses to the magic performance would have been the seagulls, and I was certain they didn't pose any threat. But Silva didn't want to risk it, so we kept the curtains closed.

Fouchard loved the sun, so I opened them all the way, allowing the warm light of the autumn morning to pour in through the glass. Only then did I dare look at my boyfriend. He was stretched out on our bed, his head supported by a pillow and his lovely naked body covered with our sheets. We had made love in this bed multiple times; it was a place of love, pleasure, and joy. There should have been no room in it for pain and sadness.

I sat on the edge of the bed and watched him.

He seemed to be breathing normally, almost serenely. I pulled my legs on top of the bed and scooted closer to him, laying my head beside his on the pillow and stretching alongside him. "I love you, Naël. Please come back to me. Don't you dare die on me, or I will kill you myself." Even though the swim in the pond had recharged me, I was still exhausted, emotionally drained. The sound of Fouchard's breath lulled me into a near-slumber, somewhere between awake and asleep. All my thoughts charged against me, taking siege of my mind and my heart.

"You're no good, Aiden," a female voice that was both familiar and strange whispered to me. "That's why we left you, your father and I. You were flawed, and I couldn't claim you as my son, the son of a goddess, the result of a forbidden affair."

"But Brother John—Dad—said you did it to protect me," I protested weakly, hating myself for the whiny voice.

Laughter filled my ears. "You're a fool, Aiden. Of course he told you that, but the truth is you are a curse to anyone who dares to be close to you. Look what happened to Vee, what happened to Cristina; twice your lover has been taken and almost killed. Do you really believe it to be a coincidence? That you have nothing to do with it?"

"But I saved them, all three." God, I hated myself for

my pleading voice, the need in my heart, the fear of aban-
donment.

"They should leave you, run far from you." A knife,
sharp and aimed straight at my heart. "You'll end up being
their demise."

"They love me. They wouldn't leave me like you did."
Wouldn't they? What if it was true, that I brought all this
strain of bad luck upon them? Could I stand by and allow
those I loved to suffer because of me? Pain flooded my being,
suffocating me. "I love them."

"You're not good enough, son. You are not nearly good
enough."

I woke up sweating, my heart running one hundred miles a minute and throbbing in my throat as if it had somehow climbed and settled there. I looked at my boyfriend, still lifeless in our bed, and sighed. "I'm no good, Naël. I'm not good enough for you."

With tears rolling down my face, I pulled away from my merman and turned to leave, but his hand shot out to grab my wrist and hold me in place. I turned to him, surprised. He was awake.

"Don't you ever say that again, sweetheart," my merrow murmured in a raw voice. "You and I are mates and good enough for each other. In fact, I would say we are excellent together, and if you ever say that again, I cannot promise I won't whack you over the head." My chin dropped. "Better yet, you say that again, and you'll have to go without sex for at least a couple months."

I laughed, or what it went for laughter at that moment when tears still choked me and the pain caused by the words in my dream still burned in my soul.

My love was alive, awake, and already giving me orders. Everything was going to be all right.

TWELVE

A POKED DRAGON NEVER SLEEPS

"Will you please stop fretting over me? I'm perfectly capable of walking the short distance from the bed to chair." The week of forced rest had not done much to improve Fouchard's mood. I had caught him numerous times trying to sneak out of the bed when his legs were still too weak to hold his body.

"Silva said—"

"I couldn't care less what the fucking warlock said." Yep, his mood was not improving at all. "I'm getting out of this bed right now."

How did the saying go? If you can't beat them, join them? Waving a very reluctant white flag, I gave in and offered my shoulder for support. He waved me away. "Don't make me use my magic on you, Naël. If you don't accept my help, I will bind you to the damned bed." I had no idea whether I could do that, but there was no harm in threats.

He huffed, his legs hanging off the side of the bed. He may still be suffering from the effects of being under fresh water for far too long, but his gorgeous legs hadn't lost their beauty. Bare all the way to his upper thighs, his brown limbs remained as powerful and sexy as ever. My mouth watered.

"Well? Are you going to lean on me or not?" I asked, feigning annoyance the best I could just as my naughty bits twanged with excitement. He grunted and draped an arm over my shoulders. "That's a good boy."

Now standing beside me, he turned his head suddenly and leaning down slightly, he bit my neck, a playful nip with more lips than teeth that caught me by surprise and almost caused me to drop him. I groaned in indignation but, in all honesty, was more than a little aroused. We made it to the armchair by the big windows without any more incidents.

Fouchard peeked outside, where the blue of the ocean stretched as far as the eye could see. "You know I will have to get in the water sooner rather than later, right?" he asked, stealing a glance at me.

"I'm a merrow. I lose my strength if I'm away from the ocean for too long."

I frowned, leaning on the window and facing him. "But you can barely walk, Naël." I had been saying this for days. The longer he was restricted to his bed, the more restless he got, itching to feel the salty waters of the ocean on his skin.

"A dip in the ocean will make me stronger." The usual argument. He could be right, but he could also be wrong, and I didn't want to risk him hurting himself further. "Please, Aiden. I'm desperate." He pretend pouted—in perfect imitation of his sister—and I rolled my eyes. "You know that when I get a bit stronger, we can make love again, right?" Playing dirty, was he? He knew my weaknesses well and obviously wasn't afraid of using them to get what he wanted.

I sighed, crossing my arms over my chest. "All right, so let's do this; I will take you down to the beach, and you can dip your legs in the water for a while. What do you say?"

His face opened into a beautiful smile. "I say, fuck, let's do it." It was as if the sun had landed inside the room. I couldn't resist that smile, the joy in his warm brown eyes. I breached the space between us and kissed him. "That was nice," he said once I pulled away. "But I want more." *Wicked man.* I did, too, but no chance of that until he was fully recovered.

"I thought you wanted to go for a swim," I quipped, stepping back so I wouldn't fall to the temptation of jumping his bones right there and then. "I guess you've changed your mind."

I felt the full blast of his stink eye. "Take me down to the beach. Now!"

"Yes, sir." I mock saluted him and threw him a smile. "Let's go."

The trip downstairs took a lot longer than it should have. Fouchard's legs buckled several times on our way down, and we had to stop to rest. When we finally got to the beach under the house, he seemed to get stronger. I helped him down as he sat at the water's edge, his legs stretched in front of him, waiting for the mild waves to wash over them. My boyfriend's smile kept growing wider every time the bubbling seawater lapped at his feet, creeping up his legs all the way to his fabulous ass. I couldn't take my eyes off him. He was beautiful and vibrant even without his full strength back, his smooth brown skin taut over well-toned muscles, and full kissable lips stretched into the most amazing smile I had ever seen. My mate was perfect.

"What the hell are you doing, fool? Don't be an idiot, and join me, will you?" Yes, he was perfect with one tiny exception—he was no sweet talker. But I was okay with that. In fact, I had learned to love that side of him. It was honest. It was raw and genuine. It was all Naël.

I dropped to the wet sand beside him, my jeans soaking up the saltwater like a sponge. Fouchard's white boxer briefs were also soaked, revealing a part of my mate's body I had a special attachment to. It was very distracting, and my eyes kept flickering in that direction despite my determination not to. My man was still weakened by his near-drowning, and I needed to be less shallow and get my mind out of the gutter. Only I couldn't. I loved my merrow so much. Not just his body either; I loved every inch of him, inside and out, including his often-cantankerous personality. But sitting there near him, watching the material of his briefs clinging to his manly parts was too much of a temptation. Unwisely and totally without my conscious knowledge, my hand found its way to Fouchard's lap. Sometimes I truly believed my individual body parts had a mind of their own.

Fouchard looked at my hand and then raised his eyes to me with a wicked little smile dancing on his lips. "Why, Mr. Mercer, what a naughty boy you are. I thought you said I was still too frail for sex."

I thought of retracting my hand, but I found it to be strangely glued to my boyfriend. I chuckled softly. "It doesn't want to let go."

"It doesn't have to," Fouchard said, the smile spreading to his eyes. His skin had a glow that hadn't been there a few minutes before. The ocean water was performing its magic on him. "Maybe I'm not strong enough for certain things, but I wouldn't say no to a little loving."

Who was I to deny my mate a little pleasure? Without delay, I rolled his briefs down his hips and legs. Wet and clingy, they got stuck around his knees, and after a couple tugs, I gave up and let them be. I had uncovered enough to be able to make my boyfriend fly. I slid my lips around him, loving the moan it drew from his mouth. His wet, warm skin tasted salty as my tongue caressed the length of him. It had been too long. I adjusted my position so I had better access to him, my hand squeezing between his legs and reaching behind so I could tease him with a finger while I suckled him slowly.

"Shit, Aiden, it feels so good." Encouraged by

his words, I doubled my efforts, moving my finger inside him while working on his naughty bits.

It didn't take long before his scream of release echoed in this man-made beach. I watched him as he closed his eyes, head thrown back and hips tilted toward me. I pulled away from him and covered his mouth with mine. His arms came around, and he pulled me down on the sand beside him as the kiss deepened. I ran my fingers across his chest, delighting in the feel of him, hard and soft at the same time.

"How's that for therapy?" I said once our lips separated. My hand was still roaming over his chest, his abs, lower still. I could never get enough of him. "Did you enjoy it?" A totally rhetorical question. One thing, and possibly the only one that I was sure of was my bedroom skills.

He chuckled and nipped at my bottom lip. "There is only one thing you must do." Oh? I wondered what that would be. "For all that's holy, can you pull my briefs all the way off? They're strangling my circulation."

I burst out laughing and did as he asked me. As soon as the undergarment was gone, his legs began their metamorphosis into his magnificent merman tail. He grumbled a sound of relief, and I knew he was feeling much better. I should have given in earlier. Just like I recharged in contact with nature, it made sense he would also grow stronger in contact with his natural habitat.

"Are you strong enough for a swim?" I asked, helping him further into the water. He raised an eyebrow, and I chuckled. "Okay, make it short though. I'll be sick with worry until you come back."

"You're coming with me." It was not a request. He held my hand and tugged me behind him. "Let's swim together for a bit." I wanted to but was afraid he was not strong enough to share his magical breath with me. I didn't want to jeopardize his recovery in any way. As if he could read my thoughts, he added, "I'm fine. A breath is not going to make me any weaker."

Giving up the fight, I stripped off my wet clothes and followed him deeper into the ocean, received his magic with a kiss, and swam into the depths alongside my beautiful merrow.

A couple hours later, upon our return, Fouchard looked like a new man. The glow of his smooth skin was back, his eyes sparkled like round pieces of amber, and his legs could now carry him without problems again. Naked and elated, we made our way to our room, took a shower together—well, a lot more happened than just showering—got dressed, and left the house. We were going to visit the coffee shop I had been neglecting for the past week or so. Vee would still be in school for another couple of hours, so we had time to check out the business and maybe stroll along the *paradão* enjoying the brilliant autumn sun.

As soon as we walked around the corner, we knew something was wrong. There was a crowd gathered in front of the store, not the kind waiting for a seat but curious about what's going on instead.

"Cristina!" I exhaled and set off at a run. *Please, gods, don't let something happen to my friend again.* I was only marginally aware of Fouchard's steps behind me as I began shoving people out of the way so I could enter my shop. Cristina was standing by the counter, leaning against Silva. I sighed in relief and stopped suddenly, my boyfriend crashing against my back. She was okay. Or was she? I noticed her paleness and the way she held on to her boyfriend's arms as if needing something to hold her steady. "Shit! What happened?"

The warlock looked up at me and scowled. "Bob happened, that's what." Anger thickened his voice.

I stepped forward and laid my hands on my friend's shoulders. "Are you all right, amiga?" She was standing on her own two legs, no visible wounds, so I breathed a little easier. "What happened?"

Cristina did look at me then. Her eyes were haunted, and her lips trembled slightly. "Bob was here," she said. "He was looking for you, but when I told him you hadn't been in a week, he started laughing like a maniac and left a note for you." She tipped her head toward the counter. "But before he left, he caused such a commotion, the whole neighborhood came to see what was going on. He may have broken a few tables and chairs."

"Fucker!" I didn't think I could ever hate anyone like I hated that idiotic god. Why couldn't he just let me and my family be? It wasn't as if I was planning on world domination or anything, so why fear me? If he and his mother hadn't been such jerks and plotted to hurt those I loved, I wouldn't even spare them a second thought. As it was, I hated them with every fiber of my being, and that scared the crap out of me.

On top of the counter was a message written in squiggly, almost unreadable script, on a dirty napkin. It read simply: "I hope you're enjoying your 'widowed' life. We are coming for you next." The little fuckturd thought Fouchard had died. I crunched up the napkin in my hand and clenched my teeth so hard a sharp pain shot up my jaw.

I turned back to my friend, trying not to allow the anger I felt to grow into a monster. "Did he hurt you?" One day I was going to make him pay for each and every little scar on Cristina's body.

Cristina freed herself from Silva's embrace and hugged me. "No, he didn't touch me. I'm just a little shaken up, that's all." I held her firmly against my chest. I was sure she could hear my heart beating furiously against her ear. "We'll get him, Aiden. The little asshole has been poking a sleeping dragon. Bad idea."

Ever since I had healed her heart, Cristina and I seemed to have a special bond. Often, she seemed to know exactly what was going on inside me as if she shared my brain or something. I wondered whether, by giving her so much of my energy to save her, I had created some kind of magical connection between us. She knew that inside me there was indeed a mighty flying lizard, one that that god and all the other turds who hurt my family had been goading. Everyone who had read Harry Potter knew you shouldn't tickle a sleeping dragon.

THIRTEEN

KARMA IS A BITCH

Even though the air was much cooler than it had been for the past week and a half, I refused to go inside. The gentle breeze brushed over my exposed skin like a caress, filling me with that titillating sensation that my recharges always triggered. I sat on the patio of my café, legs stretched over another chair, sunglasses covering my eyes, remembering a day like this a few months back when I first met my boyfriend.

It hadn't been an auspicious encounter. In fact, even though the sparks were definitely there, the fact that he seemed bent on offending me didn't quite spell a happy ever after.

Turned out the old saying was right: never judge a book by its cover.

"You look like a lizard stretched out under the sun." The male voice was one that used to rub me the wrong way, but I now had a different opinion of its owner. I cracked an eye open, raising the corner of my lips. "Don't you ever get enough of sunshine?"

I waved a hand dismissively. "Go away, warlock. You're between me and the said sunshine." I closed my eye again and crossed my arms over my chest as if getting ready to take a nap.

The warlock chuckled. It was not an amused chuckle entirely, more like a mixture of annoyance, impatience, disbelief, and a pinch of actual amusement. We had a complicated relationship. "You're such a lazy prick," he said. A chair scraped the cobblestone of the patio floor, and I knew he wasn't going anywhere. "Do you want to hear about what we got on your friend Bob and his mommy, or not?"

My eyes flew open, and I sat up straight, letting my legs drop to the floor. "You have news? The real kind?" I leaned in, supporting my elbows on my knees.

He humphed, a sideways smile lifting the corner of his lips. "I will never understand American fascination with fake news, but yes, this is real." He licked his sensual lips. The man was yummy. Pre-Naël I would be all over that, but I had quit my slutty ways for good. "What exactly is fake news? Isn't that an oxymoron? If it's fake, then it's not news. You Americans are so fucking weird." He shook his head, and I had the sudden urge to burst into laughter. Who knew that the warlock could be funny?

"Can you please keep your opinions about my compatriots to yourself?" I said, not bothering to look offended. "Are you going to share the news or not? What did you find out?"

Silva waved at Cristina, who was serving some customers inside the store. "We have Alabyron in custody."

I almost fell off the chair. "What? Where is he?" I wanted to make a fine powder with his bones and a new backpack with his skin.

"Relax, he already got his comeuppance," the cop said. I was impressed by his knowledge of English to come up with that word when I could still barely have a conversation about the weather in Portuguese. "We found him wrapped up like a Christmas gift at the bottom of a hole in the *serra*. Apparently, he made a deal with the wrong god."

"Bob got him?" I hated that I might actually

owe a debt of gratitude to the idiot demigod, however small.

"It looks like it," Silva said, leaning back in the chair. "Alabyron agreed to lure Naël to the Quinta. In exchange, Bob promised to make any allegations of the Fae's wrong doings disappear. It didn't quite work out the way he was hoping."

Would it be terrible if I cackled like a hag? The image of the Fae asshole being double-crossed, tied up, and thrown into a pit made me almost giddy. "As happy as I am to know that karma screwed Alabyron, we still don't know about Bob's whereabouts."

"Actually, we do. Alabyron overheard a conversation between mother and son while they were taking him up the mountain." I took off my sunglasses so I could better see the much-anticipated news slipping from his mouth. "They were headed to Évora."

That was unexpected. What in heaven's name was there that would interest the deadly duo? Because Évora was in a rather arid area of Portugal, the magical community was very sparse there, most of the magicals preferring the coast or wooded areas of the country. "Why Évora?"

"They talked a lot about the Capela dos Ossos,

the Bone Chapel," Silva continued. "Alabyron says they believe the chapel is some type of fountain of power."

"What do they need power for? They seemed powerful enough to me." That's all we needed: a crazy god and his psychotic mom sucking in more power than what they already had.

"That I don't know. But at least we have a location for them." Silva perked up at the sight of Cristina heading our way. "What are you going to do?"

I twisted my nose and thought for a moment. "Better talk to Naël first, but I will most likely go to Évora."

Cristina threw herself on the warlock's lap and planted a kiss on his lips. It made me gag a little. "Did you tell him?" she asked once she came up for air. She had lungs to compete with merfolk.

"What are you talking about?" I asked, not too happy with her tone of voice. She had a little smirk on her face, as if she had some deep secret she hadn't shared with me. "What did you do now?"

Silva straightened on the chair, and my friend rearranged herself on his lap. I cringed, thinking of what all that butt movement was doing to the cop. I suddenly felt like a voyeur of sorts and had an urge to flee.

"We were going to save the news until we could all be together, but it's killing Cristina, so we'll tell you now." Shit. This didn't bode well. My anxiety must have shown on my face because Silva added, "What's that face for? Nothing bad happened."

"You do look like a cat who just ate a canary," I told him. "And my amiga looks a little too excited. What are you two up to?"

Cristina bent over and slapped my knees. "Parvo, sempre desconfiado. Why are you always so suspicious of everything?"

"Have you met me? Aren't you familiar with my life story?" She stuck her tongue out at me. The more she hung out with young Vee, the more childish mannerisms she picked up. "Well, what is it? You might as well do the Band-Aid thing and spring it on me already."

She glanced at Silva for a moment, a smile on her lips, and then looked back at me, extending her left hand in my direction. I stared at her hand and then at her, confused. She stretched her hand further. "Look!"

She wiggled her fingers in front of me, and that's when I saw it. Dumbfounded and gaping, I gawked at her and then her finger again. A huge diamond ring adorned her otherwise bare hand. "What the hell does this mean?" Yes, I was having a serious brain fart.

Her voice was more like a screech. "We're engaged, stupid." I opened my eyes so wide, they hurt. "A simple 'congrats, my friend, I'm so happy for you' would be totally appropriate just about now." Her expression of excitement had turned into a glare.

"I… I…." I had been attacked by stupid. I was not sure how to feel. Was I happy that she was going to get married and obviously excited about it, or was I upset and afraid Silva was not the right man for her? I threw her another look and met her fiery eyes. "Of course I'm happy for you. I'm just surprised, that's all."

She jumped to her feet and wrapped her arms around my neck. "Please be happy for me, really happy," she whispered in my ear. "I love Tó and he loves me."

I gulped and belatedly encircled her with my arms. "I am. I'm happy you're happy, Cristina. I swear I am." I was. I wanted her to be as happy as a human could ever be, but even though my respect for Silva had grown exponentially in the last couple of months, the fact remained that he was a powerful warlock and Cristina a sweet regular. It gave me pause.

I looked over her shoulder in Silva's direction and sought his eyes. "You better be good to her," I told him, "or I will be coming after you." Even though said jokingly, it was a real threat. He knew it too.

After I recovered from the shock, we celebrated the occasion with my secret stash of coffee and giant ice cream cones from the store around the corner. Before my friend went home earlier than usual, I promised not to tell Vee yet. Cristina wanted to break the news to her herself, but she gave me permission to share it with my boyfriend. Good thing she did because I didn't think I could keep secrets from him anymore.

As soon as he came to pick me up that evening, I glanced anxiously at the back seat, looking for Vee. She wasn't in the car. "Where's the munchkin?" I asked, sliding into the passenger seat.

"I dropped her off at Cristina's. What's going on with her? She sounded weird on the phone." For such a cranky merman, my man was certainly very perceptive.

I put on the seat belt and hid a smile. "Are you

ready for this?" Naël raised his eyebrows and tilted his head. "Cristina and Silva just got engaged."

Had I looked like that when they told me the shocking news? I had to squelch the laughter bubbling up my throat as Fouchard's face contorted into a weird mix of surprise and horror. With his forehead furrowed and mouth agape, my mate stared at me, weird sounds that didn't quite form into words coming from his lips. I finally allowed laughter to go free.

"Engaged? Really?" he finally said, a comical frown on his face. "How did that happen?"

"Well, sweetheart, when a woman and a warlock love each other, the warlock buys her a diamond ring and pops the question." I couldn't help it. Not even two hours ago I had been him, flabbergasted and speechless, but now I was on the other side, and it was funny. I chuckled. "You should see your face."

He shook his head. "And you're okay with this?"

I shrugged, sobering up. "I guess. As long as he treats her the way she deserves, I'm okay with it. I just want her to be happy. After everything she went through this summer, she deserves a fairy tale."

"Cristina is not the fairy-tale type of girl," Fouchard said, putting the car into gear and moving out of the parking space. True, she wasn't, but she was in love, and love changed people. I knew that intimately. Less than a year ago, I would have never believed I would be as much in love as I was now. I'd changed my ways dramatically, from man slut to a one-man dude. Love was like a miracle cure for a lot of things.

"I wasn't a one-man kind of guy either, and look at me now." Afraid of what I may see in his face and a bit embarrassed by my admission, I turned my face to the window and stared blankly at the passing scenery.

Warmth covered my hand laying on my lap. I looked at Fouchard's big hand over mine and then raised my eyes to meet his. What I saw in them filled my heart with joy. "You're right. We are living our own fairy tale."

I chuckled softly and lifted his hand to my lips to kiss his knuckles. "Except I'm no princess, and you are no Prince Charming."

He smiled, only half looking at the road, which should have scared the crap out of me, but love was unreasonable and illogical. "Oh, I don't know," he whispered, taking my hand to his lips. "I'm sort of like the Little Mermaid, and you could easily be the prince." That gave me the giggles; Fouchard was no

Little Mermaid, and I was most definitely not a prince. "And we will get our happy ever after."

Now all I wanted to do was make him pull over to the side of the road and have my way with him, but it was still light outside, and it was a busy road. No way people wouldn't notice my lovely merman and I involved in something better suited for the bedroom—or the love cave, or that corner of the convent…. Okay, so there weren't that many places I wouldn't pleasure my man, but the side of the road seemed a bit too public.

"I want to show you how much I love you, so drive fast and try not to kill us. These pants are shrinking fast." His laughter filled the car, and I watched him, bewitched by his handsome face, the strong neck I was dying to run my tongue over, the luscious lips I wanted to be closed around my favorite body part.

Life was good.

FOURTEEN
MEET ME IN THE CLOSET

I was quickly learning that traveling when you had a child was not such an easy thing to do. Fouchard and I had to put a contingency plan in place for Vee while we traveled south to Évora in search of Bob, the idiot from India. He certainly shamed a whole nation of wonderful people and rich cultural patrimony.

Once I caught him, I would probably be hailed as a hero in that part of Asia.

Cristina had stepped up as usual and offered to take care of the young mermaid while we were gone. Vee hadn't stopped giggling and shrieking like a banshee since finding out about my friend's engagement. I could have sworn I saw Silva put in some earplugs before entering the apartment the morning of our departure.

"We'll bring you a skull or something equally morbid," I had promised my friend on departure.

She frowned and groaned in disgust. "Bring me some *trouxas de ovos* or, even better, *queixadinhas de Évora*." She licked her lips as if tasting whatever those things were. I would have to find them and hope they were something I could actually bring back with me. By the looks of it, she'd obviously murder me if I didn't.

We had been on the road for almost an hour, my eyes blurring from the lack of interesting sights to look at. Highways were all the same no matter where you were, very convenient but extremely boring. I had nodded off a few times already, and now my bladder was begging for mercy. A rest stop appeared on the horizon just in time. "Let's stop, Naël." He had given me the same kind of glare he always gave Vee when she was asking for something unreasonable. "It's either that, or I'll piss all over your nice leather seats." He immediately put on the turning lights and veered off the next exit.

Rest stops in Portugal were interesting buildings that often reflected the local traditional architecture.

This one was just plain boring, a squat building displaying the usual whitewashed walls and red rooftop but nothing else to distinguish it from any other. Not that I stopped to admire or criticize the architecture. I was on a mission, so as soon as Fouchard parked the car, I hit the ground running in a perfect imitation of the Roadrunner of cartoon fame. I may even have beeped on my way to the bathrooms.

My merman was sitting at a table, two espressos and a small plate of *salgadinhos*, savory pastries full of goodness, in front of him. "That was the longest piss in the history of mankind," he said, a mischievous smile on his lips. "I thought I may have to come and help you."

I liked that idea. "Why didn't you?" I winked and sat next to him, my hand instantly settling on his upper thigh.

His lopsided smile curved further. "Bathrooms are not hygienic enough for the kind of help I wanted to offer." My naughty bits twitched. *Damn, Naël, what's that magic you have?* "Too many germs."

"But going at it in a dirty cave is not?" The memory of what we had done in that small hole in the ground at the convent made me swell uncomfortably. *Fuck.* Now I'd be uncomfortably horny for the rest of the trip. "Is it humid in here?" Fouchard raised a brow. "Because my pants just shrank a couple sizes."

My boyfriend burst out laughing. "Unless you want to get busy under this table, that will have to wait until we get to the hotel room." As to emphasize the meaning of his words, he gave me a little squeeze where I needed release. That didn't help at all.

I began a frantic search for a hidden place, anywhere just big and private enough where I could show my merman how much I wanted him right then. Nothing came into view. I sighed, not resigned at all. "I guess *salgadinhos* will have to do." My evil boyfriend laughed.

Just wait until I get you alone. You won't be laughing then.

In my mind, I could hear him clearly, moaning and begging for more.

Shit, Aiden, think of the food on the plate instead.

Annoyed, I grabbed a croquette and bit half of it off with enthusiasm. Whoever decided to mold a food item into a phallic shape must have been either an idiot or oblivious because biting down on that cylindrical brown pastry as aroused as I was did not help matters. Much to my surprise, though, my merrow stood up suddenly, grabbed me by the hand, and pulled me away from the table into a small door I hadn't noticed before. It was unlocked, and it opened into a small storage space where the staff kept their cleaning supplies. There wasn't much space, and even as Fouchard took hold of my T-shirt and pulled me roughly against him for a kiss, we tripped and almost fell on a series of buckets and brooms. I shoved the door closed and turned around just long enough to lock it from the inside. The place was darker than a starless night, but who cared? I could feel, taste, smell—that's all I really needed.

Fouchard pulled me again into a fierce kiss that bruised my lips and sent me soaring. While our lips and tongues were connected, my hands were busy too, freeing my man from his T-shirt and unfastening and pulling down the jeans to his ankles. My boyfriend's fingers snagged my hair, pulling gently while he traced my lips, my chin, my neck with his tongue as my hand moved between us to clasp his arousal. The fire inside me was roaring, a beast fighting for release.

I moved down his body, using my lips and my tongue to trail kisses from his neck, chest, and abdomen down to his hardness. I slipped my lips over him and worked on his desire, hard and furious, putting my tongue and teeth to good use. He was quiet at first, his hands closed on my hair at the back of my head, pulling me closer, asking for more in that doggoned controlled way of his. I wanted— no, I needed him to lose control. I needed him to holler in pleasure and beg me for more of what I did best: loving him. So I spun him around, spread his legs with my feet as wide as his jeans still stuck around his ankles would allow, and for lack of any lube, suck on my finger before slipping it inside him. He groaned and tilted his ass toward my hand in offer or maybe demand—with my boyfriend, it was always a blurry line. I obliged and moved my finger inside him in small circles, in and out.

I was close to erupting like an awakening volcano, but I wanted him to scream, yell in total abandon and delight. I bent my other arm around his hips and clutched his hard shaft in my hand. We were past gentle. I worked him hard, first with my hands and then, burying myself inside him with a low moan. Things began falling around us as we rocked faster and faster against one another. People would be wondering what was causing such a racket, but we were beyond caring. Determined not to climax before my mate did, I gritted my teeth, holding on with all I had while sliding my hand up and down along his length. When I thought I couldn't hold any longer, he exploded in my hand with a scream that did me in. While he was still spilling into my hand and whatever we were leaning against, I filled him inside with my seed. I let go of him and clutched him around the waist, wanting to get even closer, needing to fill every inch of him with me.

"Está tudo bem ai dentro?" Someone knocked at the door, voice worried and wondering if everything was okay inside. We both chuckled, still connected, still trembling in the aftermath of our climax. There was more frantic knocking, and we realized we better collect ourselves before we were caught with our hands in the cookie jar, so to speak. I felt around for one of the cleaning rags I'd spotted when we entered the closet and wiped ourselves clean the best we could in the dark, hoping we had gotten rid of all evidence of our activities.

When we opened the door, and much to my mortification, there was a small crowd outside waiting to see who the crazy people in the closet were and what exactly they were doing. "Ironic, isn't it?" I whispered to Fouchard as we walked out of the restaurant, more than a little flustered but not exactly embarrassed. "I've never been in the closet until now."

My boyfriend laughed, draped an arm over my shoulders, and pulled me against him as we crossed the parking lot to our car. "It was epic. I may be a little sore later though," he said, his lips brushing my earlobe and making me shiver. "What came over you?"

"Just my god genes kicking in, I guess." It was a joke, of course. There was nothing godly about me. *He* had come over me. Being with him was the best, most effective aphrodisiac in the world. "I'm amazing, am I not? How lucky are you, having a lover like me?"

I was expecting him to say something snarky, but instead, he squeezed my shoulder and kissed my temple. "I'm the luckiest man in the world."

FIFTEEN

FLESH AND BONE

THE MEMORIES OF OUR INTENSE ENCOUNTER IN that closet kept me going for the rest of the drive. It didn't take more than forty-five minutes to arrive in Évora but another half hour to find our hotel because we kept driving the wrong way and having a hard time finding our way back. The fact we were constantly touching each other and taking our eyes off the road might have had something to do with it. Eventually, and after stopping a million times to ask for directions and being given the crazy-Americans stare many more times, we found ourselves a parking spot right in front of the hotel and a magnificent but rather out-of-place Roman monument.

"What in heaven's name are these ruins doing

in the middle of a town?" I'd been in Portugal for almost two years but hadn't traveled much out of Lisbon's suburban areas. The Roman temple, only half standing, was a sight to be seen, however incongruent.

"The Temple of Diana," my forever helpful boyfriend said while removing our suitcase from the trunk. "Leftovers from the times of the Romans and one of the very few standing witnesses to their civilization this side of Europe."

It gave me the shivers thinking that I was standing by a building that dated back at least two thousand years. Sure, it had gone through some restoration, but its power and magnificence were still alive and well in the straight lines of its tall columns and the elaborate Corinthian capitals topping them. I whistled. "Beautiful."

Fouchard came from behind me and planted a kiss right below my ear. "*You* are beautiful," he whispered. And like a schoolgirl, I blushed with pleasure. Sappy, I knew. Sue me!

Évora was crawling with churches and other religious structures. The hotel was in a building that was once part of a monastery, a fact that made me feel at home, considering we had spent so much time in another one in Sintra. Granted, this one was still in perfect condition, and the monks who once dwelled in this one were obviously not as bent on being humble as the druid monks, but it was still a monastery. We checked in and were led to a suite opulently decorated. Yes, definitely not the humble kind of monks had lived here.

The room was divided into two sections plus a bathroom. I wandered around, staring at the ceilings of the living room part of the space, awed by the walls and high arched ceilings, richly decorated with murals in tones of gold. From the highest part of the ceiling hung a crystal chandelier. Not my kind of decor, but still gorgeous. The bedroom was much plainer by comparison. Instead of murals, the walls were covered in golden yellow wallpaper and furnished with a simple bed, an armchair, and a dresser with a TV on it. Curious, I peeked inside the bathroom and was disappointed to find only a smallish bathtub in it —no way we would both fit in it together.

"Are you planning on staying long?" The bellboy was still standing by the door with his hand discreetly opened in front of him. His English was surprisingly smooth.

Fouchard dropped the suitcase he insisted on carrying by the side of the bed and slapped a few

Euros on the man's palm. "Just a couple days." We hoped. I was not looking forward to staying long in a landlocked city, and I was sure neither was my merman boyfriend. "Thank you for your help. Is there a restaurant on site?"

The man pocketed the money and smiled. "Yes, it opens for dinner at seven," he said. "Will that be all, sirs?"

I almost burst out laughing at the formality of his words, but Fouchard held it together. "Yes, thank you. We'll rest a while before dinner." Translation: we would make crazy monkey love all over the suite and work up an even larger appetite than we already had. The man left, and my boyfriend closed the door behind him before turning to me and wiggling his eyebrows like one of the Marx Brothers. "Any ideas on how to pass the next couple hours?"

I dropped to the edge of the bed, testing the soft covers and mattress. "We could go check out the Temple of Diana," I suggested with a wink. "Those Romans were fantastic architects."

He let out a loud laugh, throwing his head back. "You know what else was fantastic?" he asked, sitting next to me. I shook my head innocently.

"What we did in that closet. Think we can do it again?"

I pounced, catching his lower lip with mine and pulling it gently with my teeth. "Hell no." He started, holding the side of my arms and pulling me away to look at me. "We can do so much better now that we have a soft mattress, carpeted floors, and no buckets and brooms to fight with." Comprehension lit his face, and he yielded back into my arms and lips. My mind was already reeling with ideas of what we could do.

Almost three hours later, we walked together along the open corridors that went around what used to be one of the monastery's cloisters, lined with comfortable seats. We had taken separate long baths that required some extra hands for lathering and rinsing nevertheless, and we were now squeaky clean even in spots no one could see. I reminded myself to thank Bob for supplying the opportunity before I killed the bastard.

Dinner in the beautiful dining room was delicious and long, considering we had built quite an appetite, with many different choices of dishes. I was stuffed like a turkey by the time we left the restaurant. After talking to the monks in Sintra before we left, we had decided to visit the Bone

Chapel at night, after it was closed to visitors. We would have to figure out how to gain entrance, but we were nothing but creative when it came to doing things we probably shouldn't.

We explored the Roman temple first, trying to digest all the food we had inhaled. It wouldn't do to face the small but powerful demigod with such a full gut and not being able to move properly. I wasn't going to lie; touching stone that had also been touched by people over two thousand years ago was almost as thrilling as making love—maybe not to my boyfriend but certainly to others of the many lovers I had before him.

"You look about to have an orgasm," my mate said a bit too loudly. Several tourists still lingering around turned their heads to us. He lowered his voice. "I'm a bit jealous. Should we take a small rock with us as an aphrodisiac?"

I snorted. "Sweetheart, you are better than a two-thousand-year rock, trust me." He crouched beside me and caressed one of the stones I was diligently wooing. I could have sworn I felt his fingers on my body as he brushed them slowly over the rugged rock. I may have moaned. "If you continue touching this slab like that, I will orgasm indeed." Was this another one of my endlessly developing magical talents? Or was it the love and lust for my man creating this illusion?

Fouchard looked at me, his brows furrowing. "Really? You can feel this?" As to demonstrate, he ran the tip of one finger along a particularly deep crack in the rock, and I startled. I could feel his touch down my spine and between my butt cheeks. Holy hell, what was this beautiful new torture? My boyfriend's eyes widened as I groaned with pleasure. "Fuck me!"

The expression of surprise on his face was hilarious, but I was tingling too much to laugh. "Keep this up and I will. I don't care who's watching."

He pulled his finger away from the rock, a smile on his face. "That's new," he said, holding on to his own hand as if afraid to move it.

I shrugged, still feeling the throb of building pleasure in my lower body. "I'm a bottomless fountain of strange and wondrous magic." Bitterness tinged my words. As fantastic as this new gift was, it was yet another reminder of my origins, the product of a powerful druid mating with a goddess. A pair of very powerful creatures who didn't think twice about abandoning their spawn. Okay, I was willing to acknowledge that maybe they did indeed think twice but they still did it in the end. Same difference.

We lingered until all the tourists were gone, and the whole town was drowned in silence. It was eerie. Back home, there was always movement or some sort of noise, even if it was just the sound of the waves hitting the sand and the rocks. Here there was only silence and stillness. Even the air wasn't moving. I shivered. "Let's get this over with," I said, holding on to my mate's hand. In the silence, my voice sounded strangely loud. I shivered again. "I want to go home as soon as I can."

What did people do before GPS? Oh right, they used paper maps and had to use their map skills to find their way around. I muttered a silent prayer of thanks we had our smartphones and followed the instructions until we faced the entrance to yet another monastery, this time a Franciscan one. Everything was closed, and the only light came from the spotlights illuminating the main entrance and a few other spots along the white walls of the building. How were we going to enter this place without sounding some alarms? I listened for a moment, not sure what I was hoping to hear—the thread of a conversation or the distant sound of footsteps. Fouchard stood quietly by my side, a solid wall of muscle and comfort. After a few minutes, I thought I heard something, but I couldn't be sure what.

I sighed. "Damn it. If they are in there, they're very quiet or asleep." Or not there at all. Just because they wanted to get something from the chapel didn't mean they were staying inside it. For all I knew, they could be staying in the room next to ours at the *Pousada*. Wouldn't that be the irony to end all ironies? "Let's look around and see if there's a window opened." I knew there wouldn't be. Who was crazy enough to leave windows or doors unlocked in a sixteenth-century building full of art and religious treasures? Sure enough, after a few rounds, we gave up. "Right. There is only one way in."

Fouchard grabbed my arm to stop me. "No way. You are not going in there on your own." Shit. He had guessed I was going to do my wish-upon-a-star trick and teleport inside the chapel. "Too dangerous. You know that." I also knew that I would be more at ease knowing my merman was out of danger. The last time I had faced the Hindu ass, I had almost turned on my own boyfriend accidentally. Not to mention the time Cristina was the unintentional victim of one of Bob's attacks.

"It's the only way, Naël," I told him, turning to face him. "I will just take a look to see if they are there and if there's any indication they got something out of the chapel. I won't fight him. Simply a reconnaissance mission."

My mate shook his head and held on to my arm tighter. "No." He rarely used this authoritative tone with me. His mouth was closed tightly into a thin line, and even in the dim light, I could see his jaw muscle clenching. "You are not going in there alone. There has to be another way."

I hated myself for what I was about to do, but there was no other way. "Okay, I won't," I said, reaching out for a kiss. As our lips touched, Fouchard dropped his hand from my arm. It was now or never. I closed my eyes, visualized being inside the building, and without any delay, I was. I could almost hear Fouchard curse inside my head. Our connection had been getting stronger and stronger, and I could now guess what he felt more often than not. I knew he wasn't happy, but neither was I. I didn't like tricking the man I loved.

I looked around me, but it was too dark. The light of the moon coming through the windows was not nearly enough, so I cautiously wished some lights into existence. The dim glow didn't allow me to see very far, but I could at least move around without tripping over or crashing into things. I came upon a large square doorway supported on both sides by columns. There was some writing over the top frame, but I couldn't make out what it said, so I wished one of my lights to hover closer to it. Immediately I wished I hadn't done that. I didn't know that much Portuguese, but I knew what "We bones that are here wait for yours" said. *Not if I have anything to say about that.*

Shaking off the idea, I passed under the doom and gloom words into the chapel proper. What I saw gave me the willies; every inch of that chapel was covered in human bones. Every. Inch. Skulls, tibias, femurs, finger bones, and whatever else surrounded me. The floor felt smooth. I looked down to check out the tiles but found tombs instead. There were monks buried under the surface of that freaky chapel. All over it.

I gritted my teeth to prevent from screeching like a child in terror and made myself take a few more steps toward whatever was on the right side of the space. I walked straight into an invisible barrier —or what I thought was invisible. On further exam-ination, I realized it was just a Plexiglas barrier, undoubtedly there to prevent the tourists from trespassing too close to the walls, which I guessed after so many centuries were probably pretty brittle and fragile. Just behind it, almost within reach of my arm, there were two glass cases with something dark inside. I couldn't see what it was, and I was afraid of allowing my lights to wander too far from me and give Bob and his mother the right cover to get me. So instead, I wished myself on the other side of the glass, walked closer to the cases, and almost jumped out of my skin; inside the cases, there were two desiccated bodies, an adult and a child.

What kind of morbid assholes were these monks?

I willed my heart to slow down and took a couple more steps toward the third erect structure in that small space. I couldn't tell exactly what it was; it looked vaguely like a tomb of sorts, but it was far too small to hold a body unless it was that of a child, but judging by the poor kid whose corpse was laid bare inside one of the glass boxes, these monks preferred to leave bodies and body parts scattered around. I'd have to check online and see if I could figure out whether that thing was possibly the reason why the deadly duo was in town.

Speaking of which, where in heaven's name were those two? The place was too quiet; the silence of the dead, I guessed. All I could hear was the click-clack of my soles hitting the stone tombs beneath me. Satisfied that they weren't anywhere in the chapel, I decided it was time to hightail it out of that creepy place. We'd be back tomorrow during the day when I wouldn't be alone with all those dead people. I shivered one last time for good measure and wished myself next to my beautiful merman.

He was a sight for very sore eyes, even with the angry scowl on his face. I immediately wrapped my arms around his neck and brought his face down for a kiss.

"What's that for?" he asked afterward, rubbing his lips. I had been a little rough, I guessed. But I was so happy to see him again after all that death inside.

"Let's go back to the hotel, Naël, and let me assure you and myself that we are much alive, unlike those people in the chapel." He looked at me as if I had told him I was in love with a female. "A story for after I make love to you all night."

I felt better already.

SIXTEEN

THE POWER OF THREE... OR FOUR

I keep my promises, and I take the job of pleasing my merman very seriously, so the next morning found me sated but exhausted. It had been a magical night. I dragged myself out of bed to make some coffee for both of us. My boyfriend was still sleeping and, while the coffee was brewing, I stood there watching his bare chest rise and fall with his breath, the stoic lines of his face smoothed out by the peace of slumber. *I love you so much.* I had never thought I could love like this. Or be loved. But there we were, living the fairy tale.

"Stop staring at me like that. You're freaking me out." My lovely man spoke with his eyes still closed. I loved his grumpiness.

Coffee cups in hand, I sat on the edge of the

bed and handed him one. "Aw, I know you love when I gawk at your manly beauty." He opened his eyes and gave me an evil glare but took the cup. "Ready for a day of fantastic adventures in the world of the very dead and bony?" The memories of last night's excursion into the morbid chapel made me shiver.

His hooded eyes smiled along with his lips, a naughty curve to that delicious kissing machine. "Why go to the chapel when we have everything we need here?"

"What are you talking about?" He'd lost me.

"A bone-er?" Aw, my cantankerous merman was making a dirty joke. Naughty indeed. I laughed and planted a kiss on his nose. "You can do better than that." Yes, I could, and so I did. A few times until I spilled the damned coffee all over the sheets.

We had breakfast in the cloister under a shady canopy of vines that kept the patio cool even though summer hadn't quite left the area yet. There was an aura of serenity over the hotel that made me a bit complacent. I had a job to do. While we enjoyed our croissants and sandwiches, I googled the chapel, trying to find more information about that structure inside. "Ah! It's a reliquary," I exclaimed.

"The whole fucking place is a reliquary." He wasn't wrong. The article claimed that the bones from up to three thousand people had been used in the construction of the chapel. "What's so special about the bones inside the stone box?"

"No one knows exactly who the bones belonged to, but legend has it that they were relics from St. Francis." My voice drifted off as I kept reading the article. St. Francis was better known for his love of animals and being a stickler for poverty, shunning all worldly luxuries and comforts. "Wait! In a time when the Crusades were going full-blown, our friend Francis managed to convince a Muslim sultan to let him preach Catholicism in his lands."

Fouchard took a long sip of his orange juice. "So what? He was a good diplomat and salesman."

"He achieved something that was almost impossible at the time. Christians and Muslims were at war, and there is no way a sultan would authorize a Catholic priest to try and convert his people." I slipped the phone into my pocket and grabbed another sandwich. The bread was crusty on the outside and soft on the inside, the butter decadent, and the cheese heavenly. It was the third one I stuffed my mouth with. "Maybe St. Francis was a magical, and Bob believes that he can soak in some of his power by doing whatever with the bone fragments in the reliquary." We had a theory at least.

Fouchard called his sister, and I sat next to him, my hand on his upper thigh and eavesdropping on the conversation as I always did, now that I knew how to use this skill of mine. "Tell me you're behaving like a proper mermaid." *Wrong thing to say, my love.* What I had seen of mermaids so far was not all that well-behaved. "Are you doing as Cristina says?"

"I'm doing just fine even though I'd be doing better if you had taken me with you guys." I could almost see her, arms crossed in a pout. "You keep promising me you will take me on a trip, but you never do."

I felt my boyfriend tense up. "This is dangerous, Vee." For a child who had been kidnapped and almost killed, she didn't seem to have a keen sense of danger. "I will take you on a trip once things settle down and we can enjoy a relaxing time together." In separate rooms. The last time we had to share sleeping accommodations, I hadn't been able to touch my man for days on end.

"You always say that, but I bet you're having a good time anyway." She was not far from the truth. As long as I had her brother with me, even the bad times turned into something good. I could hear her stomping her foot. "I'm so mad at you, always leaving me behind."

The tight line of Fouchard's lips told me he felt as guilty as he was angry at his sister for having yet another meltdown about things he couldn't control. My heart filled with guilt too; after all, if it weren't for me and my capers, Fouchard could be leading a quiet life besides the young mermaid he loved so much.

I intervened, taking the phone away from him. "Don't be mad at your brother, Vee. He's here to protect me, you know that." She humphed on the other end. "When we come back, I will buy you every mermaid accessory we can find in that favorite store of yours. What do you say?" It was slightly shameful that I was trying to buy her forgiveness, but I couldn't stand knowing she was angry at Fouchard because of something that was really my fault.

Fouchard opened his mouth to protest, but I raised my hand to his lips. He groaned in frustration.

"Okay, I know he's there to help you out, Aiden," she said, more warmth in her voice. "I know he's your boyfriend and all, but he is also my brother, and I miss doing things with him." *Ouch. Knife straight to the heart, Vee.* "Besides, I love you too and also want to do things with you."

Fouchard took the phone from my hands. "When we get back, we'll go on a weekend together, okay?" Barring any maniac gods trying to kill us both. She humphed again, but there wasn't as much determination in it now. She couldn't stay angry at her brother for long. "I love you. Aiden loves you, and we both miss you, my little bratty mermaid."

"Don't you call me a brat, bro," she said indignantly. "I'm more like a princess mermaid, so treat me accordingly." The Vee I knew and loved was back. That kid could dish out sarcasm almost as well as me. "Love you both. Please try not to get killed."

Before we left to go to the creepy chapel, we also called Taz. We needed her to ask the druid monks whether they knew anything about that small reliquary in the chapel since we couldn't find much about it, and we were going on a hunch rather than facts. It was time to face the music—a funeral march in this case.

We walked to the chapel hand in hand, ignoring the stares of the locals. The small city was extremely sedate. With the tourist season on its last legs, there were mostly locals wandering the streets. We had left a gaggle of school children behind as they explored the Roman ruins, undoubtedly on a school field trip. They would most likely go visit the chapel next, and I wanted to have our business taken care of before that happened.

Resisting the urge to sit at one of the coffee shops on the way, we soon arrived at our grim destination. "Are you ready for this?" Whatever *this* was. Fouchard nodded, and we walked in together. There were a few people already milling around, taking selfies with the bones and skulls as the background—what were they thinking?

I made a beeline to the small white tomblike stone box close to the altar. The Plexiglas separation was still in place, and I couldn't wish myself over it like I had done the night before so I got as close as I could, leaning over the half wall, pretending I was taking a picture. In fact, I was "feeling" it, searching for some kind of magic vibes. That was one of my oldest superpowers, being able to detect magic even when no one else could. Afraid I would fall headfirst over the barrier, my mate held on firmly to my hand and remained silent, scowling at the other visitors who clearly couldn't care less about being in a place where the dead and silence reigned. I chuckled quietly at his usual protective streak and leaned in closer.

After a few seconds, I did feel something: a humming of sorts, like the sound of a vibrating singing bowl, calm and yet full of energy. Magical energy. I snapped my head toward my mate. "Magic," I whispered, straightening. "Powerful magic. This is what the god of stupidity wants. Whatever it is, he hasn't gotten it yet. It's still in there, letting out wave after wave of magic vibrations."

Fouchard slipped an arm over my shoulders. "What do we do now?"

I had no fucking idea. "We wait, I guess. Bob won't try to steal it during the day, not with his mother with him. She might be crazy but she's definitely smarter than he is. So we have to come back at night and wait some more." Not my favorite option, but the only one that seemed promising. I rubbed an incoming headache from my eyes with the back of my hand.

"Couldn't you try to steal it before he did?" My eyes flew open. "Well, that way, he couldn't get it."

"Are you fucking nuts?" Wow, that sounded much harsher than I'd wanted it to be. I softened my voice. "If I touch that thing, whatever it is, I may end up with more power. I can barely handle the power I have, much less more. No way. We just have to make sure he can't get to it."

My boyfriend was quiet for a moment. "We could probably use the help of the monks." The suggestion came hesitantly, almost fearfully. He knew that any mention of my father or his druid mates helping us would cause me to lose my cookies. "They have certain powers we don't have. Maybe they could enchant the reliquary so that no one could open it."

It made all kinds of sense, but I was not going to call any of my father's cronies, as kind and welcoming as they had always been. However, his suggestion gave me an idea. I pulled out my phone and dialed Silva's number. Fouchard gaped at me, confused.

"Silva? I was wondering if you could do us a favor." I didn't waste time with pleasantries and went straight to the crux of the matter. I wondered if he could come up with some spell that would do just what my wonderful and clever boyfriend had suggested. After all, that was Silva's specialty, right? Magic spells.

The warlock listened to me without interrupting, then thought for a moment before answering,

"Not a bad idea. We'll be there this afternoon. Meet you at the door of the chapel at three o'clock." He didn't give me time to ask who *we* were and hung up.

"It looks like we have a few hours to be tourists," I told my merman, sliding the phone in my jeans pocket. "Where do you want to go first?"

I could have guessed his answer but still smiled when he said, "Coffee first."

At three on the nose, we were sitting on a bench across from the entrance to the Franciscan church that the chapel was annexed to. I felt it before I saw it—the air wavering as if the ground was emitting heat, then a subtle flash of light and poof, there they were, all three of them. My jaw dropped. *Fuck!*

Silva stepped forward, shaking some invisible dust from his black sweater. "I brought help," he announced unnecessarily. Behind him, Taz and Brother John waved as if we were meeting for a party. "Your father and Taz insisted on coming to lend us a hand."

I ground my teeth. "I asked *you* not *them*." My voice slipped out between my clenched jaws. "Especially my fa—Brother John." My mate squeezed my arm in warning.

Silva smiled that dazzling smile of his and

shrugged. "The power of three. Ever heard of it?" He called the others with a wave of the hand. "Put on your big girl panties, Aiden, and let go of your personal grudges."

How dare he call what I felt for my father a grudge. I had a grudge for the freaking Troll who stuck my head in a toilet in DC or the butcher down the road who had consistently charged me more than what he should. With my father, it went way beyond that. I didn't know what to call it, but I guessed it was like a mixture of hate and love, denial and yearning. I stepped forward with full intent of punching the warlock, but Fouchard held me steady. "Cool it, sweetheart," he whispered in my ear. "It will be okay."

Taz, clueless as usual, skipped her way to us. No hat for her today or sunglasses. Even her shoes had shorter-than-usual heels. She did mean business then. "This is like a family reunion." *Oh no, it isn't, witch.* I fulminated her with a look. "Ouch, Aiden. That glare melted my eyelashes. I love you too."

Clueless, totally clueless. I took a deep breath, trying to compose myself. This was for the greater good. We needed to stop Bob before things got out of hand, and if my dear absentee father could help, then I needed to be an adult and let him.

"Let's go seal the freaking box," said Silva, rubbing his hands as if excited. We followed him inside the building, but my mind was churning with questions; how in heaven's name were we to do what we were about to do when there were so many regulars out and about? This would make a perfect joke: a warlock, a witch, and a druid walked into a church….

Our weird and unlikely group arrived inside the chapel and, not-so-discreetly, positioned ourselves close to the reliquary. Oddly enough, we didn't seem to be attracting any attention. Then it dawned on me; one of my magical companions was charming us into invisibility or something equally crazy. Despite my unease with my own magic, I couldn't help but be impressed by it. My father, still in his brown robes, wiggled his fingers and chanted something I couldn't identify. In a wink of an eye, the barrier between us and the reliquary vanished as if by magic—oh, wait, it *was* magic.

Fouchard was still holding my hand as if afraid I would do something nuts, which I totally could. But by now, I was entranced by the whole thing. I was able to put aside the fact my father was one of the three trying to seal the box to watch in fascination as they moved in an eerie choreography of movements, words, and finger-wiggles. When my mate gasped and retracted his hand from mine suddenly, I stared in confusion. There were thin ribbons of what looked like electricity sparkling between my fingers. I lifted my hand and gaped.

"What the hell is that?" Naël asked, shaking his hand as if he had been burned.

"Magical energy?" I had no idea. It looked as if watching the other three creating a magical web of some kind had triggered my own powers. I felt this compulsion to join them even though I had no clue what to do. "It wants to join them." There was no better explanation; I could truly feel its desire to join forces with the others' magic.

"What are you waiting for?" my pragmatic boyfriend said. "Join them. One more hand in the pot might make a difference." I wanted to, but the idea of joining forces with the man who had abandoned me as a baby was holding me back. "You have to move on, Aiden. Even if you can't forgive him, you can at least decide to work beside him."

The electric threads zapping between my fingers grew stronger, and with a last look at my mate, I stepped forward to join the magic circle they had created.

"Hear now the words of the witches," Taz

murmured, her green eyes so intensely focused on the reliquary, I didn't think she saw me as I joined hands with her. "The secrets we hide in the night. Oldest goddesses I invoke thee and your powerful magic I beseech." I had never heard Taz speak like that. It was a bit unsettling. I realized that I had never witnessed her doing her voodoo. It was both disquieting and wondrous. "In this night and in this hour, I call upon your ancient power."

Unlike Taz, Silva was silent, his hands moving in a hypnotic dance, and my father, the druid, had his eyes closed and his arms wide open as if willing the reliquary to come to him. The energy releasing from my fingers joined Taz's as soon as our hands touched. I didn't feel I was actually doing anything, but the smell, the feel of magic in the room changed, became stronger, more focused. After a few panicky heartbeats, the stone box shook and groaned for a moment before settling back into stillness. Taz dropped my hands and looked at me finally. "It's done."

Brother John and Silva took deep breaths, their shoulders relaxing and arms falling along their sides. "It should be good," Silva said, throwing me a look. "Thank you, Aiden. That boost you gave us helped a lot."

I widen my eyes. "Me? I didn't do anything." I didn't. I had simply stood there and held Taz's hand.

"Your power is subtle but mighty." It was my father who stepped forward, his hands now hidden inside the wide sleeves of his habit. "You don't feel it because you were born with it, but it resonates loud and clear for any other magical creature."

I refrained from scowling and instead took Fouchard's hand in mine. My anchor, my lifeline. "I just don't understand how no one could track me if my powers are as noticeable as you say they are."

"Most of the powers were dormant until recently," Daddy dear said. "Your mother and I were able to suppress your most unusual powers until such time as you needed them, not to help yourself but to protect those you love."

I bit my upper lip, still not convinced. "You're sure that thing is sealed and that Bob and his mommy won't be able to retrieve what's inside?"

All three nodded emphatically. "I suggest we go celebrate," said Taz, the clueless witch. "Where can we get a good glass of wine? Make that a goblet."

"I'm in no mood to socialize," I said with a grunt. Especially with my father.

Surprising me, my mate came to their defense.

"Let's go at least have a bite to eat. Using magic works up an appetite." Taz nodded enthusiastically. Then, he lowered his voice to a whisper only I could hear. "Sweetheart, you need to do this. They did come to our aid."

I twisted my lips before letting out the breath that had been pressing inside my chest. "All right, let's go. We can ask at the hotel for a good place to go to."

We walked together back to the hotel, Fouchard's arm around my waist and my head leaning casually against his shoulder. Maybe he was right. Maybe I needed to do this, to get used to the presence of my druid father in my life. The way things had been going, it didn't look as if we would be able to avoid each other ever again. Whether I liked it or not, our paths were entwined.

I turned to my lover and smiled. "That troll in DC would have crapped his pants if he had known he was sticking the head of a mighty godly creature in the toilet."

My mate laughed. "He was dumb as fuck, sweetheart. I have always known you were a force to reckon with."

SEVENTEEN

GODS, TEMPLES, AND RELICS

THE MEAL TURNED OUT A LOT MORE PLEASANT THAN what I had thought it would be. I managed to work my way through a platter of *chorizo assado* without turning the small roaster flames into a weapon against my father, and I was also successful at not using his head as a target for the olive pits. When my father twisted his nose at a plate of *pataniscas*, small deep-fried salted cod cakes, I realized that besides the blue eyes, we shared the same taste for food.

After the light dinner, we walked back to the hotel. It was getting dark, but the night was warm and quiet. Taz insisted on checking out the Roman ruins because she was convinced there was something magical about them. No matter how many times I told her there wasn't, she wouldn't believe me. While she was investigating the matter under the spotlights, Fouchard and I sat on a rock enjoying the quietness of the evening. Brother John and Silva were involved in some philosophical discussion about earth spells, and for the first time that day, I felt at peace. I had survived a meal with my father, a witch, and a warlock. Miracles were real, after all.

"Hell is going to break loose when our teeny god finds out we screwed his plans." I leaned against him, grateful for the solid support of his body. "He's going to blow a gasket."

Fouchard chuckled softly. "I'd pay good money to see it."

We fell silent again. The dark veil of the night had fallen, and with it, an eerie aura that muffled every sound. There was magic abroad, and it wasn't coming from my friends. I straightened, every sense in full alert. "Something's coming."

Taz jumped off the edge of the temple and sprinted to us almost at the same time my words left my lips. "Something is coming." It was unsettling, to say the least, that I shared the same premonition with the red-haired witch.

We all stood up and gathered closer together in silence, listening for anything out of the ordinary. I heard it first: a sizzling sound as if the lighting in the temple had shortened. Then, darkness—deep blackness in a starless and moonless night. We closed our circle, instinctively gripping each other's hands, creating a circle of magic and power. Protection against whatever was coming.

A blinding flash of light cut the darkness. "The *brahmachakram!*" I yelled, opening my arms to protect my merman. The little god had once almost killed me with it. I'd recognize that sound anywhere. "Take shelter."

My father stopped me from fleeing, holding my arm in a viselike grip. "No, we need to stick together. Our united power is stronger than his." I begged to differ. I still remembered clearly how much that damned ball of fire hurt when it went through my shoulder. But the druid monks had once protected us from Bob, so I chose to trust him. Stepping back into the circle, we bound hands again and waited.

Another flash illuminated the square, and I watched apprehensively as a ball of energy flew too close to my boyfriend's head. I pulled on the hands and forcibly moved the circle a few steps to the right so that my merrow was not in the line of fire, but I was.

"Hey, little fucker," I yelled out into the darkness. "Don't be shy. Come out and play if you have the balls." I wasn't sure it was a good idea to goad him, but I preferred fighting a foe I could see than one who hid in the darkness.

Bob didn't disappoint. With another dramatic burst of light, the diminutive god appeared before us, dressed in full traditional garb—ears, arms, and nose heavily decorated with gold. "You think I'm scared of you?"

I scoffed. "Well, we did mess up your plans for St. Francis's relics. You must be pissed off. Understandable, I guess, but you have been a very bad boy, my friend."

An animal-like growl escaped his throat. I was definitely pissing him off. "Still hiding behind Daddy's skirts, are you?" It was his turn to royally tick me off.

I moved to free myself from the circle and charge him, but Fouchard on my right and Taz on my left held fast. "Let me go," I hissed, wanting nothing but to smash the little weasel's face in. My friends were a lot stronger than I gave them credit for. I grumbled like a bear and gave in. They weren't going to let me do something stupid.

He waved his hands in the air, and a glow grew

in intensity within one of his palms. It swelled to the side of a soccer ball before he released it toward us. Taz began chanting some weird-ass spell while Silva hissed something unintelligible. I set my chin to my chest, clenched my jaws, and threw poisonous darts at the irritating god—okay, they weren't really darts. More like killer glares. There was a buzzing in my ears, and for a moment, all I could see was that ball of energy in Bob's hand. Next thing I knew, the ball was gone, and so was the glare and the buzzing. Bob was nowhere to be seen, and I felt as if I had run a marathon. I collapsed to the ground, and Fouchard kneeled beside me, holding my head on his lap.

"Sweetheart, are you okay?" I couldn't talk. All my muscles were numb and felt heavy as lead. My mate glanced at the others and yelled, "Quick, he needs to recharge." Fouchard's arms went under my legs and arms to lift me.

I must have passed out, but when I came to, I was lying in a grassy patch. I didn't recognize the spot, but I didn't care. Someone—hopefully Naël— had stripped me naked and covered me with dirt. I was still heavy and brain fuzzy, but new energy was already running in my veins. I could feel it pumping through my heart and dashing to other parts of my body. "Naël." My throat was sore and scratchy, and the words felt as if I was regurgitating sand. I coughed, suddenly anxious but soon calmed down as my mate's hands covered mine on the dirt. "What happened?"

My eyes were not working right yet, but I could discern the beloved form of my boyfriend kneeling beside me. "Whatever you did to stop Bob depleted you of your energy." His gentle, warm lips brushed my forehead. "You gave us all a scare."

"You must learn to control your power, my son." So, my father was here too. *I would have learned, Daddy dear, if you hadn't abandoned me.* The words, however, never left my lips. Not because I didn't want to hurt his feelings, but because I didn't think I should waste the little energy I had sassing my absentee father. Not worth it. "When you are well, you must come to the convent and let me train you." And hell might just freeze over.

"Why don't you all go home, and I will take care of Aiden," Fouchard said. My vision was finally realigning, and a quick look around told me that I was lying somewhere in one of the hotel's cloisters. The area must be under a charm of some kind so other guests couldn't see me naked and half-buried in the dirt. "Bob won't be coming back tonight."

I grabbed my merman's hand tighter, remembering something. "Where did the idiot go?" We still had to capture him before he did anything even more messed up than what he had already.

"Évoramonte," Taz said, coming to kneel beside me too. "In his rush to get out of there, he left a receipt behind from an inn in town. That's most likely where he has been hiding. Quiet place, not a lot of people around; the perfect place for staying out of sight."

I opened my mouth to say something, but my mate stopped me. "I know, I know. We'll have to go there," he said, resigned. "Tomorrow, though. Tonight, you rest and recharge." I wasn't going to argue.

After our cohort of magicals left, Fouchard dug me out of the hole I had been lying in and, being a bit overzealous, carried me to our room. I didn't fight him even though I was recovered enough to walk on my own. Instead, I cuddled against his chest, my hands clasped behind his neck, and head nestled in the crook of his neck. He smelled heavenly, the fresh scent of the ocean still lingering on his skin even though he had been away from it for a few days already. I took a deep sniff and sighed.

"Are you smelling me?" he said, amusement obvious in his voice. "That's not creepy at all."

I sniffed him again. "I'm half druid, sweetheart. Nature completes me, and you always smell of the ocean and the sun."

He snorted. "Are you telling me I complete you?" He hitched me up a bit more, rearranging his hands under my legs.

"At the risk of sounding like Sid the sloth, you do complete me, my love." I planted my lips where my head had been and kissed him. "In so many ways."

He didn't say anything, but I felt his heart beat a bit faster inside his chest. "Get the key from my pocket," he said as we arrived in front of our door.

Swiveling a little in his arms, I slipped a hand inside his jeans pocket to get the key and found an extra hardness underneath the fabric. "Whoa, sweetheart. Do my words affect you that much?" I pulled out the key card and waved it in front of his face. "Not that I'm complaining or anything."

He scoffed. "Don't be so cocky, Aiden." He bent down just enough so I could reach the lock and wave the card in front of it. The door opened. "I just happen to get a little excited every time Bob is in town."

"Maybe you should ask for his hand in marriage then." My playful tone betrayed a note of jealousy. I knew he was joking, but the very thought of him with anyone else made me see red.

Fouchard kicked the door shut and carried me across the suite into the bedroom, where he deposited me onto the bed with a gentleness that totally belied his size. "I'm already taken," he whispered in my ear. He let go of me, and I felt bereft without his touch. "I'll be back."

My mate had covered my nakedness with a blanket to carry me across the common spaces in the hotel, not that there were a lot of people around at that late hour of the night. I threw the blanket aside and leaned back on the clean, cool sheets and pillows, crossing my arms behind my head and legs at the ankles. I wanted him to get an eyeful of me when he came back from the bathroom. Suddenly I needed to remind him he had me any way he wanted. I wanted to remind him he didn't need anyone else. Chiding myself for allowing my old insecurities to creep up again, I closed my eyes and took a deep breath. *You're being stupid, Aiden. Naël loves you.* I didn't doubt it for a minute, and yet, that fear of abandonment popped out of nowhere once in a while to haunt me.

Naël could be stealthy as a cat when he wanted. I never heard the bathroom door open or close, and neither did I hear his footsteps across the carpeted floor, but I felt the mattress give in to his weight beside me, his warm—and very naked—body yield against my side, and his sweet breath caress my cheek. "A penny for your thoughts, love."

My eyes now open, I turned my face toward his, our mouths inches apart and glances locked. "I was thinking I must be the luckiest man on earth." I smiled and touched his nose with mine.

"Lucky that you fished out such an amazing specimen of merman?" he said with a chuckle, making lazy circles on my abs with his fingers.

I laughed. "I was thinking more along the lines of me having such a righteous bod, but I guess we can go with what you said." He tried to tickle my waist, but I wasn't ticklish at all. Instead, he fanned the flames of my desire. "I'm so lucky I found you, the most obnoxious, cranky merman in the Atlantic Ocean—and possibly beyond." He pinched me on my side. Hard. I flinched and chuckled. "Ouch."

In one of his cat-like moves, my mate rose from his side-laying position and straddled me. I gasped as our overly excited naughty bits touched. "Well, sweetheart, this obnoxiously handsome merrow is about to make you very happy. Are you ready?"

Was I ever! If having sex with my merman was a sport, we would so make it to the Olympics.

EIGHTEEN

DESPERATELY LOOKING FOR BOB

Évoramonte was a sleepy town built within castle walls, much like Óbidos. But where Óbidos was busy and crawling with visitors, Évoramonte was quiet, even giving the vibes of being abandoned despite the houses with their immaculate whitewashed walls and bright-colored painted windows. We walked along the cobbled streets, slick with the rain that had been falling all morning, scouting for any sign of the annoying god and his mother.

"Is this place even inhabited?" Fouchard asked, water dripping down his brow and rolling to the tip of his nose. I had a sudden urge to lick it dry, but I had to focus on tracking the asshole who wanted me dead.

Unlike other magicals, my sense of magic—or what I started calling my magical spidey sense—was enhanced when it rained. Since my magic was earth-derived, anytime the elements were making themselves heard or seen, whatever weird power I had inherited from my parents grew stronger and more precise. I couldn't sense any magical presence in town. Either Bob had a new way of shielding himself from me—doubtful since he didn't know I could sense his presence and, well, his lack of ingenuity—or he was not in town anymore.

"Let's walk around the other side of the town," I told my merman, my hair dripping wet. The rain hadn't stopped falling yet. It was light but insistent, soaking everything in its wake. Every villager had disappeared under the protection of their roofs, and the town looked like a true ghost town. "I can't sense him anywhere."

Fouchard held on to my hand tighter and pulled me closer. "What if they aren't here?" His clothes were soaked, but so were mine.

I could hear our shoes sloshing with each step, so soggy and heavy I was afraid they would dissolve in the water. I stopped for a moment to remove them, sticking them inside the backpack I was carrying over a shoulder. It felt good to walk barefoot over the rough rocks that paved the street. Energy coursed through me. I sighed.

"If they aren't, we'll just go home and follow their trail."

Our walk around the full length and width of the town didn't yield any results. If they had been here, they were long gone. With no reason to linger in the sleepy town, we got in the car and drove away. Neither my boyfriend nor I was bothered by the fact we were dripping wet, but the leather seats of Naël's car were not happy. More than once I had wiggled on the seat and cracked up laughing about the sound I made. Fouchard looked at me, an eyebrow raised, and I laughed even more. I guess I was not too old for bathroom humor.

We got home late because I insisted on stopping every ten miles or so to either drink coffee and eat or make out with my mate. All that contact with the rain had made me hungry for more than food. Vee and Cristina were waiting at the door and eyed us with disapproval as we climbed out of the car, our clothes and my hair in total disarray. The mermaid believed our explanation of not having had time to get properly dressed that morning, but Cristina pinched her lips and tapped her foot. She knew exactly why my T-shirt hung halfway untucked, and the zipper of my jeans just happened to be open. I looked at her, smiled, and shrugged. She shook her head slowly, but I could see a tiny smile pulling at the corners of her lips.

"Where's the mighty warlock?" I asked, accepting the coffee she offered me when we got to the kitchen.

"He actually works, unlike you." *Ouch!* "I called him after you told me Bob wasn't in Évoramonte anymore. Tó's trying to pin down his location."

The doorbell rang and Vee, always the nosy one, ran to open it. "You have visitors," she yelled out from the door. Visitors? We never had visitors. Cristina and Silva were frequent sights, but even Taz had never set foot in Fouchard's house.

Curious, I cradled my hot coffee mug and peeked around the doorway. "Who is it, Vee?" I felt my merman's presence behind me, his warm breath on the back of my neck.

Three figures appeared; Vee led a pair of familiar faces, but only one was welcome. I must have blanched because Naël laid a hand on my shoulder and whispered, "Are you okay?" He couldn't see what I could: my father walking along the hallway on his way to the kitchen.

I sidled away from the doorway into full view.

"What is he doing here?" I asked Taz, who walked beside Brother John, her red, messy hair gathered in a wild bun on top of her head. Her high heels tick-tacked their way over the tiled floor, but her usual mischievous smile was not there. Instead, she chewed on her upper lip and stared at her hands as if they were the most interesting thing on earth.

"Don't blame the witch," my father said, raising a hand between us. "I was coming with or without her. She thought it would be wise if she came along to be a buffer."

I shot a glance at the witch, full of sharp edges. I did not want to see my father, much less talk to him. Yes, he had helped us in Évora, but I wasn't ready to let go of the anger I had held on to my whole life. "What do you want?"

Fouchard stepped around me and placed himself discreetly between us as if afraid we would attack each other. "Maybe we should take this to the living room," he said, the perfect host and way more levelheaded than I would ever be. We all followed him silently. My anger roared in my ears, hot and furious. My body was still overloaded with energy, and my emotions were too intense and too close to the surface. *Bad timing, Daddy dear, terrible timing.*

Taz came to my side as we walked across the hallway. "I'm sorry, Aiden. He said he had something to tell you that couldn't wait," she whispered. I didn't look at her, afraid I'd kill her with my eyes. It was never a bad idea to be cautious with these new and improved powers of mine. "Do you hate me?"

I did look at her then. I couldn't hate her. A few months ago, I wouldn't hesitate to tell her to fuck off, but I had grown to like her, to think of her as a close friend, someone I could trust. Besides, she was one of the few people in this world who actually understood my pop culture references. "I don't hate you, stupid." Okay, maybe I could have been a bit nicer, but she *had* brought my father to my haven. "Remind me to cross you off my will."

She made a move for my arm and hung from it like a besotted girlfriend. "I'm in your will? I'm touched, Aiden," she said, feigning excitement. "But do you even have anything of worth?" She meant it as a joke, but it somehow hit me hard. I didn't have anything of value other than my books and my coffee shop, and even that was rented property, not really mine. Taz noticed the change in my expression. "You may not have any material things, but you have people who love you, me included."

My heart melted a bit, and I managed a smirk. "Don't try to butter me up, witch. I'm still not sleeping with you." She humphed comically but didn't let go of my arm until we were in the living room.

Fouchard had offered a seat to my father, and Vee, her eyes bulging and zigzagging with curiosity, had perched herself on the arm of the couch to the right of him. When no one else moved to take a seat beside the monk, Cristina offered herself as the sacrificial lamb. "I do hope you guys are going to put on a good show," she said. "I haven't been to the theater in ages." I berated her with my eyes. It didn't faze her; she just shrugged and smiled at me. *If I didn't love you so much, woman.*

Fouchard sat on the armchair, and I followed Vee's example and sat on the arm, next to him. "Well, Father," I said, embedding as much sarcasm as I could in the word. "What is so urgent you must invade the privacy of my home?" Of course it wasn't my house per se, but it was indeed my home. Naël *was* my home.

Brother John smoothed an imaginary wrinkle from his robes and cleared his throat. "The Oracle sent me to tell you two things." So not his idea. I wasn't sure whether to be happy or disappointed.

I'd spent a lifetime wishing my parents would show up and show some interest in me. "One, he wants me to train you on how to control your powers." *Aah! Fat chance.* "Second, he had a bad premonition."

"Isn't that what he does? Have premonitions?" I quipped, more harshly than I'd meant. I knew better than scoff at things like that. I'd experienced the foreboding visions myself and knew they were real. "What exactly did he foresee? Bob coming after me? Old news, Father. I think we all know that."

The druid looked up at me then, his eyes burrowing into my soul. "No, not exactly that, even though it is indeed related." Fouchard leaned in, his hand seeking mine over my upper thigh. "He had a vision about Bob and his mother procuring a weapon."

I think we all looked at him dumbly. Wasn't that what the fucking mini-god was always doing? Looking for weapons to defeat me? "He already has the most powerful weapon in the world. What can be worse?"

He cleared his throat again, clearly uncomfortable. "This time, the weapon he is seeking to obtain —and if the vision is correct, he will very soon—is more of a preventive type." What? I shook my head, confused. "He is looking for a weapon which will render you powerless and thus vulnerable to his attacks."

Well, that was indeed new. "Does such a thing exist?" I asked, hoping I didn't sound too cocky.

Brother John nodded. "Yes, everyone has their kryptonite, and you are no exception, my son." That last word rankled, and I swallowed an insult. He was here to help so it'd be smart not to alienate him too much. Below all my anger, frustration, and sense of loss there was a spark of hope, of wishful thinking. Maybe he would end up training me, and maybe, just maybe, we could get close enough to, if not erase, at least blur those defensive lines I had built around me.

"And what is, pray tell, my kryptonite? Hard work? A world without beaches? Commitment?" I felt my mate's hand tense up. *Shit! Why did I say that?* I didn't mean it at all. Yes, months ago, I was so not the kind of guy to commit to anything, relationship or otherwise, but that had changed radically; I now was one hundred percent committed to my relation-ship with Naël. That was my number one priority in life, further up on the list than even my business or getting laid as often as humanly possible. I loved him and wanted to be by his side forever. I tried to hold on to his hand, but he pulled it away, leaving me bare and in a panic.

"Son, on earth everything has a balance," he said, wringing his hands on his lap. "There is darkness to balance light, evil to balance good, and your powers are no exception. When you were conceived, both your mother and I immediately realized you'd have more power than any creature alive. That you'd be able to control and use the elements as a weapon. We also knew that just as you were growing inside your mother's womb, the universe was creating something else to balance this shift within the elements."

Still feeling bereft without my merman's hand, I gaped stupidly. "Where is this weapon? What is it?"

For the first time I noticed that none of my friends, including Vee, who always had something to say, were saying anything. I looked around me, surprised at the looks of concern each one of them had plastered on their faces. I turned back to the monk.

"We have never been able to find out, but we think it's something related to your mother's life in the Milky Sea." *Wait. What? Milky Sea?* What the fuck was he talking about? My confusion must have been obvious because he explained, "Lakshmi was once the God Vishnu's consort. One day she was angry at the corruption and arrogance of humans and gods alike and went into exile in the Milky Sea where she stayed for over one thousand years." Could this woman—goddess—be my mother? For real? "She's been connected to that sea ever since, and she thinks that the counterpart to your powers must be somewhere under it."

Cristina broke her silence for once. "Where is this Milky Sea? I never heard of it."

My father turned his face toward her. "It's the Indian Ocean. Not exactly a sea but the way the ocean looked while she was living in it. A luminescent phenomenon on the surface of the water that creates the illusion the ocean is creamy white like milk."

Despite all that had happened, this story grabbed my full attention. As hard as it was to believe that it had anything to do with me, it was fascinating, like a story I would read in a fantasy novel.

"How does Bob know what it is if you don't?" Taz asked. I was glad my friends were more with it than me and asking all the proper questions.

"I don't know how he figured it out." My father

rubbed a hand across his mouth, looking suddenly much older than he was. "Baburaj's mother was promiscuous enough that she might have somehow gathered that information from one of the other gods. Maybe even Vishnu himself."

"Well, can't we just ask this Vishnu guy?" Vee asked, much to everyone's surprise. Good question, my young mermaid. "If he knows, why not share that with his wife?"

Brother John winced. "She's not his wife anymore and hasn't been for a thousand years." His skin flushed at his abrupt comment. "Vishnu has been, er… gone, for a long time. No one knows where he is hiding."

"What about Lord Rama?" Taz stood up and crossed her arms. Who was Lord Rama? These people kept talking about people I'd never heard of. "He was Lakshmi's husband as well. Maybe he knows something." How many husbands had my mother had? And was she even married to my father, or was I the product of an illicit affair? Now was probably not the right time to ask.

"Dead end," my father said with a sigh. "He knows nothing."

We all fell silent. You could hear our breaths and the sound of the ocean outside, and I had a ridiculous and totally inappropriate urge to go on a swim with Naël. I stole a glance at him, and my heart fell; his lips were set into a thin line and his eyes on the ground. I slapped myself mentally for being so stupidly impulsive and never thinking before I spewed words I didn't mean.

"Well," Taz dropped her hands along her sides and twisted her nose before continuing, "We're just fucked, aren't we?"

There was a moment of surprised quiet, and then we all burst out laughing—everyone except my merman who stood up and left the room without saying a word.

NINETEEN

SISTER AND MOTHER OF PEARL

I DIDN'T SEE MY MERMAN FOR THE REST OF THE DAY. I guessed I should have been flattered by the fact he trusted me to take care of his sister, but I was mostly worried. I knew he was mad at me and with good reason. Sometimes I needed someone to muzzle or gag me so I would stop spewing shit. After Taz and my father left, Cristina lingered for a while until Silva called her, telling her he was on his way home. Even though they hadn't officially moved in together, the warlock cop spent most of his free time in my friend's house. Vee had homework to do and a whole series of *Riverdale* to binge on Netflix. I doubted that was an appropriate show for an almost twelve-year-old to watch, but I was far too anxious about Fouchard's whereabouts to pay much attention. I made her a bucketful of buttery popcorn with unicorn sprinkles and sat beside her while she indulged in teenage drama and romance while my eyes frequently wandered to the door.

The car was in the garage so I was guessing he had gone for a swim. A long swim that was frazzling my nerves and making my heart shrivel inside my chest. The talk I felt was coming loomed over my head and conscience, but anything was preferable to this waiting game.

"Will you stop fidgeting?" I had yet again stood up to wander to the hallway and stare at the basement door. "Sit down, Aiden. He'll be back soon enough."

I sighed and dropped down beside her. "He's mad at me." I wasn't sure why I was starting this conversation with the young mermaid. Probably my need to talk, period.

Vee turned her head and looked at me with her emerald green eyes. "You shouldn't have said you didn't want any commitment." For such a young creature, this girl was sometimes a bit too observant. "Why did you say that? May I remind you, you once promised me you were with my brother for the duration? You promised me you wouldn't leave."

I shook my head, the sting of tears making me

blink like a loon. "I won't. I have no intention of leaving your brother. Or you." That tight fist around my heart squeezed even tighter. "I never wanted commitment before your brother, but that has changed. I love him and want to be by his side for the rest of our lives."

The young mermaid cocked her head, stuffing her mouth with popcorn. "You know merfolk live very short lives, right?" Bits of chewed popcorn flew out of her mouth into my T-shirt. Blood left my face. "He'll die way before you."

The thought of him dying and leaving me alone in this cruel world was too painful to contemplate. "What?" It came out as a sob.

Vee laughed. "You're too easy, Aiden. Just kidding. Merfolk live about as long as humans, maybe a little longer." I glared at her. *Cruel little wench.* "I wanted to see your reaction. You *do* love my brother, don't you?" Was there ever any doubt? But if even Vee had her misgivings, what did that say about how Naël thought? Was he also not too sure of my love?

I covered my face with my hands and grunted. "Shit. I gave him the impression I didn't love him enough to stick around, didn't I?" I looked up. She nodded, still chewing on the rainbow-colored popcorn. "I'm so stupid."

She waved her hand and then patted me on my shoulder. "You'll kiss and make up," she said. "If you promise me a lifetime supply of ice cream, I will talk to him too."

"You're a little mercenary." Despite my anxiety and frustration, I had to smile. A glance at the wall clock told me it was way past her bedtime. Tomorrow was a school day, and her brother would be livid if he found out I let her stay up that late. "Bed with you, silly mermaid." She protested but turned off the TV and stood up to go up to her room.

"I'm taking the popcorn," she said, hugging the huge metal bowl. Taking me by surprise, she got on her tiptoes and kissed my cheek. "Don't worry too much. He loves you too." I watched her climbing the stairs humming "Kiss the Girl" from *The Little Mermaid* movie, except switching the word "girl" with "boy." Cheeky.

I checked all the doors and windows—with a wild canon god after us, I didn't want to make it easier for him—and then went down to the base-ment. The underground beach was drowned in soft light and so serene I felt immediately calmer. For a minute at least. Then I remembered why I was there and why my lover was nowhere to be found, and my stress punched me in the gut with the power of a heavy-weight champion. I slunk down to the sand, my misery choking me.

"I should have my tongue cut off," I yelled out, my words echoing throughout the cavernous beach. Then I threw myself face-first into the sand.

"I couldn't agree more." I almost jumped out of my skin before I realized it was the beloved voice of my mate. I jerked up, my eyes hurting and blurred by bits of sand. I wiped them urgently away and watched as my merman appeared out of the shadows. His beautiful body glistened under the artificial lights, and I fell in love all over again. "You can be such a prick sometimes, Aiden."

I nodded, still kneeling on the sand. "I am, I really am," I admitted. "But I didn't mean it, Naël, not even a smidgen."

Wearing only his swim trunks, Fouchard dropped to his knees before me. "Then why say you didn't want to commit?"

"Because I'm a dummy, and every time I open my mouth, crap comes out," I said, shuffling closer to him. "I love you, sweetheart. You know that. I want to be with you forever, no matter what it takes."

Silence fell and our eyes locked. I must have stopped breathing for a moment because I was winded by the time my mate lifted an eyebrow and asked, "Are you one hundred percent sure? You really want to be with me for the duration of our lives?" Yes, yes I did, even if my life didn't seem promisingly long at the moment with a god in pursuit. I nodded like a dog with fleas. He dug in his pocket and pulled out a small bag with something inside. "I had this made for you out of an oyster." He showed me a ring made of mother-of-pearl, simple as it reflected every color around us. "I love you, Aiden, and want to be your husband." What? Suddenly my brain was filled with explosions and incapable of rational thought. He wanted to marry me? "Will you be my husband, sweetheart? Will you marry me and make our commitment official in the eyes of the world?"

I sputtered something meant to be words, but that had no resemblance to them at all. My thoughts raced. Did I want to get married? Fuck, a few months ago, I wasn't even sure if I wanted a relationship that extended past a roll in the hay, and now… did I? Did I want to make this huge commitment to a man who could be as sweet as he was obnoxious? An alpha who was anything but when we were alone, someone more than willing to be vulnerable and give me his all. Did I?

"Fuck yeah!" I exclaimed, echoes reverberating against the rock walls. "I so want to be Mr. Fouchard." I threw my arms around his neck and brought his face close to mine in a collision course with a kiss. I swallowed him whole, his seaside flavor filling me with a joy I couldn't describe if I wanted to.

When we drew apart, breathless from our kiss, my mate chuckled and said, "You do realize you won't really be called Mr. Fouchard, right?"

"Okay, so you can be Mr. Mercer then," I said, laughing and pulling him into another hug. "Or Mr. Husband. I don't care. I just want us to be together forever."

Fouchard guffawed and pulled me away for a moment to slide the ring into my finger. "It's official; we're engaged."

"You may kiss the groom," I said, and just as he was opening his mouth to protest what I'd said, I covered his mouth with mine and slid my tongue against his. I was an over-the-moon happy groom.

TWENTY

THE WELCOME COMMITTEE

"Hey, blushing groom, will you stop gushing over your engagement ring and come help me?" Cristina balanced a tray packed with dishes on one hand and a pitcher of lemonade in the other. She didn't look pleased, but I'd been having trouble concentrating for over a week now, since I had gone from single man to an engaged man. Half the time, I wanted to be like a peacock and strut my tail feathers—if I had any, of course. "We're out of clean coffee cups."

Reluctantly, I pushed away from the wall I was leaning against and headed to the kitchen to wash some dishes. I refused to take off the ring, so I pulled out a pair of plastic gloves from the cupboard and slipped them over my hands. I'd been walking on clouds for days, my focus never forgetting the moment my merman had asked me to marry him, even knowing that Bob, the dickwad, could be in possession of a magical artifact that would render me vulnerable to his attacks.

Vee had been even more excited than me, if that was possible. The child had not stopped making plans for our wedding even though we hadn't set a date. The last time she talked to me about it, Fouchard and I were getting married in a god-awful room, completely decorated with mermaid paraphernalia and a couple of unicorn-inspired frills. It was horribly tacky, and there were zero chances either me or my merrow would ever accept such a setup. But it did keep her little hyperactive imagination running wild and busy. Since she insisted on "planning" with Cristina almost every day, my mate and I'd had plenty of alone time to indulge in what we enjoyed doing the most—each other.

"I never thought you'd be this starry-eyed moron." Cristina walked into the *copa*, expertly setting the tray, now filled with dirty dishes, down on the small counter. "Who would have thought that love could turn you into a teenage girl."

I glowered at her, flipping her the finger. "You're

just jealous because you're not the only one engaged anymore." Shit. I did sound like a petulant teenager. What was happening to me? "I thought you'd be happy for me."

She smacked my shoulder with the kitchen towel. "*Idiota,* of course I'm happy, but you've been intolerable for the past week, staring at the ring as if expecting it to perform some kind of miracle and being even less helpful around here than usual." She clicked her tongue. "That alone is a huge problem. In case you haven't noticed, we've been pretty busy."

She was right. For the past week or so, the coffee shop was almost as busy as during the summer. The area had been inexplicably swarmed by Swiss tourists who couldn't get enough of coffee, pastries, and the lingering warm fall sunshine. November had started fabulously with great weather, great business, and now my engagement.

Life was good.

"Sorry, amiga, but—" I removed the glove with my teeth and stuck my ring finger in front of her. "I can't stop staring at it." The ring was indeed as beautiful as it was simple. The band of tungsten carbide was inlaid in black mother of pearl, waves of blue and green aquamarine mingling and melding with the black flat exterior. It was perfect. My boyfriend—fiancé—had bought a matching band for himself, another thing that made me giddy with happiness, however irrational that might be.

Cristina wrinkled her nose and then smiled. "Okay, it is gorgeous," she admitted. "But can you please start pulling your weight around here? We have a room and patio full of Swiss waiting to be served. I have a feeling they won't stay neutral for much longer if we don't do something about it."

I removed my other glove and towel-dried the last few cups I'd washed before grabbing a tray and heading out into the store to take some orders. I almost fell flat on my ass when my eyes landed on the beautiful woman by the window. Jhanvi, Bob's mother, dressed in a beautiful red sari, shiny raven black hair tied into a long thick braid, sat by the window, her thin, heavily adorned forearms resting on the table and her onyx eyes trained on mine. My eyes trailed to her bare feet, heavily decorated with rings around her toes and bangles around her ankles. What the hell was she doing there? And where was her asshole of a son? I looked around, a bit frantic, looking for Bob, but he was nowhere to be seen. I relaxed enough to breathe normally again and face her.

"What are you doing here?" Belatedly I cursed myself for not having asked the witches to place a protective spell around Bicas R Us. "You're not welcome."

She made a funny whizzing sound with her mouth. "Like I care," she said, scratching the tile inlay of the table with a long scarlet nail. "I came as a courtesy to a fellow magical."

I scoffed. "Courtesy? Do you even know what that is?" She scowled. "Just get on with it. What do you want?"

She giggled like a young girl, a sound so ludicrous coming from her I almost burst out laughing myself. "Well, I want you dead, of course. But today is not the day," she said with a pucker at the end. "It's coming, though. Soon. In fact, that's what brings me here; I might as well let you know that Baburaj has acquired a magical item that will prove your undoing."

Not going to lie, my heart dropped a few inches. "What are you talking about, old yaksha?" I goaded, deflecting the fear creeping into my soul that very moment.

Jhanvi's lips flattened, and her nostrils flared like those of an enraged cow. "I'm telling you, *dusht*, that my powerful son traveled to the Milky Sea and found the one thing that will bring you to your knees."

I had no idea what she'd just called me, but it didn't matter. The little prick had found it. The one magical item or weapon or whatever you wanted to call it that would render me powerless. I was fucked. The joy that had filled my every cell for the last week dissipated like the morning mist and was replaced by dread, heavy and thick. What was I going to do? Was Naël going to be a widower even before he was a husband? Or was Bob going to take my loved ones down along with me? The thought paralyzed me.

"No snarky jokes? No insults?" The Indian woman brought her hand to her chest in mock surprise. "I'm almost disappointed." Her eyes hardened, and her lips curled into a sneer—the smile of a viper. "You are going down in smoke, Aiden. And your fish man will fry along with you." I half expected her to cackle like an evil witch, but she just vanished.

My limbs refused to move. I was frozen in place by fear—fear for myself but mostly for my mate. I was no martyr or hero, but I was willing to die to protect my man. He'd given me the one thing I'd always wanted but could never have: love. I was not going to allow anyone to hurt him.

Cristina bumped into me as if she hadn't seen me standing there. "What the hell? Where did you come from?" She *hadn't* seen me. The wicked hag must have put some charm over us while we talked. "You look pasty, more than usual," she said, furrowing her brow. "What's wrong?"

"They have it." Cristina frowned and opened her mouth in a silent question. "The weapon my father told us about. Bob has it."

It was her time to blanch and almost drop the dishes she was carrying. "What? How's that possible? Even your mother doesn't know where it is."

I lifted and curled my arms over my head, shaking. "Somehow they found it. The one thing that will defeat me."

We stared at each other for a moment, and then my friend dropped the tray on a nearby table, rattling the dishes and attracting the eyes and ears of customers. "We'll figure it out, amigo." She hugged me. At first I just stood, too shocked by the turn of events to react, but then I lowered my arms and wrapped them around Cristina. A thread of comfort weaved itself into my soul as I rested my head against hers, my faithful friend, a regular with the courage of a magical.

A realization slammed into me like a solid wall; I would have to ask my father and the other druid monks for help. I couldn't do this alone. I needed all the support and magical help I could muster. Only six months ago, I would have been all alone against this danger, but I now had friends in the magical community. Friends who were willing to risk their necks to help me. As much as I didn't want to involve my father in this, I had to swallow my pride if I wanted Cristina, Vee, and my man protected. If Bob could indeed rob me of my powers, who would be able to defend my loved ones?

"Can you hold the fort for a few minutes?" I asked Cristina. "I need to call Taz." And Naël, of course. He would be all manly bravado and anger, wanting to protect me, but he couldn't—not against a god. He would only get hurt, and I couldn't allow it.

Cristina nodded, and I hid in the *copa* to make the phone call. Taz jumped into action right away and told me we would meet later in Fouchard's house. My heart sank. Just a little bit ago, I'd been over the moon, gazing stupidly at my engagement ring. Life sucked sometimes, and fate seemed to love hitting us mercilessly over the head.

When I went back into the coffee room, Cristina was staring at something she was holding in one hand. "What's that?" I asked, closing in.

"I don't know. Look!" She shoved the small item in front of my face. I stepped back a bit so my eyes could focus on it. It was a toe ring, the same kind I noticed in Bob's mother's toes earlier. She must have dropped it in her hurry to leave. "Jhanvi's toe ring." I took it from Cristina and slipped it into my pocket so I didn't have to see or think about it anymore. I had more important things to worry about.

After closing, Cristina drove us to Fouchard's home in Cascais. I hadn't given him any details, keeping the bad news to only a hint. He wasn't happy about my reluctance to share details over the phone, but he had no other choice than to wait. By the time we got there, we had a surprise welcome committee waiting for us. My father, a couple of the other monks, Silva, Taz, and most surprising of all, Dona Moreno, the high priestess. Wow, things must indeed be dire.

The living room felt a lot smaller than usual, as

if by their presence, our magical visitors had shrunk it.

Taz pulled a youngish man toward me and said, "I brought a date." Leave it to Taz to make this meeting about my impending doom a good place and time to bring a date. "This is Oisin." The young man, looking barely twenty, offered me his hand with a smile. His red hair, a mass of unruly curls, was a halo around an ivory and freckled face. I shook his hand. "He's one of the Tuatha Dé of Ireland." A what? "When he found out what was going on, he kindly offered to help." The witch batted her eyes and smiled as if besotted by the tall Irishman.

"Very glad to meet you, Mr. Mercer." He spoke with the light Irish accent of someone long exiled elsewhere. "It's an honor to help you."

I wanted to ask what in heaven's name could a wiry young thing like him do to help against a maleficent pair, but I thought it would be rude, so I shut my mouth, smiled, and thanked him for any help he could provide.

Taz caught the subtle sarcasm behind my words. "Don't be so patronizing, Aiden," she said, frowning and shaking her head in disapproval. "Oisin may look young and green, but he is one of the mighty Celtic gods. He is powerful and a true magician in bed." I gave her a look. I had no wish of talking about her sexual adventures. "And if you think he's too young for me, think again. He's not quite an immortal, but he will live a couple decades more than you or me."

I stand corrected. Could Taz be in love? In some ways, she was a lot like me, not taking anything too seriously and playing the field. "And how exactly can you help?" I asked directly at the young Celtic god.

Oisin had a pleasant face, his pale blue eyes so transparent I felt as if I was looking straight at his soul. "Since your foe is a demigod, having a full god on your side will most certainly tip the scales in your favor," he said in a sensual baritone voice that somehow belied his wiry, youthful frame. "I have some skills that may prove very helpful in your battle with this—what did you call it, Taz?—oh yeah, Bob."

I wouldn't turn down any help I could get. I wasn't going to lie; I was terrified of what Bob could potentially do not just to me but my family and friends. "I'm very grateful for your help, Oisin."

"Oisin could prove to be your best ally yet."

The beautiful, classy Dona Moreno approached, impeccably dressed, as usual, her lips covered and perfectly contoured in the reddest of lipsticks. "I'm so happy to see you again, Mr. Mercer. I just wish it was under better circumstances." I nodded. "But all is not lost, and you have amassed quite the powerful army of friends. I believe I'm not lying when I say we've got you covered." Her lips stretched into a charming but sincere smile. I did like the high priestess a lot. There was something about her I couldn't put my finger on, something that spelled trust and strength. "And you even have your father on your side," she continued, unaware of or not caring about my cringe. "John is a strong, capable druid who will always be an ace in anyone's pocket."

Much to my mortification—I felt as if I needed to puke my heart out—they exchanged a look, one of complicity and familiarity I hadn't realized existed between them. Was my dad a man-whore like me? Or was whatever the relationship he had with my mother a nonexistent thing anymore? Did goddesses get divorces? There was still so much I needed to learn about this world I been born into but had been kept out of for so long.

We all milled around the room, in small clusters

of people, talking and munching on the snacks Vee and my merrow had laid out on the tables. It all had the feeling of a cocktail party rather than a war room, and I had the insane urge to burst out laughing. We were talking about everything except the reason we were here.

"Are we ever going to make any plans of attack?" I finally asked, my nerves frazzled and my patience running short.

My father opened his mouth to answer but didn't have the chance to do it because from behind me, a familiar voice echoed, "They are waiting for me, of course."

I turned around, my mouth wide open in shock. What the hell was the Einstein lookalike oracle doing here?

TWENTY-ONE

THE WAR ROOM

THEY COULD HAVE KNOCKED ME DOWN WITH A feather. The little, always half-high, old oracle was standing right there in the middle of Fouchard's living room—my living room. The others, with the possible exception of my mate, didn't look too surprised, so this must have been planned.

"It's been a while since I left the convent grounds." Hell, I thought it had been a lifetime since he left that library room, much less the convent. "But this demanded some unprecedented actions." He looked around appreciatively, looking much like a tourist in a museum except for his clothes. Standing, the monk looked even thinner and smaller in his brown habit and scapular, but there was a light in his eyes I'd never seen before in all my visits to the *Convento dos Capuchos* in Sintra. "This is a beautiful home, Aiden."

I shifted on my feet. "Thank you, Brother Serafim, but it's not my house."

Naël sidled beside me, his hand going around my waist. "Aiden is right," he said. "This is not his house. It's *our* home." Good thing he was holding me tight because my legs went to jelly beneath me. *Our home.* It had an incredible ring to it. "I think I speak for my fiancé too when I say we're very surprised to see you here."

Behind the old monk, two younger men stood, their eyes on the floor and hands inside their wide sleeves. They advanced in unison with the oracle, who was looking a lot sprier than I ever thought possible, toward the couch. "Mind if I sit? My legs are not young anymore." He could have fooled me. I gestured toward the seat, and he dropped onto it, helped by one of the younger monks. "We are all here then?" He directed his question at my father, who nodded and invited everyone else to take a seat.

We couldn't all fit on the set of comfortable couches, so I pulled a few chairs from the neighboring dining room. My mate, ever the gentleman, had offered his seat on the overstuffed chair to

Dona Moreno, who graciously accepted, crossing her shapely legs at the ankles. I scooted to the side to make room for him on my chair despite the fact that both our butt cheeks would be half hanging out. I needed my merman close to me.

The oracle raised his hand to my father in an invitation to speak. The man with the same exact eyes as me cleared his throat. "We are all here to come up with a plan to protect my son and make sure Bubaraj never hurts anyone again." Duh, I think we'd all figured that much. My father, Captain Obvious, locked eyes with mine, making me wiggle uncomfortably in my seat. "He now possesses the weapon created upon Aiden's birth, which means my son won't be able to stand up to him."

I opened my mouth to protest, but Naël covered my hand with his. "Hear him out," he whispered. Reluctantly, I settled back into my seat.

"Among all of us we have enough power to defeat him even if he renders Aiden powerless," my father continued. He looked around the room, inventorying our forces. "One witch, two gods, a merman, a warlock, and a whole convent of druids."

"Hey, you forgot a mermaid," Vee yelled out,

outrage in her voice, "and a regular." Cristina nodded.

My fiancé turned to his sister, who had sat cross-legged on the rug. "You won't be participating in this, sis." She huffed and crossed her arms in a sulk. "Don't give me attitude, young woman. You are not going, and that's that."

Cristina, sitting next to her, held her by the shoulders and pulled her closer. "We will be like those nurses during World War I. They were just as brave and essential as the men who fought in the front line without actually ever setting foot on the battleground." Vee relented ever so slightly but still mumbled something under her breath. I could only imagine what she was saying. Despite the situation, I smiled. "We'll be heroes of another kind."

Everyone returned their attention to the druid monk who claimed to be my father. "I say we preempt his attack by attacking first." Great idea—except we had no clue where the idiot was hiding. I snorted, and when everyone looked over as if I had grown two heads, I rolled my eyes like the teenager I had apparently grown into. "That's where Oisin comes in. He has many magical powers, one of which allows him to track creatures across space and time. All he needs is an item that belongs or has been touched by Bob or his mother."

"He's been to Bicas R Us, but the place has been cleaned since, so I doubt if there are any traces of him left behind," Cristina mused, chewing on her nail.

Something tugged at my memory, but I couldn't quite retrieve it. "Shit. Not sure we have anything."

Cristina raised her head suddenly, her eyes lit and a smile on her lips. "The toe ring, Aiden." What was she talking about? "The one Jhanvi left behind earlier today."

I slipped my hand in my pocket and felt the circular shape of the ring cold against my fingers. Pulling it out, I held it aloft as if it was a trophy. "She left this behind this morning." We all stared at it for a moment before I handed it to Oisin. "Will this work?"

The red-haired man smiled, the skin around his eyes and his mouth crinkling in delight. "Perfect." We were on to something now.

It was Naël's turn to speak. "Once we locate them, what do we do? He will surely use the weapon against Aiden right away and then try to kill him with the brahmachakram. What do we do to prevent that?" I wiggled closer to him, wanting to feel his heat against my body.

"Oisin is also in possession of Claíomh Solais, the Sword of Light." My druid father said this as if I was supposed to know what that was. Well, I didn't. I raised my eyebrows, and I could have sworn his shoulders slumped a bit as if he was disappointed in my lack of Celtic lore knowledge. My inner child wanted to stick my tongue out at him, but for once, the adult part of me won. "In simple terms, it's an unbeatable sword. Whoever yields it, wins."

"Kind of like Excalibur." Everyone turned their heads to Vee, surprised. "What? I read. I watch movies." She looked so outraged, we all burst into laughter. "Fine, keep laughing, but you know I'm right." She crossed her arms and pouted.

"The girl is not too far from the truth," Oisin said. Vee smiled, placated. "I don't need the sword to beat Baburaj, but you can use it. That way, once he takes away your powers, you'll still be able to have some of an upper hand." It sounded better than nothing, but I didn't want to fight to kill. My own powers had terrified me with their lethal strength and my lack of control. I'd rather fight him with my fists than wield a dangerous weapon.

I shook my head vehemently. "No, I don't want the sword," I said, seeking my merman's hand and lacing my fingers through his. "Give it to Naël. He's the big scary ex-marine. He will handle the sword better than me." Fouchard gave my hand a pointed squeeze. Every eye turned to me, uncomprehending. "I have a weird aversion to weapons." The truth was the idea of killing another sentient creature scared the crap out of me. I was not sure I could live with myself if I did kill someone, even a hateful idiot like Bob or the king of the Fae—but I'd be totally okay with punching their faces to a pulp.

Oisin threw my father a look as if asking for permission. My father nodded, so he turned to my merrow and said, "All right, the day of the battle, I will hand you Claíomh Solais then." Fouchard opened his mouth to protest, but I pulled on his hand forcefully, and he closed it without a sound. I could be bossy too.

The white-haired oracle had been happily munching on Vee's macarons and sipping tea, seemingly oblivious to the conversation going on around him. I was almost shocked to hear his voice echo through the room. "That's settled then. In my vision, I saw Aiden be brought down by Baburaj."

What? That was not good, right? "The images became murky after that, so there is no telling what happened exactly, but we must be ready to protect him. Aiden is a future leader of our community, a crucial one to our survival. We can't lose him."

What? "Wait, wait a second," I interjected, my hand raised in front of me. "I'm no leader of anything," Except maybe my sexual life. "And have no wish of being one. But even if that's true, why would I be crucial to everybody's welfare?" I didn't like this one bit.

My father stepped in. "It's been written in the stars since you were born." What a crock full of shit. Written in the stars? Who the hell was I? The new redeemer? I could barely keep myself out of trouble, much less take care of a whole community of magical creatures. Probably reading my expression of disbelief, my father threw an SOS glance at the oracle.

Brother Serafim stopped his macaron-filled hand halfway to his mouth to squint at me. "Aiden, my boy, why are you always so cynical? Your father is telling the truth." Little bits of a half-chewed cookie flew out with his words. "The day you were born, your destiny as the leader of our people was written across the skies. Only magicals could see it, but it was there, nevertheless. We've been waiting anxiously for your coming of age." I had come of age a long time before this. I was practically middle-aged, and here I was listening to this insane tale that sounded like something out of a young adult fantasy novel.

I wasn't buying it. "Stop the bullshit, will you?" My voice came out a lot louder than I had planned, and even Fouchard tensed up beside me. "I am no leader or savior or anything remotely of that caliber. I am a coffee shop owner with a few magical powers who wants to live a life of anonymity. Is that too much to ask?"

Cristina hopped to her feet and came to stand by my side. "Maybe you are all reading too much into it," she said. "Maybe it just means that he will be able to rid the community of Bob, the idiot, and his bitch of a mother. Maybe that's how he will protect the community." My best friend, always ready to give me the benefit of the doubt and jump in to be my knight in-not-so-shiny armor.

The oracle looked at her intensely for a moment or two, then said, "Nuh, the stars were pretty clear about it," and stuffed his mouth with a pink macaron.

A flood of heat climbed my neck into my face,

not of embarrassment but of anger and frustration. Now I was a fucking savior of my people. It wasn't only cheesy; it was totally and utterly preposterous.

"I need to talk to Aiden in private," my merrow said, standing and pulling me up with him. He didn't wait for an answer, leading me out the living room door into the hallway. I was more than happy to leave that room full of people who apparently were expecting me to be some kind of hero I had no wish of being. My merman took me all the way to the corner by the staircase before stopping, laying his hands on my shoulders, and peering deeply into my eyes. "You don't have to do this. Get rid of Bob and then tell them you are out."

His luscious lips were very close as he bent down slightly to my height, and I wanted to kiss him and forget the whole conversation of the past hour. "How do I do that? It would have been easy before because they didn't know me, but now they've got my number." As much as I wanted to, I didn't see a way out of this mess.

"We can hide in our cave until they give up looking for us." I smiled at him. I'd love to hide where we had quite a few wonderful memories, but it was not viable. Who would take care of my store?

Who would watch Vee? No, as much as I hated it, I had to face this challenge face on.

I crossed the few inches between us and kissed him. "I love you for saying that, but I can't. I have to grow up and face the fact my life has taken a detour into crazy and just run with it." He lowered his lips on mine again, and we remained in a lip-lock for a while, taking comfort in each other's flavor and heat. When we pulled apart, I was breathless but as ready as I was ever going to be to accept the idiotic, insane challenge the magical community was laying on my shoulders. "Let's go face the music," I said, holding on to Naël's hand and pulling him toward the living room. "However out of key and scratchy it might be."

TWENTY-TWO
DEAD MAN WALKING

THE REST OF THE WEEK WAS A BLUR. I GOT UP every morning, ate, went to work, ate some more, walked on the beach for a while to recharge, ate again, went home, and buried myself in my loving merman—the only thing I looked forward to these days. Fear and doubt hung over my head every minute of the day, and it was turning me into a very boring—however sexy—man, or whatever I was. Fouchard made my days bearable, gave me something to live for with his tender loving and big strong arms. His love was the light at the end of the dark tunnel I had managed to get myself into, and I soldiered on relentlessly toward it, hoping to leave the darkness behind once and for all.

I woke up that morning tangled up in Naël's

arms and legs, blinking furiously at the bright fall sunlight coming in through a crack in the curtains. Today was the day. Doomsday most likely, considering I would be rendered totally helpless against the little evil Hindu god, my life left solely in my friends' hands. The fact I had a bona fide god plus had a bunch of powerful druids on my side notwithstanding, I was still in a sucky position. And then there was that whole bullshit about my role as some sort of savior of my people, the same ones I had spent most of my life avoiding. The universe had a sick sense of humor.

I watched my mate sleep, his rock-hard chest rising and falling, his dark eyelashes fanned over his smooth brown skin, a smattering of a scruff covering his face. I ran my thumb over the line of his lower jaw, delighting in the scratchy feeling against my skin. I scanned the rest of his body with my gaze, from the delicious neck I loved running my lips over, down to his lower body, naked and glorious in the morning light. I loved morning sex with this man, and that morning I needed it more than ever to distract me from what was about to happen and focus only on the love of my life. I slipped from under the arm that anchored me beneath him and slowly, so as not to wake him up, turned around the opposite way so I could kneel beside his hips and take him with my mouth. If I was going to die, I wanted my merman to have one last unforgettable memory of us together.

As soon as my lips latched around his hard length, Naël stirred and moaned softly. I suckled him, using my naughty tongue the best I knew how—and gods knew I'd had a lot of practice—until his eyes flew open and a loud groan of pleasure escaped his lips. He looked down, and his dark eyes met mine in a silent greeting. A lovely, wicked smile curled his mouth, and I doubled my efforts, quickening the pace of my mouth's ebb and flow rhythm. He arched his back, throwing his head back onto the pillow with a scream of pleasure, his knuckles turning white as he closed his hand on the white sheets. *I'm going to make sure you remember me, sweetheart.* I didn't want to be forgotten like I had been by my own parents and the world in general. I wanted my fiancé to remember the way my lips felt on his sensitive skin, how I felt inside him, how my tongue tasted and played against his own. I wanted him to love me even after death.

I slipped a hand between his parted legs and filled him with one of my fingers. He cussed and pressed himself harder against my hand. "Ready?" I mumbled, my mouth still full of him.

"Hell yeah." I pulled out from him and climbed up his body until our bodies were flush with each other, his hardness against mine. "Do you want me to…?

"No, this is all for you today, sweetheart," I said, my lips over his. "All about you, my love."

I closed in on his delicious mouth, my tongue sliding along his while I rubbed my lower body on his, my hand sliding between us to caress him. I wrapped my hand around him and coaxed him into a climax I was hoping he wouldn't soon forget. I felt him pour his seed over my hand and my own arousal, gasping into my mouth. I was right behind him, spilling myself on him even as his body still trembled from his orgasm. I collapsed on top of him, spent and sated, my ear over his chest listening to the music of his heart.

"Not that I'm complaining," he said after a while, once both our hearts had settled into a regular beat. "But what was that all about? You shouldn't exhaust yourself like that before battle." Ever the marine.

"Does it matter whether I'm tired or not?" I said, resting my chin on his chest to look at him.

"Bob is going to suck out all of my powers until I stand totally vulnerable to any attack. Tired or well rested, the result will be the same."

His arms went around me, enfolding me completely. "I'm afraid too, but we have fucking awesome backup. I choose to believe we will be fine, that you will be fine."

I was quiet for the next five minutes or so, my chin still resting on his chest, lost in thought. "I know I will be," I finally said, planting a kiss on one of his pecs. "Besides, I will have my manly man of a boyfriend beside me, wielding the fucking sword of light. What could possibly go wrong?" Everything, really. But I was not going to ruin this moment with negative thoughts, even if my mind was reeling with them.

We later met with the Scooby gang, now expanded by a few more members. My father raised his eyes to me as soon as he saw me getting out of the car. We were all meeting by my coffee shop and departing from there to wherever we were going to battle the not-so-great Bob. I was still having trouble looking my father in the eye, but I had to admit my chest no longer exploded with anger every time I saw him. Instead, anger had been replaced by a strangely soft feeling that I didn't recognize but was guessing was the path to forgiveness.

Taz, dressed in sweats, came out from behind the red-haired Oisin, and I did a double take. "What the hell are you wearing, witch?" I said, shocked by the absence of high heels and stylish clothing. "Who are you and what have you done with Taz?"

She scoffed. "Funny, Aiden. How can I go into battle dressed like the gorgeous woman I am?" I snorted, and she gave me the stink eye. "Why aren't *you* dressed for a fight?"

I was wearing my usual getup: jeans, a black T-shirt, and flip-flops. I had considered wearing sneakers, but the weather was still too nice for closed shoes, and to be honest, if I was going to die, I didn't want my last minutes on this earth to be with painfully restricted toes. If worse came to worst, I could always kick off my shoes and go bare-footed. It would be as if I connected to an electric outlet, charging me with the energy I needed to face the monsters.

Oisin wore a strange shirt with high stiff collars that had to be pretty uncomfortable. I nodded in their direction. "What the fuck are those for? There's a fashion statement if I ever saw one."

The Celtic god laughed. "Protection. They are made of a special material imbued with magic. Don't want to stick my neck out too much, if you get my drift." Taz encircled his waist with one arm and pulled him to her with a familiarity that surprised me. "Are you ready, Aiden?"

As ready as I would ever be, I supposed. I nodded and looked behind him where my father and a few other monks sat cross-legged on the ground, chanting something weird and unintelligible. Right next to them, observing everything with eyes opened wide in awe, was my best friend Cristina and her fiancé, the warlock cop. The only one missing was the oracle, but I didn't expect him to be directly involved in the battle. It was shocking enough to see him at our home a week ago.

Fouchard exchanged a few words with Dona Moreno, who, like Taz, had forgone her classy clothes in favor of stretchy and comfortable yoga clothes. After a while, he came back to me, draping an arm over my shoulders. "So, Oisin, you have located Bob." It was not a question. I gaped. When had that happened?

The young-looking god smiled wider, his freckled face a true ray of sunshine. "Yes, that ring was perfect. I was able to track them straight to where they have set up camp." I squinted, confused by his words. "Literally. They have pitched a tent in an isolated area of the Guincho beach." Fuck. They had been practically in the neighborhood all this time. Guincho was just a few miles down the road from Cascais where my fiancé lived with his sister.

Speaking of which. "Where's Vee?" I asked, looking around, knowing all too well the little mermaid would do anything to be there with us. "How did you manage to convince her not to come?"

Naël laughed. "You got to be kidding. I haven't convinced her of anything. She's in Cristina's car, texting her mermaid friends about how she will be on the front line of an epic battle."

A quick glance at the car parked a few yards away told me he was right. Vee's almost white hair was visible even from this distance. "She's not staying, is she?"

"Fuck no. She's going home in a few with Cristina," my fiancé said. "Cristina needs to be far from us herself when this thing goes down." I exhaled a breath of relief. I didn't need to be worried about my two favorite girls while I was being decimated by a demigod. My face must have betrayed my thoughts because my merman pulled me closer and whispered in my ear, "I will repay your most delightful morning surprise after the battle. With interest." He was obviously trying to make me feel a bit more confident, and he succeeded. Nothing motivated me more than a promise of earth-moving sex. The cunning merrow just had given me ammunition to avoid certain death.

Not wasting any more time, Oisin pulled the magical sword from its scabbard and handed it to Naël. "Don't drop it. As long as you have it in your hand, you're invincible," he said. Fouchard closed his hand over the pommel and weighed it. "Drop it and you're most likely dead."

"Cheery, aren't you?" I quipped. "What am I supposed to do, other than wait patiently to be slaughtered?"

Taz slapped me in the back of my head. She had been spending way too much time with Cristina. "Silly, you're not going to be slaughtered. Maybe a little thrashed, but you can totally survive that." *With friends like this, who needs enemies?* "You'll be fine."

Cristina approached, worry contorting her face and making her scars stand out— a reminder of why I needed to get rid of Bob. "You will be careful, won't you, Aiden?" She tried to smile, but it came across more like a frown. "No heroics, you hear? Não sejas parvo."

I snorted. "Have we met? I have no ambitions to be a hero of any kind, amiga. I will always be the guy who runs instead of fighting." Not true, I had found out. Funny how I didn't seem to know myself too well until first Cristina and then Naël walked into my life. I was not the coward I had always believed myself to be.

She threw herself in my arms, practically tearing me off Fouchard's. "You better come back alive and in one piece. Or we'll have words." I scoffed, and she slapped my ass. "I'm not kidding." I didn't think she was, but I didn't want her to worry too much about me.

I watched as her car disappeared into the horizon. We all jumped into our respective vehicles and headed toward Guincho. The day had started sunny, but it was quickly changing, a worrisome reflection of our mood. Dark clouds were gathering high in the sky, and the wind picked up speed the closer we got to the sandy dunes of Guincho. As we drove along the coast, I watched the ocean get wilder and wilder, the dark waters churning into giant waves that crashed mercilessly into the beach, throwing showers of salty mist flying into the air. Beautiful but deadly.

"Do you really think we can defeat Bob and his mother?" I asked my fiancé in a small voice that betrayed my worry.

"Sweetheart, we are heading to battle with the best army anyone can hope for," he said, placing a warm hand on my upper thigh. "There are no ifs or buts; we will win this."

I loved that he was so optimistic, but the weather itself didn't look too auspicious. I wanted to be that hero that muttered, "This is a good day to die," except I did not want to die or see any of my Scoobies dead. Hell, I didn't even want Bob dead, just trussed up like a turkey and thrown into a deep hole from where he would never hope to climb out.

I covered his hand with mine and squeezed gently. "I know, we'll be fine." There was no point in worrying him more by letting him know how my insides shook, or about the bile in my stomach that threatened to erupt at any time. *Believe it, and you will achieve it.* What a crock of shit! Tell that to my shriveling, churning innards.

By the time we parked the car behind a dune in one of those secluded corners of this never-ending beach, I was so nauseated I was certain I must have turned green. *Grow some balls,* my inner self kept saying to no avail. I was pretty sure I had left them at home. Or maybe I just never really had them.

Stepping out of the car, I inhaled deeply, the crisp ocean air filling my lungs with energy and relieving some of my anxiety. I breathed it in again. Gods only knew I would need all the earth energy I could get. My lovely merman came around the car to stand beside me, his hand seeking mine. I raised my eyes to his and sighed.

"We can do this," he said with a confidence I wished I had. He leaned over to kiss me, and for a moment, everything was well with the world.

When his lips left mine, the world came crushing down on me again. I shivered, watching the others approaching. "All right. Let's do this," I said, more to myself than anyone else. "And may the odds be ever in our favor."

A voice emerged from the humming sound of the wind. "Idiot! Couldn't you have chosen a happier movie quote?" No, Taz, I couldn't because I now knew what Katniss felt.

TWENTY-THREE

THE BIG REVEAL

I'D KICKED OFF MY FLIP-FLOPS A WHILE BACK. MY bare feet felt better buried in the cold sand, the gritty grains supplying me with the kind of energy I needed to face the little monster. If I was going to be divested of my dubious powers, I might as well at least be in the best physical shape possible. As I walked toward the area where Oisin had seen the deadly duo, my muscles tightened, my breathing became easier, and my step lighter. I said a silent thank-you to Mother Nature and all her elements for gifting me so generously and kept walking.

Beside me, Fouchard's military boots crunched the sand, his face locked into an expression I hadn't often seen since the first time I met him—stoic determination mixed with a pissed-off sneer that didn't bode well for anyone who dared cross him. In his hand, the Claíomh Solais caught the pale rays of the sun and reflected it like a mirror. Or maybe the sword of light did indeed hold light inside it.

Taz, Silva, and Oisin walked directly behind us, a strange trio of magicals with the warlock's raven black hair in shocking contrast with the flaming hair of the other two. There were no visible weapons on them, of course; their magic came from inside them, not from some enchanted object. As if keeping a safe distance, the three monks, my father, and the high priestess walked a few yards behind all of us. Like me, the druids wore no shoes, their steps buried and muffled by the sand. Dona Moreno, surprisingly enough, had also removed her shoes and walked like an experienced soldier toward war.

I sighed again. My backup was a formidable lot indeed. My chest relaxed a bit, positive vibes replacing the dark clouds that had been hovering over me for days. Bob might have the weaponry to defeat us, but we had the element of surprise and the sheer numbers on our side. We stood a good chance of winning after all.

If I hadn't been so stressed, I would have laughed at Bob's expression as he laid eyes on me and my small army of magicals. His chin dropped so low I was afraid he may have dislocated his lower jaw. Whatever he was holding fell soundlessly to the sand, and he stood, paralyzed. His mother was quicker to recover from the shock and reclaimed the fallen object, a white sphere that emitted an inner light. Was that the weapon that would turn me into a sitting duck? It didn't look like much of a weapon, but it was beautiful as an object; jeweled tones of light appeared and vanished on its surface, giving the impression it moved on its own. It was mesmerizing, and knowing I was looking at my kryptonite made it impossible for me to look away.

"Don't look straight at it." The priestess placed a hand on my shoulder and pulled me around to look at her. I blinked, freed from the invisible strings that tied my gaze to the pearl-like object in Jhanvi's hand. "It will hold you prisoner and suck out all your energy." No one else seemed affected by it. "It is tuned specifically to you, Aiden. It won't work with anyone else." *A custom-made weapon tuned in to me alone. Awesome.*

Jhanvi held it high over her head and cackled—what was with her and the dramatics? "Behold your undoing, Mercer."

Her attitude really rubbed me the wrong way. "You dumb bitch. Have you noticed I brought reinforcements?" My sarcastic bite was back. Yes, sarcasm was my ultimate weapon and the one I wielded the best. "Put that stupid hippie gadget down before we smite and pulverize you."

The hate in her eyes was bone-melting. Holy shit, what had I done to her to deserve such loathing?

"You think we're scared by your troop of freaks?" she yelled, still holding the damn sphere aloft. "My son has the brahmachakram. Nothing and nobody can stand a chance against it."

I scoffed, unwisely maybe. "May I remind you that your son had no luck using that same weapon with the druids a while back? I brought them with me, as you can see."

"Hiding behind Daddy's habit again, are you? Coward." Her words rankled, and I made as if to walk to her, but Fouchard grabbed my wrist and held me in place. "My son will kill you and all your friends without breaking a sweat." Right. He did have a very powerful tool at hand. I needed to be more subtle, except I didn't know how. Subtlety was not my forte. "Come if you dare."

I looked at my comrades in arms—yes, I was starting to imagine myself in one of those war movies—waiting for a sign. Oisin stepped forward to stand beside me. I guess that was as good a sign as any. I gathered my anger and wove it into an invisible ball in my hands and then let it grow until it caught on fire. I lifted it up on one hand and pulled my arm back to throw it at the mother and son duo.

"Do it now, Baburaj!" Jhanvi's scream was muffled by the wind, but the little man heard it and opened his hands to catch the lightning sphere his mother threw at him. I hurried to throw the ball of fire before he could neutralize me, but he moved with unnatural speed. I had just released it when I felt all my strength wan away like the retreat of the low tide. My aim was affected, and the angry ball of fire sputtered and took a detour to the left, crashing into a dune and sending millions of grains of sand flying into everything, including us. Belatedly we protected our eyes with our hands, but the particles blinded us for a few seconds. Thankfully Bob and Jhanvi had also been affected by the side effects of the explosion.

We recovered first, but I was facing my worst enemy bare of any magical powers. I heard the funky buzzing of the Claíomh Solais as Fouchard raised it over his head and took a fighting stance. Behind me, the druids had already started their mumbo jumbo, and next to me, Oisin was performing some weird choreography with his hands and mumbling something in a language I did not understand.

"Get the brahmachakram," Bob's mother yelled out in the voice of a general commanding her troops. Now we knew who the mastermind of that operation was. The little god didn't have the brain-power to plan and implement anything remotely effective. His talents were all limited to drinking.

Like the totally whipped moron he was, he didn't delay doing as Mommy dearest commanded. Turning around, he picked up the destructive weapon from its perch on a rock and pointed it at me. I froze. What did I do now? What I really wanted to do was run and tackle him so I could acquaint him with my fists, but I knew he would get me first. And without my power, I would be as good as dead.

"Aha! Not so cocky now, are you, Mercer?" he taunted, waving the weapon in my direction. "Maybe I should start with your fishy lover."

Big mistake. Huge. Mistake. Threatening me was one thing, but targeting my man was another thing altogether. He pointed the weapon at my merman, and I lost all sense of self-preservation.

With a battle cry that shocked even myself, I charged at the demigod, startling him into almost dropping the brahmachakram. The sudden realization that I wouldn't get to him before he discharged the weapon in my direction didn't deter my trajectory. Alive or dead, I was going to wrap my hands around that scrawny neck of his and squeeze until his eyes turned backward in their sockets.

I fully expected to get hit by the fiery orbs of the deadly weapon, but somehow Bob fired them upward into the sky. It baffled me a bit but not enough to stop me. I reached my foe and had no trouble closing my fingers around his air pipe. He sputtered, and his eyes widened in panic. Whatever was going on around me, I was too far gone into protection mode to care; I squeezed harder and took morbid pleasure in the choking sound I extracted from the weaselly creature. Something hit me over the side of my head and threw me a few feet away and onto my ass. Confusion muddled my thoughts, along with a loud ringing in one of my ears. It took me a moment or two to be able to focus my eyes on what was happening in front of me. Even then I couldn't move, still stunned from the hit.

Fouchard was chasing Bob with the sword of

light, silent and deadly. It would have been comical if I didn't know how dangerous the situation was. That's when I noticed the yaksha retrieving the weapon from where Bob had dropped it and pointing it at me.

At least she wasn't aiming at Naël.

In the back of my mind, I knew I should be scrambling for safety, but my limbs didn't obey me. The blow to the head had affected my ability to move, and I sat there like a giant bull's-eye begging to be hit. I threw a last look at my boyfriend, wanting to see him one more time before dying— because I was sure I couldn't survive this. He had given up on the chase and turned around to run toward me, doing something I had never seen him do; he was screaming, a terrified, heart-wrenching scream that made my eyes fill with tears. He knew what was coming too.

"I love you." I couldn't be sure he heard me among the confusion of the battle, the sound of the wind, the chanting of the druids. I couldn't even be sure I actually uttered the words. But I had to say it nevertheless. I'd never be his husband now, but at least he was alive and well. I closed my eyes, ready for the blow.

But it never came. The ringing in my ear

blotted a lot of the other sounds, but I was certain the brahmachakram had not been fired. I opened my eyes, one at a time, and thought maybe I was hallucinating; standing between me and the weapon was Dona Moreno, her elegant body surrounded by a halo-like glow and, next to her, the young Celtic god glowed as well. I couldn't see Jhanvi because they blocked my view, but I heard—or thought I did—a static sound, like electricity through a live wire. Not the sound of Bob's weapon but something just or even more powerful. I didn't know how I knew that, but I just did.

Someone dropped on the sand beside me and wrapped me in his arms. "Aiden, my god, are you all right?" My sweet merrow bookended my face with his hands and checked my eyes. I tried to smile but couldn't be sure I was successful. Every move I made was labored and painful. He ran a hand over the side of my head where I had taken the brunt of the blow, and his fingers came back bloody.

"Fuck, you're bleeding." He peered into my eyes again. "Can you hear me? Do you know who I am?" I managed a tiny nod, and he smiled, his lip trembling. "Okay, okay, your eyes are a bit unfocused. Maybe a concussion. Lay down, rest." How could I do that when a battle was raging around me? I groaned against his hands as he tried to push me down onto the sand. "The others have the situation in hand. Stop fighting me. Lay down."

A blast echoed through the beach, and even my buzzing ears heard it. A flash of light erupted between the priestess and where the yaksha was in a starburst heading to the skies. It vibrated the earth beneath us in waves that could not be mistaken for anything other than pure energy. My contact with the cool sand allowed me to absorb some of it, and I felt immediately stronger. The ringing was still there, but I could now move a little and speak. "What was that?"

Fouchard looked as confused as I felt as we both stared in the direction of Dona Moreno and Oisin, who were no longer glowing. They lowered their raised hands and turned around to face me. The priestess smiled, and my pain eased as if by magic. They both crossed the space between us, Oisin gallantly offering her an arm for support.

"What the hell just happened?" Naël asked, cradling my aching head against his chest. "Where's Bob? I—shit, I let him go."

"No worries, merman," Oisin said, pointing behind me toward the druids. "Taz and Silva got him. The druids have him in a confinement spell."

I licked my parched lips. "And his mother? The brahmachakram?" I couldn't see her anywhere.

"She's been taken care of and won't be bothering you ever again," Oisin said with a chuckle. Hardly the time to laugh, I thought, but who was I to judge a god? "We're not sure about the weapon. One minute it was there, the next it wasn't."

Dona Moreno dropped to her knees beside us and touched my face with gentle fingers. "How are you feeling, Aiden?" Her voice soothed the dull pain in my head further. "I didn't get to you on time, I'm sorry. It was quite a blow."

"I've had worse," I managed to mumble. Not true, but the pain was going away, and the ringing had faded a bit. "Is everyone safe?"

"Everyone is doing fine," my merrow assured me. "We have to get you to a hospital though. You're bleeding profusely, and I'm almost sure you have a concussion."

"Let me take care of him, Naël," the priestess said with a tilt of her head. "I can heal him."

I admit I looked at her suspiciously. I still had my doubts about witches and was not sure how their healing powers worked—or if they worked at all. However, every time I looked at her, I felt better, as if by her very presence she was already healing me. I nodded, and Naël relaxed against me.

Dona Moreno placed a cool hand on my cheek and held it there for a moment, peering deep into my eyes. "You've always been brave in the face of hardships and trouble, Aiden. Your mother is very proud." I sat up so suddenly my head swam. She held me down with a gentle but firm hand. "Lay back into your fiancé, Aiden, so I can restore your health."

"Why did you say that? About my mother?" I asked, making her work of checking my head difficult. "How would you know she's proud of me? Have you met her?"

Giving up on examining the wound on my scalp, she lowered her hands to her lap and smiled. "Yes, I do know her very well," she said, a strange sadness in her eyes. Both my merrow and I fixed our gaze on her, waiting for her to continue. "But that's a conversation for another time. You must take care of that wound."

I grabbed her hands, stopping her from resuming the healing process. "No," I said firmly. "With all due respect, Dona Moreno, I think I have the right to know who my mother is, don't you?"

She hung her head as if pondering. A moment

later, she raised her eyes back to me and sighed. "Of course you have the right to know," she said, sitting back on her calves. "And since there is no reason to hide it from you anymore...."

My father had materialized behind her, hands inside his sleeves and eyes suspiciously shiny. "Tell him, Penny. Tell him the truth."

The familiarity between them surprised me and not for the first time. I bounced my gaze between them, a nagging idea beginning to slowly coalesce, the memory of my father's earlier words echoing in my mind, "One witch, two gods, a merman, a warlock, and a whole convent of druids." Two gods! I only knew of one. Who could possibly be the other? Was it possible that Dona Moreno was...? No. Couldn't be. I swallowed the dry lump in my throat.

Penelope Moreno smiled at my father and then at me. "Okay, you might as well know," she said with another sigh. "I'm Lakshmi. I'm your mother."

TWENTY-FOUR

NEW BEGINNINGS

IF I EVER WONDERED HOW IT WOULD FEEL TO BE HIT by a stampeding herd of elephants only to be immediately attacked by a cast of hungry, sharp-beaked hawks, I could now describe it in great detail. Penelope Moreno's claim left me flatter than a tire that had just crossed over several rows of police traffic spikes.

The last few hours between the time she had dropped her bomb and the time we had returned home were nothing but a blur. I had no memory of how I had gotten to my merrow's house—most likely the same way I had gone to Guincho in the first place—or what I said to the priestess in response. My life just kept getting weirder and weirder.

"Blink twice if you can hear me, sweetheart." Naël sat on a chair facing me, his eyes level with mine and his hands clutching my biceps. His attempt at humor didn't go unnoticed but fell flat nonetheless. He clicked his tongue like a mother hen, something that would normally send me into a fit of laughter, but this time only made me blink. "Oh, good, you're alive after all. You must speak to me, Aiden. Tell me what's going through your mind."

A quick robotic scan of the room told me we were alone. "Where are the others?" I asked, slowly awakening from my near-catatonic state.

"We got here first. They'll be in soon," he said, still frowning in worry. "I called Cristina, and she should be coming soon too. Let's talk before they get here."

"What can I say?" My head was still reeling from the news, and I honestly didn't know what to think. The only thing that was clear-ish in my mind was the sudden understanding of why the high priestess's voice was always so soothing to me—the voice of a mother, maybe something I remembered from my early days.

Fouchard exhaled loudly, rubbing my arms. "Sweetheart, you must be feeling something. You must be angry or confused." He bent down lower to have better access to my eyes. "You have to talk about it or it will eat you up inside."

I took a couple of deep breaths and then raised my head. "I don't know how to feel, Naël," I confessed. "First I find out my father is a druid who lives a few miles away from me, and now I discover that the witches' high priestess is actually my mother, who is also a fucking goddess. What the hell happened to the normal life I wanted to have? Why can't my parents be a poor farmer and his wife who couldn't afford to keep me? Someone regular and simple."

My merman switched seats so he could be next to me on the couch. He draped an arm over my shoulder and pulled me to him until my head was resting in the crook of his neck. "I know it has to be a shock to the system, but it could be worse." I cocked my head and widened my eyes in disbelief. He chuckled nervously. "It could have been someone like Jhanvi. At least Brother John and Dona Moreno are the good guys in this story."

I widened my eyes even further. "Good guys? Have you forgotten how they abandoned their baby son shortly after birth and left him to figure out his way in this big and cruel world?" My voice came out sharper and louder than I had planned. It wasn't Naël's fault that I had such a sorry excuse for parents. If anything, he'd given me the love and stability I had always craved but never had. "Sorry, Naël. I'm just very confused and frustrated right now."

"I know, sweetheart, I know." He placed a gentle hand on my head and pulled it down to his shoulder again. "You don't have to talk about it now if you don't want to, but I'm here for you when you're ready. I love you."

I sighed again, hating the way I was feeling. I was far from a child and felt as if I was whining like one. I had to grow up and put on the big boy shorts. "You will be the first one to hear my rant once I figure out how I feel." It was a promise, and I knew it would come. Sooner or later, this confusion, this shock would wane, and I would be able to finally voice whatever it was now buried under an ocean of doubt. "We should have some food ready for the team. After all this fighting, they must be hungry." Focusing on the practical was better than the alternative.

Together we prepared sandwiches and threw a couple of frozen pizzas in the oven. I filled a bucket with ice and buried several bottles of beer in it.

After staging a bunch of coffee cups by the Nespresso machine and the canister of coffee pods, I stacked a pile of napkins and silverware on the counter and wiped my hands on my very dirty and sandy jeans.

"Maybe we should change before they get here," Fouchard said. "We're tracking sand all over the house. The cleaning lady is not going to be very happy with us." She was most likely used to it, considering we often tracked wet sand from the basement beach after our swims and exploits in our love cave, but getting rid of the scratchy grains that were invading some private areas of my body was a great idea.

By the time we returned to the kitchen, Taz, the warlock, and Oisin were already standing there, drinking coffee and munching on sandwiches. "We took the pizzas out of the oven," the witch said, staring at me intently. "How are you doing, Aiden?"

"Why is everybody worried about my psyche? I'm not as weak as I look." My outburst made Taz flinch.

"Dude, I was talking about the possible concussion," she said, filling me instantly with remorse. "What the hell happened for you to be this touchy?"

Shit, she didn't know. I'd forgotten that of the three, only Oisin had witnessed the big reveal. He looked sheepishly at me and shrugged. "I didn't tell them anything, Aiden," he said. "I figured it's not my place." He figured correctly, but on the other hand, that meant I would have to do the honors of telling everyone about my strange, however powerful, parentage. I didn't want to have that conversation.

"What didn't you tell us, Oisin?" Taz was on full red alert, her green eyes round as saucers. I swear her ears had perked up. "What happened?"

I shook my hand dismissively. "Not ready to talk about this, witch." Her eyes were so pleading, I sighed and added, "Oisin, you tell her or she might explode. I don't want witch gunk soiling the house."

Taz had the nerve to look offended but immediately grabbed the young Celtic god by the elbow and steered him out of the kitchen. Poor Oisin. But better him than me.

The front door opened, and Cristina walked in with an overly excited Vee, who ran and yelled like a banshee all the way to the kitchen. "Aiden, Aiden, I found the perfect outfit for your wedding." *Gods, give me patience!* What horrifying thing had she dug up now? She waved a magazine over her head, which she slapped on the countertop in front of me. "Look at this." My gaze drifted to the open magazine with a certain trepidation. I almost gagged. The picture showed a jewel tone suit made entirely of fabric covered in fish scale sequins. Who in their right mind would wear that?

"Vee, that's not quite my style, you know?" I really wanted to be married in jeans and a T-shirt, even though I'd be willing to compromise by wearing a blazer over it. But not that monstrosity I was looking at. "Can we talk about this another time, Vee? I'm not in the right mood." All right, I would make an excuse since I couldn't very well tell her what was really in my mind. "I got hit over the head and am feeling a little dizzy." Moreno—or Lakshmi—had done an amazing job at not only healing the wound on my head but also the effects of the concussion. I was a bit lightheaded but nothing else. Did I get my healing powers from her?

The young mermaid pouted for a moment, but then she saw Taz talking to Oisin and decided to join the duo. She had been acting all starry-eyed around the red-haired man. Could she have a crush on the young god? That's all we needed now, first crushes and heartbreaks.

The front door opened again to reveal an

unlikely pair: my parents. My mother, still wearing her comfortable but stylish clothes, and my father in a rustic brown habit were the most mismatched couple I had ever seen. My stomach churned. Those were my parents, the people whose genes had formed into whatever I was and then left me. A powerful druid and a goddess. Sometimes I wondered whether all of this was a dream.

"We need to talk, Aiden," Dona Moreno said. "In private."

I nodded, unable to deny her request. "Naël comes too."

"Of course, he is part of the family." Mine yes, but my parents and I were nothing remotely resembling a family. Not yet. Maybe never.

The four of us retired to the small study in the back of the house, a space rarely used but quiet and private. My father stood at one corner of the room, his hands hidden inside his sleeves and an unreadable expression on his face. Afraid my wobbly legs would fail me, I sat on one of the two small armchairs with my boyfriend standing right behind me, his hands casually resting on the high back of the chair as close to my head as they could be without touching me. His presence strengthened me in ways I couldn't explain.

Dona Moreno pulled up a chair but, at the last minute, let it go and walked up to me. "How's your head?" she asked, her gentle fingers probing my scalp. A shiver ran through me and filled me with a warmth I didn't recognize. What was that sense of comfort, of safety her touch filled me with? "Does it still hurt?"

I closed my eyes, relishing that unfamiliar feeling. "I'm okay. It's just a little sore." Her fingers left my scalp, and I felt bereft.

"I know this is all upsetting and hard to process," my father said. Gross understatement. "But we have to find a way for us to reconnect."

I bristled, straightening on the chair. "Reconnect? When did we connect to start with? Hard to do that when you don't even know who your parents are."

My father had the good sense to lower his eyes. Moreno spoke up, "This must be so difficult for you, Aiden. I can only imagine. But allow me—us—to tell you how it was for us." I nodded, however reluctantly. Fouchard squeezed one of my shoulders. "I had other children, gods the whole lot, disconnected from real life and not interested in family. I loved them all and was pleased to see them into adulthood and leave the nest. But then Pavarti cursed all gods to never have children, and for hundreds of years, there were no little ones in the world of the gods."

Was this for real? Was I really sitting here listening to Lakshmi telling me about how she and the other gods in Hindu mythology had lost their ability to procreate?

"Almost forty years ago, I decided to take on human form and live among the magical community," she continued, crossing one leg over the other knee. "I had long been separated from Vishnu, who had lost all touch with reality. I wished for nothing but a normal life. The local coven had been left without a leader when their last priestess died suddenly of a heart attack, so I stepped in and made them believe I could replace her. Then, one day I met your father, John." She looked up at my father with yearning in her eyes. Holy shit, they were still hot for each other. How gross and beautiful at the same time. "We fell in love. Imagine my surprise when, after hundreds of years of infertility, I conceived another child. A very special child who was half god, half human but one hundred percent magical. With both our magical genes, you were born with amazing latent powers that would be feared and coveted by many other gods. We had to hide you until such time when your powers would be realized and impossible to hide anymore."

Brother John stepped closer to her and laid a hand on her shoulder. She smiled at him again and covered his hand with hers. "Your father is a good man and a very powerful druid, intimately connected with the elements, and so are you. I am a goddess who draws powers from the ocean and the rivers, one who can heal, and so do you. We wish we could have been there for you growing up. We watched you from a distance with broken hearts. You have no idea of how many times I went to bed and cried all night, my heart craving you just like lungs crave oxygen. Your father was my anchor, my strength, but I know this was as hard on him as it was on me. As it was on you, my son."

Silence fell, my heart beating noisily inside my chest. I wanted to love them. Fuck, I did love them, but I couldn't forgive them yet. The wound in my heart had not healed yet. I made a strangled noise, and my fiancé stepped forward. "Dona Moreno, Brother John, thank you for sharing this with us— with your son. I'm sure Aiden understands now why you did what you did, but you must be patient with him. He has been alone for a long time, and he needs time to think things through, to get used to the idea he is not alone anymore."

"We understand," the druid monk told my fiancé. "We hope he'll forgive us and allow us back into his life, but we understand he needs more time. Of course we will give him all the time he needs. We will wait for as long as necessary and be here anytime he needs our help." He turned to me. "We'll be here for you, son. You let us know what we can do, anytime, anything."

I nodded again, a silent and hesitant thank-you. The actual words had caught in my throat, strangled by a feeling that was half happiness, half sorrow. I had my lost parents back in my life, so that was reason to be happy, right? But this old pain, this hole in my soul that had grown in tandem with the natural growth of my physical body, was still there, yearning to be filled but cautiously shying away.

A memory flashed in my head. "When I met you at the beach two months ago, you didn't look at all like yourself." The image of the beautiful Indian woman dressed in a sari and barefoot on the sand had haunted me for weeks afterward. "How come? Or was I wrong in thinking she was you?"

Dona Moreno smiled. "It was me. I have lived many lives, many different reincarnations. The woman you saw is just one of them—really just a projection of one of them but still me." How strange to have a goddess for a mother, an individual who could literally change her appearance at a snap of her fingers. "Now that you know what my current reincarnation looks like, I won't change it again." That was a good thing. I was confused enough as it was. "Thank you, Aiden, for listening to our side of the story. We do love you very much." I couldn't help it; I smiled like an idiot who had just been told he was a genius.

My mother—how lovely she was—stood up and walked out of the room hand in hand with my father. For a brief moment, I wondered what kind of a childhood I would have had if I had grown up with them in my life, but I couldn't visualize it.

"Are you okay?" my boyfriend asked, crouching before me. I shook my head, still unable to say anything. "Okay, time for some earthy therapy." I raised my gaze to him. What did he mean? "Let's go." He laced his fingers through mine and pulled me up.

Like thieves or, as I prefer to think, spies, we sneaked past the kitchen on silent steps and hushed voices and quietly opened the door to the basement. The fresh ocean air hit me and revitalized me right away, only getting stronger as we went down the steps and onto the cool sand.

It was getting chilly, and I shivered. "We don't have to do this if you're cold." Naël looked at me, worried.

"No, I want to." I did. I needed to take my mind off gods and druids, of lost childhoods and found enemies, of life and death, of what the future might still be hiding from me. I needed it to be just me and my merman, my fiancé, my love, the one who made me feel worthy and wholesome, capable and loved. We began stripping our clothes as we sauntered over the sand, discarding them behind us like unwanted old skin. The ocean water bit into my skin, first shocking and then soothing as we waded into it, holding hands as if to a lifeline. I closed my eyes, took a deep breath, and plunged, allowing the salty water to cover me fully.

Let this moment be a new beginning.

TWENTY-FIVE
SAINTS AND SINNERS

I NEVER THOUGHT I'D SAY THIS, BUT I SURE MISSED my powers. It had been over a week since our epic beach battle and the effects of Bob's beautiful but evil power-sucking orb still lingered. My mother assured me they'd be back, now that they had returned the kryptonite ball to its watery tomb in the deepest depths of the Indian Ocean, but that now-familiar spark of magic inside me was still off. Thankfully, my sexual endowments had not followed suit or life would have been unbearable.

"Damn, Aiden," Naël exclaimed as his upper body hovered over mine. "How can you be ready to go again so soon? One of these days you're going to kill me." I widened my eyes, slightly alarmed, but he quickly added, "But what an awesome way to go."

His lips descended on mine and worked their magic as they lingered there for a while, teasing, licking, suckling…. Oh yes, it would be such a lovely way to die. I groaned in protest when he pulled away. "Unfortunately, I have to go to the embassy to take care of some papers."

He slipped off the bed, leaving me panting and forlorn. My naughty bits were frustrated and aching for him. I rose on my elbows to follow him around the room, that lovely hot body of his moving gracefully from one side to another, picking up clothes here and there. I almost swooned when he bent over to retrieve his shoes from underneath a chair across from our bed. That was a sight I would never get enough of. It looked as if I'd have to take a warm shower and make friends with my favorite appendage since my boyfriend wouldn't be able to oblige.

"What do you need those papers for? Come back to bed." He stole a glance at me with a wicked smile. I waggled my eyebrows suggestively. "I'll make it worth your while."

He chuckled, slipping into his jeans. "Tempting, but if I don't take care of these documents, we won't be able to get married." He shoved his feet inside his shoes and sprinted to the edge of the bed to deposit a kiss on my lips. "Save it for later, sweetheart." His whisper almost did me in. He laughed again and left but not before brushing his fingers along that aching part of my anatomy. Wicked man. I would get him later for this.

After spending some time getting reacquainted with myself, I took a long hot shower, got dressed, and went to work. Fouchard and I had stayed in my condo overnight while Vee spent the night with a friend from school. Cristina was already at the store, getting everything ready for the day. The Swiss tourists were gone, so business was back to normal, still busy but sedate compared to before. I welcomed the distraction of serving tables, making coffee, washing dishes, all the while bantering with my best friend. If I really tried, I could pretend everything was back to normal, but every time Cristina smiled at me, the scars on her face reminded me nothing was and never would be normal again.

My phone rang, and I answered automatically, my thoughts still on what Cristina had to go through because of me and my crazy background. "Hi, sweetheart." Like a balm, Naël's voice washed all my regret and worries away. "We're going out tonight. It's time we start acting like normal people dating do." The problem was we were not regular people. "It's São Martinho, and I can't wait to show you how the natives celebrate it."

"Does it involve sex?" I asked wistfully.

"Better, okay, maybe not better, but pretty great." We hadn't been on a proper date in a long time and god knew we had certainly earned it. "Be ready at closing. I will swing by to pick you up."

As soon as I pressed End, Taz and Oisin, who had been inseparable lately, walked in. My eyes veered to their connected hands. So their friendly relationship had developed into something more. Interesting. "What are you two doing here?" I asked, heading behind the counter to get the coffees and pastries the two would most certainly ask for.

"I have a message from the high priestess," the witch said, sitting down and crossing her legs, her stiletto shoes hanging precariously from the tip of her toes. My heart contracted. My mother. The thought of her existence still filled me with contradictory feelings. "She wanted to know whether you are still suffering from headaches and if you have any of your powers back."

The terrible migraines that had haunted me for days after the battle had finally faded away—a fact that made me giddy—but my powers, other than the ones I had had all my life, were still missing in action. "No to both questions," I said, coming back with a plate packed with pastries. Taz might be skinny, but she could eat like a lion. "Why the sudden concern?"

Taz puckered her lips and eyed the pastries with delight. "Ooh, the *bola de Berlim* looks amazing." I gave her the large fried pastry ball and waited for her to go on. "And she's concerned because she is your mother, idiot." She took such a large bite off the *bola* that I was afraid she would lock her jaw. She didn't. "I still can't believe it. What are the odds that my high priestess is both your mother and a goddess? It's true what they say: reality is stranger than fiction."

Oisin picked on a *pastel de nata* as if afraid it would bite him. "We also came to invite you and Naël to come with us to a little celebration by the beach," he said, still twisting his nose. "The bar just down from here is throwing a party tonight."

Cristina joined the conversation, setting a tray full of dirty crockery on the counter. "Shit, almost forgot that today is São Martinho." At my eyebrow rise, she added, "Amigo, this is the day for a *magusto*, to eat roasted chestnuts, and drink *jeropiga*." The woman was speaking in some alien language I could not make heads or tails of. "How can you have lived here for almost two years and not know what that is? *Que vergonha*, how shameful."

"You guys are always finding excuses to drink and eat," I said with a chuckle. "And the worst part is that you do it all in the name of the saints. You basically turn a cardinal sin into a virtue." One of the many reasons I loved this country and its people.

We were still sitting around that table when it was time to close. Punctual as a Swiss clock, Fouchard showed up just as I was turning off the lights. What had begun as a date quickly evolved to a three-couple outing. A while back, I'd be upset not to have my merman all to myself, but I now had a totally different perspective; being around people who I could call friends was one of the few changes in my life I was grateful for. We strolled along the *paradão*, heading to the beachside bar that was offering the *magusto*, whatever that was. It was a typical evening for this time of the year—comfortably cool, clear star-studded skies, with the regular susurrus of the ocean waves lapping the shore. My fiancé had me sheltered against his side, his arm over my shoulders and his body heat keeping me snug as a bug in a rug. Perfection.

The bar owners had set up on the beach instead of the actual restaurant site, loungers and small side tables sprinkled the sand around a roaring fire. A delicious scent tickled my nose. Chestnuts! Man, no one did roasted chestnuts quite like the Portuguese. My taste buds did a little happy dance as I watched the two servers behind the makeshift counter by the fire scooping the hot nuts into cones made out of newspaper pages and handing them to the customers. A couple other servers walked barefoot on the sand, large pitchers on hand as they poured a tawny drink into every-body's cups.

"What's that they're serving?" I asked my merrow as we made our way down the steps to the beach.

Taz called out from behind me, "Jeropiga, idiot. Prepare to be awed." Drunk was more likely. Judging by the size of the cups, it wouldn't be long before many of the bar patrons would be seriously buzzed. This could be highly entertaining. I couldn't wait to see Oisin lose his godly dignity to a good dose of alcohol. Or the ever-righteous warlock for that matter. I made a mental note not to drink more than a glass so I could truly enjoy the show.

"Should we place a bet on who's going to be

wasted first?" I whispered in Naël's ear. He chuckled. "Unless it will be you."

He shook his head. "No way. Merfolk's livers can handle a lot more alcohol than a human's. I'd have to drink my weight in booze to get a buzz." I admit, I was a bit disappointed. I was very curious to see how my stoic merman would act under the influence. "Besides, alcohol stunts sexual potency. You wouldn't want to miss our planned afterparty activities, would you?"

The sweet stirrings my man always incited made me wiggle in my seat. "There are planned activities afterward?" I squeaked, my throat constricted by sudden desire. He looked at me and winked. "Fuck. Can we scarf down a few chestnuts and go home now?"

His hand sought mine. "Just chestnuts? No jeropiga or beer?" He seemed genuinely surprised. *Man, I thought you knew me better.*

I leaned over to whisper, "I love a beer or two, but nothing can live up to you and me in a compromising position." He burst out laughing, throwing his head back into the lounger, exposing his sexy neck. I leaned a bit more and placed my lips right below his ear to slide them down his neck. "You think I'm kidding?" Rhetorical question, of course.

He had known me now long enough to know I took our sex life very seriously. I felt him moan softly against my mouth.

"PDA alert," Taz yelled out like an eleven-year-old. "Stop that. It's gross but strangely erotic." She threw Oisin a look that spoke volumes—in fact, I would rather not have seen it. "You just might get lucky, my sweet Tuatha Dé." I pulled away from my beloved's neck, gagging. "Well, Aiden, you had your chance with me, but you chose the merman." Like I was complaining. I flipped her the finger, and she reciprocated with the same enthusiasm.

Despite my pants growing tighter every time I thought about whatever my fiancé had planned for afterward, I stayed with my friends for an hour or so. Turns out jeropiga was a sweet, highly alcoholic wine that went surprisingly well with the hot chestnuts, warming up my insides and stirring up the flames already flaring in me. When I couldn't focus on anything else but the way my mate's lips moved when he talked or the way his tongue flickered out to lick a runaway drop of wine from his finger, I jumped to my feet, grabbed his hand, and unceremoniously pulled him away from my friends.

"Well, that was a bit rude," Fouchard said,

feigning outrage. "You barely gave us time to say goodbye."

I circled his waist with my arm and pushed him against the wall. "They'll live." I crushed my body against his, hidden by the shadows of the building behind us. "I, on the other hand, might have exploded, and that would be very, very inconvenient."

His nose touched mine, mouths merely a couple inches away from each other. "And that would be bad because…?"

"Because I want to explode inside you, beautiful merman." I captured his mouth with mine, thrusting my tongue roughly between his lips. Something was different tonight. I suddenly felt renewed, stronger, reckless. With my tongue still dancing with his, I pushed a hand inside the front of his pants and rubbed him hard. Not that he needed much help. He was there already. Energy ran through me, from my heart and lungs to the tip of my fingers, toes, and other unmentionable parts.

"What's got into you, sweetheart?" Naël's words were chopped by his ragged breathing. He pressed himself onto my hand.

Yes, what was this surge of energy? Was it possible my magic was coming back? An idea popped into my head. "Hang on to me, Naël. Let's see if this works." Hanging on to him with an iron grip, I closed my eyes and wished myself in my apartment. A breeze and a gasp from my mate told me it had worked. When I opened my eyes, we were standing just outside my front door. "It worked. My magic is back."

"What the hell was that, Aiden?" My merrow looked baffled and a bit taken aback, still holding on to my arms as if afraid to let go.

"I wasn't sure I could do it, bring someone along with me when I teleport," I explained, a frisson of magic climbing my spine. "I guess I can." I smiled like a fool. So satisfied with myself it was truly disgusting. *My magic is back.*

"Your magic has returned?"

I nodded, incapable of wiping the smile from my lips. Why was I so happy to have my powers back? The same ones I had hated in the past. I was a complicated bastard, that's for sure.

A wicked smile stretched along my mate's lips. "Now I'm wondering what other new things you can do with your magic."

Oh, he was wicked indeed. "I have no idea, but what do you say we go to our room and try it out?"

TWENTY-SIX
HIDDEN OBJECTS

If I was a turtle, I would be retreating into my shell and never coming out again. If I was an ostrich, I'd have my head buried in the sand. But I was the great Aiden Mercer, odd magical creature extraordinaire, the love child of a powerful druid and a Hindu goddess. I couldn't hide however much I wanted to. So instead of lingering under the blankets, giving my mate yet more proof of how much I loved him, I was on my way to magical prison for a face-to-face with my worst enemy. Life sucked sometimes.

"Tell me again why I have to talk to the little turd." Cristina's fiancé was not happy with my very vocal reluctance to see Bob. I had been badgering him since we left my condo, shooting him with every excuse I could possibly find in angry outbursts. "We kicked his butt; he tried to steal my powers and then kill me. I think we've said all we could say to each other."

"Can you stop being a child, Aiden? For once." How dare he call me a child? I had valiantly fought the idiot god and his mother even after I had been robbed of my magic. I could have died. I almost did. I was not a child, even if I sometimes acted like one. "We need to know where he has the brahmachakram hidden, and he won't speak to anyone but you."

"Well, he and I aren't on talking terms anymore." I did sound like a brat. Fuck, I thought I had matured, but apparently, the simple mention of Bob brought my inner child back with a vengeance.

Silva parked in front of a nondescript one-floor building with whitewashed walls and a couple windows. *This* was the prison? It didn't look very secure. Silva turned his head to me when I let out a gasp of surprise. "It's glamoured, Aiden. Not what it seems." Wait! I could see through glamours and my magic was back, so why couldn't I see through this one? Before I could ask, the warlock answered, "Specialized glamour your mother came up with some years ago. It holds well, right?"

My mother was a woman of many talents, apparently. Shit, of course she was. She was Lakshmi, a goddess of such power she was often portrayed as having four arms—which I was sure came in handy when keeping her children and ex-husband in line. As soon as we crossed the front door, the glamour faded, and reality appeared. There was not much to see on the inside. I could feel the wards set along the gray walls, wards that reminded me of the protective circle the druids had conjured that day Bob came to attack me in the convent. There was a basic reception area with one small counter and a desk where a dour-looking warlock sat staring at the blank screen of a computer.

"You do realize there's nothing on the screen, right?" I couldn't help telling him. He raised his eyes to me, scowled, and went back to what he was doing.

"He's scrying to make sure none of the prisoners are planning an escape," Silva explained as he led me to the back of the room. The computer was a fucking crystal ball? Ingenious, I hated to admit. There was a lot I still needed to learn about the world of magic. Silva wiggled his fingers, and a door that hadn't been there before came into view. "Through here."

As soon as we'd crossed the threshold, the door disappeared again. It worried me a bit. "If I needed to get out in a hurry, would the wards hold me in?" I asked, following the warlock down the corridor dimly lit by magic globes along the walls.

"Who knows? Your magic is different from all other magic, so your guess is as good as mine." That was not an answer, at least not a helpful one. I was still the weirdo, even in the magical community.

He opened another previously invisible door, and we entered a small space void of any furniture. He wiggled his fingers again, and the opposite side of the room lit up to reveal an unwelcome vision; Bob was sitting on a cot facing us. I started until I realized an invisible force field separated us. More magic.

"I will leave you with him," the warlock said, much to my surprise. He was going to leave me alone with this monster. "He's perfectly harmless right now. Your mother was able to put a restraint on his magic powers." He shimmied his fingers once more, and a chair popped out of nowhere. "Get comfy and talk. Ask him about the damned weapon he hid. We need to neutralize it before another crazy gets a hold of it."

I nodded, sat down, and watched him leave me alone with my would-be assassin. Not a comfortable feeling, even knowing I was protected by all kinds of magic. Hating myself for being so nervous around the little prick, I turned my eyes to the lit part of the room and faced Bob. At first, it looked as if he hadn't seen me, but after a moment or two, his thin lips curled into a nasty smirk. He could see me after all.

"Look who's here," he said, voice so thick with hate my stomach lurched in instant fear. *You have nothing to fear, Aiden. He's restrained and powerless.* I pushed that dread down and replaced it with the hatred he had nurtured inside me by hurting those I loved—first Cristina and then Naël. "Are you coming to apologize for killing my mother?"

"I didn't kill your mother, as much as she deserved it." I was glad I hadn't been the one doing it. I didn't think I could live with myself if I had taken a life, even if a despicable one. "I was out of commission, remember?"

He actually growled like a rabid dog—not that I'd ever seen one. "She died because of you, moth-erfucker." Well, that was totally unnecessary, wasn't it? "If you hadn't been born, we wouldn't be in this situation now, would we?"

I shook my head, trying to process his insane reasoning. "You do realize that I didn't have much to do with the fact of being born, right? Your mommy dear did explain to you the birds and the bees?" Sarcasm, my weapon of choice, was locked and loaded. "Must I remind you that I was not even aware of my powers until you decided to kill me?"

"You were doomed the moment you came out of your mother and threatened me." God, were all villains this deluded? I didn't know he existed; how could I have threatened him in any way? What a stupid asshole. "You had to die."

I cackled like a hag. "Well, I got news for you, Bob; I'm alive and well. You failed, buddy, big fat fail." I had to refrain from throwing myself against the invisible wall and closing my hands around his scrawny neck. I didn't want to kill him; I just wanted to squeeze his air pipe until his eyes popped out of their sockets.

"Not thanks to you, Mercer," he said, his face contorted into a mask of hatred. "If it weren't for your parents sheltering you your whole life, I would have got you long before now."

What was he talking about? My parents hadn't

been around since shortly after my birth. "That's where you're wrong, jerk. My parents abandoned me as a baby. I had no one to protect me but myself." I wasn't sure why I was telling him that, but it was as if those words had to burst out.

Bob laughed then. "You idiot. They have always been hovering around out of sight, protecting you from powerful creatures like me. They warded every place you lived, every spot you visited. How do you think you managed to hide for this long?"

"My powers were latent, not visible to others until recently." Despite it all, I was deadly curious. What was he talking about? My dad had mentioned watching me from afar, but he hadn't mentioned anything else other than the time he stepped in to help me with the troll in D.C.

"Bullshit. Yes, you hadn't come to full realization, but anyone with enough skills could smell you. You reeked of power from the moment you were born." What? That wasn't how the story went. "Your parents made sure no one could find you by hiding you among the regulars and keeping you unaware of your true identity."

I fell silent, thoughts running through my brain at the speed of light. Was that true? Had my parents been telling me the truth all along? "If that was true, they would have kept me with them and brought me up instead of leaving me in the regular world."

"It was easier to hide you that way," he said, a low growl under his words. "Close to them your powers were even more visible, magnified, and fed off their own."

So my parents had not totally abandoned me after all. They had still denied me a home, the security of feeling loved, but they had been secretly protecting me all those years, making sure creatures like Bob wouldn't find and eliminate me. I was even more confused now, my thoughts all mixed up in a swirling tornado of contradictory feelings. I needed my mate, my tether to sanity and happiness. I was here for something else, but I couldn't remember what. My mind clouded with all this new information.

I was about to stand up and leave when I remembered my original reason for the visit. "Where is the weapon, Bob?"

He stopped snickering and gave me the evil eye. "Wouldn't you like to know?" Yes, why else would I ask? Oh wait, little Bob was trying to be funny, but he couldn't beat me at my own game. "Not telling you, sucker."

"I beg to differ, you sorry-ass excuse for a god," I said, pushing myself to my feet and locking my gaze with his. I could do so many things by just wishing them to happen, so maybe I could do this too. I focused on the question and held his gaze until panic colored his eyes. He could feel it, my prodding of his mind. "Tell me, Bob, where is the brahmachakram hidden?" I wasn't sure if I actually said the words out loud, but I got an answer right away. The location of the deadly weapon came to me despite Bob's valiant efforts to keep it hidden. I let his gaze and mind go. "Well, thank you. How kind of you to share this information with me. Maybe I will come and visit you again soon, Bob."

I turned around and headed to the door behind me. The door cracked open, and Silva stuck his head inside the room. "Ready?" I nodded, and he moved aside to let me through.

I was just closing the door behind me when I heard the imprisoned god yell out, "Fuck you. And don't call me Bob!"

TWENTY-SEVEN
CASTLES IN THE AIR

IF THE CHILD HAD BEEN ANY HAPPIER, SHE WOULD have exploded. In an accurate imitation of a crazed kangaroo, Vee bounced and hopped on her tiny feet from one end of the living room to the other, squealing all along. "I can't believe it, Naël. You're really taking me there?"

My mate shrugged in obvious defeat. "I promised you I would, didn't I?" Vee nodded vigorously. "Well, today, I keep my promise. You're coming with us to the Castelo de S. Jorge in Lisbon." Vee hopped around a few more times, shrieking. "Child, go get dressed if you want to go. I'm starting to have second thoughts." Magic words. She stopped and ran out of the room to go upstairs.

"That kid has some pipes," I said, uncovering

my ears. "Are you sure there's no siren genes in her blood?"

Fouchard laughed and dropped beside me on the couch. "I've wondered that myself." He twisted on the seat so he could face me. "Are you ready for this?"

My smile died on my lips, and my stomach did a little flip-flop. "Yes, as ready as I'll ever be. Not a conversation I'm looking forward to, but it's time I talk to my mother. If nothing else, I have to thank her for helping us." The worry I saw in his beautiful brown eyes melted my heart. "I will be fine, really."

Despite my confident statement, the drive to Lisbon was riddled with anxiety. For once, I was grateful Vee filled the heavy silence with her nonstop chatter. I kept my focus outside the car as the scenery sped by, looking but not seeing. My mother had requested I visit her so we could talk. My first instinct was to say no, but after what Bob told me, I had second thoughts. I couldn't avoid my parents forever, so I might as well grab the bull by its horns.

My mate parked the car in an almost-empty parking lot. It was still early in a rainy morning that heralded winter's arrival to the land of eternal sunshine, and both the natives and tourists had taken shelter indoors. Impervious to the misty rain, Vee ran in front of us, neglecting to grab the umbrella from the back seat. I was slower, taking my time to get out of the car and sludging my way behind her, holding my boyfriend's hand. I was grateful to the rain for infusing my body and my spirit with the extra energy I needed to do something so simple and yet so colossal.

One server greeted us at the door of the restaurant and led us across the large space to the staircase that descended to my mother's quarters. We had been here before and were familiar with the way. Vee couldn't stop oohing and aahing at the rock walls, the beautiful tiles, and the paintings as she followed us down the steps. I hesitated by the high priestess's door, my hand poised to knock. I threw a glance at my mate, who nodded encouragingly.

"Come in, please." My mother's voice was soothing as usual, a subtle tenderness in her tone.

We all walked into the large room, Vee almost trampling us in her excitement. "Dona Moreno, this is so cool," she exclaimed, twirling on her own feet.

The goddess chuckled softly. "So glad you think so, Vee. Would you like some chocolate?" The mermaid stopped and widened her eyes. "Help yourself to it. There's a box on the table." Vee sprinted to the table and wasted no time locating the promised chocolates.

"I trust you're doing well," I said, not recognizing my own voice. Why was I being so formal?

My mother smiled and the whole room brightened. "I'm well, thank you, Aiden." She gestured at the couch facing her chair. "Please, sit down. Let's talk, shall we?"

"Dona Moreno, I'm sure you'd like to have your son to yourself for a bit," Fouchard said, touching my arm. "I'll take Vee for a tour of the castle while you talk."

I was about to protest when she said, "Thank you, Naël. Give us twenty minutes. Then join us for warm drinks and a light meal, okay? Take some chocolate with you, Vee. I bought it especially for you."

With her cheeks puffed up like a chipmunk, Vee scooped a few more pieces of individually wrapped chocolates and followed her brother out the door. "You be nice to your mom, Aiden," she said before closing the door, chocolate bits flying out of her mouth. "You're lucky you still have one."

Damn, Vee. Straight to the heart. That child could be a pain one minute and wiser than her years next.

When I looked back at my mother, she had an amused smile on her face I couldn't quite explain. "That child is a hoot." I would have called her something else, but yes, she was definitely that too. "Why do you look so nervous?"

I took a deep breath. "Do you have to ask?" She smiled again as if encouraging me to elaborate. "I'm almost thirty-seven, and I just now discovered my parents. I'm not going to lie; I've harbored some less than filial feelings for you and Father." Was that too harsh? I didn't want to hurt her. "Sorry, I *am* very nervous."

She stretched across and patted my knee. "I don't blame you, Aiden. It was a lifetime." I almost wanted her to be mean so I wouldn't feel so guilty resenting her. "I don't expect you to forgive us right away, but I am hoping we can keep moving in the right direction." I did too. After my conversation with Bob, I was not so solidly set on hating them forever anymore. "But I called you here today to talk to you about something else."

That surprised me. "Oh? May I ask what?"

She licked her crimson lips before she answered, "I have no right to ask this, I'm well aware of it, but I will nevertheless and hope you won't bite my head off." My mother had a sense of humor.

"I only bite during full moons," I quipped, feeling suddenly at ease in that room with a beautiful goddess who happened to be also my mother. Her laughter was like small crystal balls rising, falling, and crashing against the furniture. I had to smile.

"I understand you and Fouchard are now engaged." Shit, was she going to make a fuss about same-sex marriage? I had never stopped to wonder how she'd feel about it. I knew my father was okay, but my mother…. "Naël is a lovely man, and he obviously loves you very much. My heart rejoices for you, son. It's rare to find someone worthy of our love, even rarer to find your true soul mate like you did. Have you set a date yet?"

I blinked. "Not really. With everything that's happened, we haven't had the chance to sit down and think through it. Except for Vee's totally insane plans, of course."

She burst out laughing again. "Oh yes, she showed me some of it the other night. Interesting concepts she has come up with." Interesting was not the word I was looking for. "She's a bit mermaid crazy, isn't she? You'd think that a mermaid like her wouldn't be so into mermaid stuff."

It was my turn to guffaw. "She was already a big

fan of everything aquatic before she found out about her other half. I think it's still all too new to her. I'm sure it will wear off after a while." I scratched my chin. I needed a shave, but Naël liked the feeling of a scruff against his skin. "I'm certain my mate agrees with me when I say we want a simple ceremony with no mermaid decor or unicorns or rainbows. Just us and our family and friends."

"I would love to be there when you get married." I was floored, my lower jaw dropping. I wasn't expecting that. "I know I shouldn't, but I waited so long to be a real mother to you, and now you're marrying your mate, and I can't help it: I want to be there with you." Tears glittered in her eyes, and I found it very hard to swallow all of a sudden. "I'm not normally this emotional, but ever since I took on a human form, I seem to wear my heart on my sleeve. Hormones, I've been told."

I chuckled, and she tried to smile through the tears that had begun rolling down her face. "Of course you're invited." Did those words come out of *my* mouth?

The high priestess, who always seemed so together, fell apart and cried in earnest. I couldn't stand it. I quickly switched seats so I could be beside her and pulled her against me, laying her head on my shoulder.

"I'm sorry, Aiden. These are happy tears, don't worry." I wiped some of her tears with my thumb and she covered my hand with hers, pressing her cheek against it. "I'm so happy to be in your life, my son, and I do hope that we can grow closer with time because I do love you, you know? And so does your father. He has suffered much not being able to bring you up, to teach you the ropes, watching from afar, helpless, as you grew into an amazing man."

What could I say? Inside me, that part of my heart frozen from years of neglect and loneliness, the part that had not yet thawed under the warmth of my man's love, began melting. If I wasn't careful, I'd soon be forgiving everything I'd always blamed my parents for. So I kept silent, enjoying the feel of her skin under mine and allowing her love to slowly but surely take root in my soul.

Naël and Vee came back a while later, soaking wet and laughing. "Had a good time?" My mother handed them towels and gestured for them to sit by the fireplace. "You must be frozen."

"We're merfolk. We can handle cold water." My mate wiped his short hair with the towel and leaned over to kiss me. "Did you have a good talk?" I nodded, the knot in my throat still preventing me from talking without bursting into tears. Despite the emotional upheaval this meeting caused, I felt lighter, as if a great weight had been lifted from my heart and soul.

The high priestess had a table set with all kinds of goodies that a server had brought in right before my man came back. We all sat around the table, spirits running high and starved. Vee attacked the food as if she hadn't eaten in years, and we all laughed at her enthusiasm. She wasn't happy, but that didn't stop her from eating more.

My hand had found my merman's on top of the table between us, and we exchanged a glance. I didn't dare to say it out loud in front of my mother, but I was hoping the "I love you" came clear across in my eyes.

"Any idea of when the wedding will be?" my mother asked suddenly. Both Fouchard and I raised our eyes to her in surprise. "So I can plan accordingly." Her beautiful ivory face was flushed, giving her the look of one of those Botticelli women. My heart filled with love for her, and it almost choked me. Shit, when had that happen? When had I quit blaming and started loving her?

I was glad Naël answered because I didn't think

I'd be able to speak. "We haven't talked about it, but since you asked, I might as well put this out there." Vee stopped chewing and looked at her brother with interest. Oh shit, she was about to come up with some other crazy idea. "Aiden, sweetheart, why don't we get married this Christmas?"

A Christmas wedding? I'd never been the romantic type, but somehow that idea sounded amazing to me. Especially considering it wouldn't involve any snow or heavy clothing. "That sounds great," I managed to squeak out. "That's less than a month away. Do we have time to get ready?"

Vee jumped in with her usual gusto. "Of course, there is time. I have a great idea—"

"No!" Fouchard and I shouted at the same time. We exchanged a panicky look, and then he added, "We love all your ideas, sis, but we prefer to have our kind of wedding, okay?"

She crossed her arms and pouted. "Your kind of wedding? What's that exactly?"

"Sweet Vee, it's their day," my mother said, rescuing us from Vee's ire. "It is important that things go the way they like best because it's a day to remember your whole life. When you get married, then you can organize it the way you like, but for now, let them do it."

I swear my mother had magic in her voice because Vee, who was always so hardheaded and tough to crack, immediately replaced her pout with a smile. "I guess that makes sense, Dona Moreno. Are you coming to the wedding?"

My mother glanced at me and Naël and then back at the young mermaid. "I wouldn't miss it for the world." Those few words meant everything to me, but the question remained: Was I building castles in the air?

TWENTY-EIGHT

HORMONES AND WATERFALLS

"No fucking way, Aiden." I hadn't seen Cristina this agitated in a long time. She paced the floor of Bicas R Us like a caged lioness, complete with a mane—her hair had grown to alarming puffiness these last couple of months. "Tó and I are getting married at Christmas, not you."

She was being totally unreasonable about this, not what I was used to when it concerned my best friend. "Are you kidding me, Cristina? You are getting married next year, so what difference does it make if we both get married during Christmas? We'll be a year apart, for fuck's sake."

"You'll steal all my thunder, and people will think I snatched the idea from you." Seriously? Had we now reverted to childhood pettiness? I was about to tell her exactly what I thought about her cocka-mamie reason when I noticed the shine in her eyes. She was crying. What the hell was wrong with her?

Making a concerted effort to lower my voice, I cupped her neck with my hand and made her look me in the eyes. "What is going on, Cristina? This does not sound like the reasonable, rational amiga I love." Her eyes were flooded and her lips quivering. "What happened?"

She burst out crying in earnest, tears cascading down her face. "I don't know what's wrong with me, Aiden. Everyth-thing ma-makes me emotional," she said, hiccupping against my shoulder. "Yesterday, I almost sucker punched the butcher because he insisted that fried steak was better than grilled."

I covered her face with my other hand and laughed softly. "Next thing you know, you'll be brawling with the mailman because he left you too much junk mail." She laugh-sobbed. "Don't kill me for asking you this, but is your little red friend visiting?"

She raised her head and stared at me incredu-lously. "My little red friend? Who the hell is——" Her eyes widened, and I had to duck so she wouldn't smack the back of my head. "You *idiota*, no, it's not my period, and I have never in my life called it that.

Who the hell taught you that ridiculous euphemism?"

"It made you laugh, didn't it?" She shook her head and smiled. "Now, seriously, what's wrong with you?"

"You are," she said, her smile belying her words. "Maybe I am a bit hormonal, who knows? I didn't mean it, Aiden; of course you can get married at Christmas. I will be there with bells on. Literally."

I pulled her closer again. "Have I told you lately how much I love you? Even when you're a pain in my ass?" She tried to push me away with a snort, but I held her tightly. "Kidding aside, Cristina, thank you for being my first ever friend and making my life one hundred percent better."

"I thought Fouchard made your life better," she said, flattening her hand on my chest.

"Well, he does and with fringe benefits," I said with a chuckle. "But you did it first and without sex. That's one for the books."

She pushed me away, feigning disgust. "You are still such a man-whore. But I do love you. Now, can we go back to serving our customers?"

Whatever had been bothering her was gone. I watched my friend zoom from table to table with a tray balanced on one hand, as impressive as a circus performer, and I smiled. I must have done some-thing right to get such a good friend.

Vee came busting through the front door later that day, closely followed by my merman in all his glory. "Cristina, can you please tell my brother that a unicorn horn would look awesome over the wedding arch?"

Cristina looked at me, a question in her eyes. I shook my head and whispered, "No, she has no idea what symbolism the unicorn has in the LGBT community." I turned to my soon-to-be sister-in-law and added, "We'll consider it, all right? Now, go get yourself a *nata*." She was more than glad to comply.

Fouchard snorted at his galloping sister and kissed my forehead. "She's driving me crazy." I kissed him back, and we both watched Cristina scooping two *pasteis de nata* from the display and give them to Vee. "Are you ready?"

My fiancé had a surprise lined up for me but refused to tell me what it was. "It's hard to get ready for something you don't know what it is."

"If I told you, it wouldn't be a surprise, now, would it?" I guessed that made sense, but surprises made me a little nervous. "You don't need much; bring a change of clothes and a toothbrush. I will take care of the rest." I arched my eyebrows, and he added, "I'll bring the lube as well." Now we were talking. I already loved this surprise.

The weather had made a sharp turn to winter in the last couple of days. The temperature had dropped to the lower fifties, and I had reluctantly replaced my flip-flops with closed-toe sandals and covered my T-shirt with a plain hoodie. My body was not too happy being covered and not in contact with nature, a fact that made me crankier than usual. I was looking forward to this outing with my boyfriend, now that we didn't run the risk of being shot at or kidnapped when we least expected it.

After closing, Cristina took Vee for a girls' night out with Taz, and I left with my man. Closed lipped as he could be, Naël drove his car with a steady hand and a smirk on his face. He was up to something. I was surprised when he parked the car by the Convento dos Capuchos. "*This* is the surprise?" I exclaimed. "May I remind you we have been here many times?"

He laughed and climbed out of the car. "Be patient. I promise you, you will be pleasantly surprised." Something fishy was going on.

We entered the convent through the glamoured greenery and met with a welcome committee of sorts. My father and two other monks were waiting for us on the other side of the invisible wall. "Greetings, my son," he said. Even though I had let go of most of the resentment and opened up to the possibility of actually loving this druid, I still had trouble when he called me son. "Naël, everything is as you requested. I will guide you there."

Fouchard had a wide smile dancing on his lips as we followed the three druid monks through the convent proper and into the woods. We were going in the woods this time of night and in this temperature? We walked for a while, following a beaten dirt path that climbed and meandered through the woods until we reached two large boulders.

"We're here," my father said. "Brother Serafim said that you can stay for as long as you want. The magic will hold until you are ready to leave."

Magic? What magic? I was getting nervous with all this cryptic talk. "What's going on, Naël? Are you finally going to take me behind a rock and murder me?" Not that I thought that for a minute.

My merman sighed. "Idiot. If I wanted to kill you, don't you think I have had plenty of occasions to do it and get away with it?" Okay, that was true. "I thought you'd grown smarter since you met me in early spring, but it looks as if your brains couldn't handle it."

Wait. Was he emulating his old self, the cantankerous merman I first fell in love with? I squinted at him, twisting my nose as if smelling something rotten. "What are you up to, Naël?"

He thanked my father and the other monks who left without another word. I looked around me. It was dark, the only light furnished by the full moon. *Oh great, full moon.* Hopefully there were no werewolves around. I thought I heard the sound of falling water, but that couldn't be right. There weren't any bodies of water nearby, but the closer we got, the louder the sound was.

"What is that sound?" I asked, not able to hold my curiosity any longer. We had gone off the path and were now roughing it through wild vegetation like two explorers in the jungle.

"What does it sound like?" Infuriating man. Would I be asking if I knew? "You'll see in a minute."

With one shove, Fouchard pushed a large bush out of the way to reveal a vision. I mean, it had to be a vision, right? There were no waterfalls or lakes in the property, yet there it was, lying right in front of my eyes. I glanced at my boyfriend, hoping he would clarify it for me, but he just laughed and stepped into the clearing. I couldn't believe my eyes;

it was a small area, mostly taken up by a smallish lake fed by a gorgeous, if small, waterfall. I turned my eyes to him again, my mouth agape.

He chuckled and pulled me over to where there was a large rock. "Magic," he said, as if that explained everything. Which I supposed in a way it did. "Your father and mother helped me create this mini-paradise for us to celebrate our love and your birthday."

Birthday? I had no clue when my birthday was. It was a mystery how I even knew how old I was. "I don't have a birthday." I turned my back on him and stared at the lake, a twinge of sourness filling my stomach. I used to make up days when I was in school so the other kids wouldn't make fun of the boy without a birthday. Not that anybody ever came to my made-up birthday parties, but I felt I had to keep up appearances, try not to stick out any more than I already did.

"Yes, you do, sweetheart." He turned me around to face him. "Your birthday is November twenty-third, my lovely Sagittarius fiancé. Your parents told me a week ago. I've been plotting this with them since."

I had a birthday? "But today isn't the twenty-third yet." I wasn't sure why I was protesting. A minute ago, I didn't know when my birthday was, now I did so what did it matter that my birthday was in two days and not now?

Fouchard drew me into his arms. "I know, but the others are planning a surprise party for you, and I didn't want to ruin their pleasure." My merman kissed the top of my head. "You'll have to pretend you didn't know, okay?" I nodded against his chest, my heart beating so fast I couldn't catch my breath. Was I happy or sad? I couldn't tell. "This is my gift, a celebration of our relationship and your thirty-seventh birthday. Do you like it?"

Of course I did.

They had somehow created a mini paradise. Even the temperature was summerlike warm. There was such a lovely stillness to the air around us, the moon illuminating the water into a sparkling moving surface. I swallowed my unshed tears. "And what exactly are you planning to do here?" I managed to say.

He pushed me away to look into my eyes. "Tonight is all about you, sweetheart. Why don't we start by shedding these cumbersome clothes?" I liked the sound of that. I liked it a lot. My lips curled into a smile, and my merrow snorted. "I thought that would bring a smile to your face."

Fouchard grabbed the edges of his T-shirt to pull it up, but I stopped him. "No, let me do it." I was swelling inside my jeans, but so was my heart. This was the man I loved—heart, body, and soul. There wasn't a bit of him I didn't love, even his cranky side.

I started peeling clothes off him, first the T-shirt, then the shoes and pants. As I stripped him of his underwear, I made sure my fingers brushed along his skin and closely followed it with my lips, trailing kisses from his waist down to his knees. I loved the way he shivered at my touch. Once he was as bare as when he was born, we both stood face-to-face, drinking each other in. I began walking slowly around him, one hand flattened on his chest, trailing it across his pecs, his upper arms, his back. I paused there for a moment, watching the muscles in his strong shoulders and back contracting as I brushed my fingers down his spine and cupped one of his perfectly shaped buttocks. I lingered there for a while, touching, watching… and chuckled.

"Are you laughing at me?" Naël asked. As if! A memory of a movie scene had popped into my head and tickled my fancy—so to speak.

"I just imagined you as Patrick Swayze and me

as Jennifer Grey." I laughed again, my hand still trailing on his ass.

"What?" Fouchard was not as well versed in pop culture as I was. Or Taz, for that matter.

"From *Dirty Dancing*," I explained, my lips finding a sweet spot on his shoulder. He still seemed perplexed. "The big sex scene? You're fucking kidding me, Naël. You've never seen the movie?"

He laughed, grabbing my free hand and taking it to the part of his body that was obviously craving me. "But I like this Jennifer, whoever she is." My merman was the loveliest creature on earth, I was sure of that. He could utter the most idiotic nonsense, and I would still melt into a messy puddle. I knelt behind him, my hands on either side of his hips, and I kissed him over and over again until my naughty bits were so strained inside my jeans it hurt.

I let him undress me then. He wasn't as methodical as I was, and, in a blink of an eye, I was butt naked and gloriously aroused. "You're beauti-ful," my merrow said, his lips nestled in the nook of my neck as he stood behind me. "And tasty." He chuckled against my skin, his tongue flickering between his lips for a moment. I pressed my ass against his erection and groaned. "Not yet, love. Let's get under the water."

The magically created water was warm and soothing as we waded into it, making our way to stand under the waterfall. I rather expected the water to whip me with its power, but instead, it caressed me as it fell on my head and shoulders and rolled over the rest of my body. That waterfall had been magically coerced into gentleness. Fouchard came from behind me and encircled my waist with his strong arms, planting a long kiss on the back of my neck. He turned me within the circle of his arms until I was facing him and glued to his front side.

"Happy birthday, sweetheart," he whispered against my lips, water cascading over both of us. "Can't wait to legally claim you as mine for eternity."

"Whoa there, merman. I'm not something you own." It was a feeble protest because I loved him so much, I couldn't care less about semantics. I knew him well enough by now to know he didn't mean it that way.

He let out a guttural groan as my hands slid down to his nether regions again. "I know that, but neither am I, and yet, you totally own my heart and my body. I will be yours and yours alone forever." I liked that very much indeed. He nibbled on my earlobe, sending electric shocks through me. "Are you saying you don't feel the same way? That you can't pledge your fidelity to me?"

Silly merman. Who else would I ever love that much? "Don't be thick, Naël. Faithful is my middle name. I gave up on the whoring the moment you laid your hands on me." He smiled and then nipped me again, a little harder this time. I shivered. "I love you, beautiful merrow."

He pulled away from me and offered me his hand. "Come, let's swim together." Swim? Now? I was not sure I could even walk properly, much less swim. "There's a little cave underneath this water-fall, specially created for you." Oh, that was much better. "It's your birthday. You can do whatever you want to me today."

"Anything?"

"Within reason." He smiled wickedly. "Well, shall we go?" He didn't wait for my answer. In a quick fluid move, he dove underwater and vanished from sight. I searched for him but couldn't see where he'd gone.

When I was beginning to panic, a big splash gave me pause. A beautiful iridescent blue tail broke the surface and remained almost airborne for a moment before falling on the water again with a great big splash. My heart must have stopped for a second because I was breathless.

I was the luckiest man alive.

TWENTY-NINE
FORGIVING IS NOT SO DIVINE

Fouchard had made me close my eyes and walk into the room as if I didn't already know there was a surprise birthday party beyond those doors. "You'll hurt Vee's feelings if you don't pretend you don't know."

For the little mermaid I would do just about anything, so I walked into my boyfriend's darkened living room under the pretense of making out while his sister was with Cristina. "To make this really believable, I should at least take off my shirt and hang from your neck as we walk in." I was just teasing. Maybe.

My tall and often forbidding merman raised an eyebrow in warning, and I shut up as he pushed me through the doorway. As soon as we turned on the lights, several people jumped from behind the couch, yelling, "Surprise!" I staggered back a few steps, taking my hand to my heart and gasping. Who knew I could be such a good actor?

Vee, wearing a funny party hat and blowing on a whistle of sorts, ran to me and threw herself in my arms. I was not quite prepared for the onslaught and almost dropped her. "Happy birthday, Aiden," she yelled in my ear, loud enough to make it ring. "You're now thirty-seven years old. You're pretty ancient like my brother, so I promise to give you the respect we owe seniors." *Fat chance of that, little imp.* "Aren't you happy you have a birthday now?"

I planted a kiss on her forehead and put her down. "I'm ecstatic with happiness, girly. Who wouldn't be happy with a new way of driving home the fact you're getting older?"

She screeched and jumped into her brother's arms.

Cristina replaced her in my arms. "Happy birthday, amigo. Parabéns." She looked at me with honeyed eyes, and I sighed at all the scars marring her beautiful amber face. I would never stop feeling guilty about those. "Vee is right; you're starting to look a bit long in the tooth."

I laughed and gave her another hug. "How's the

stomach bug?" She refused to take a day off from the coffee shop, but there had been many runs to the bathroom in the past couple of days. She shrugged. "Go to the doctor, please. I won't pay you worker's compensation if something happens at work." She stuck her tongue out at me and walked away to join Silva by the makeshift bar my mate had set up in a corner of the living room.

The witch was the next one approaching and throwing her long skinny arms around me. "Damn it, every time I take a step in the direction of the bar, I get interference. This is why I never played football." That and the fact I liked my pretty face and my bones a bit too much to risk damaging them. "What do you want, witch? You're giving me witchy germs."

She laughed as she pulled away, not wasting the opportunity to slap me across the back of the head. "You love it, and you know it." Maybe a little, but I would never, ever admit it to her. Not even under torture. "Happy birthday, fool. Are you happy you're a normal person now with a celebrated beginning?"

I grabbed her hand and began pulling her along with me toward the bar where my fiancé was busy preparing everyone's drinks. "I'm dying for a beer, witch." She blocked me. Not again. "What? It's my birthday, and I want a fucking drink."

She leaned in, and I stepped back, startled. She tsked and leaned closer again. "Don't tell anyone, but you don't only have a birthday now, but you'll be an uncle soon."

That made zero sense. I had no siblings. Or did I? "Don't mess with me, Taz. Are you going to tell me I have some secret brother or sister I had never met?"

She placed an index finger on her temple as if thinking. "Hmm, you do have a bunch of half-siblings who are gods." Shit, I'd never thought of that. I didn't want any more gods in my life. "But that's not who I mean." She leaned in again and then stretched on her tiptoes to reach my ear. I took pity on her and bent down slightly. "Cristina is pregnant."

I straightened so fast I almost knocked her off her high heels. "What?" She waved her hand and shushed me. I lowered my voice. "You're crazy. She has been sick with a stomach bug…." My voice dragged as I realized what the alleged bug really was. I closed my hands into fists. "That son of a bitch. Warlock or not, I'm going to punch his teeth in." I made as to charge on Silva, but Taz held me in the spot. "Let me go. That idiot has never heard about condoms?"

"Will you calm your ass down? They're engaged, what's the big deal?" The big deal was that Cristina would now have a small one to complicate her life. "Just be happy for them." Easy to say.

I was hyperventilating, clenching my hands at my sides and biting my lower lip for lack of something better to release my anger. But Cristina did love kids and was amazing with them. Vee was so smitten by my best friend she couldn't go a few days without spending some time with her. And Silva, despite being a warlock and fiendishly handsome—and a moron who did not use condoms apparently—had proven himself to be a reliable, caring guy. The way he looked at her when he didn't know I was watching spoke volumes of how much he loved Cristina. My breathing slowed down, and I relaxed. Maybe she would be happy; in fact, I could almost guarantee she would be. Fuck, maybe this was intentional. I had never known Cristina to be lax when it came to birth control.

"This is why Cristina asked *me* to tell you; she was afraid you'd go ballistic on her man. She figured I could control you with my magic." She giggled-chuckled. "Promise me you are not going to attack Silva." Taz was still holding on to my arm. "Promise."

I nodded. "Okay, okay, I promise. But if the asshole hits the road when he finds out, I will smite him with my fireballs." That seemed to trigger a massive laugh attack. "What are you laughing at?" She couldn't stop laughing, folding onto herself, her arms across her middle. She mouthed the word "fireballs," and I got it. "Funny, very funny."

I walked away. I needed a beer now more than ever or a triple espresso, whatever was available. Taz yelled across the room, "Balls of fire, Aiden. That's you all right." I was going to kill that little witch and take great pleasure as I did. Fouchard looked up from what he was pouring in a tall glass and laughed. "See, even your boyfriend agrees."

I flipped her the finger and took whatever it was Naël had been preparing from his hand and gulped it down. Bad idea. Whatever it was burned like molten rock going down my pipe. I began coughing, and he tapped me on the back.

"What did you do that for? That was straight *aguardente*," Naël said with a chuckle.

Damn, that thing was called fiery water for a reason. I was not much of a drinker, other than a beer or two, so the strong alcoholic liquid scorched my insides as easily as fire. But it did distract me from the irksome subject of my best friend's pregnancy. Maybe they were wrong, but women had like a spidey sense for that kind of thing, and a witch had it ten times over. I shook my head and coughed a few more times.

"You really have a death wish, sweetheart." Fouchard's lips curled up at the corners, and his eyes spelled mischief.

Okay, my sweet lover, you don't need to be so amused about my blunder. I was hoping he could hear my telepathic message, but he kept smiling so I figured he didn't. Damn it! I had to practice my skills.

I turned around, still coughing, and I almost crashed into my mother and father huddled together like two old compadres sharing a secret—which, come to think of it, they probably were. For a brief moment, I wondered whether I could get away with pretending I didn't see them but quickly realized I couldn't be that subtle. I decided to face them head-on. "Well, hello, parental units." Shit, now I sounded like an idiot, which I was, of course, but that didn't mean I wanted to sound like one.

My mother, beautiful and serene as always, smiled, and my heart slowed down to a leisurely pace. "Hi, Aiden. Happy birthday, son." She took a step toward me, and I didn't miss the slight squeeze she gave my druid father's arm. "Can I give you a hug? I understand if you don't want me to."

I wanted to say no, but my mother had an enchanting quality I couldn't quite explain; I always found myself incapable of refusing whatever she asked. I nodded, speech-impaired, and she enveloped me in her warm arms. Every muscle in my body softened, and, as if made of Play-Doh, I molded myself into her soft body. I closed my eyes and inhaled her scent: ocean breezes, and starlight. My mom. This was my mom, holding me the way I'd always dreamed of being held.

"I've dreamed of this for thirty-seven years," she whispered in my ear. "I love you, son, and I am so, so sorry we had to leave you like we did." I understood that now. If the day came when I had to leave Naël to protect him, I would, no matter how painful it was. Now that I knew what love felt like, I understood. I yielded further into her embrace. "I hope you will forgive us one day."

I sighed and took another deep breath in. "I forgive you, Mother. I think I forgave you that day at the battleground." I pulled away to look into her eyes, glittering evergreens in the snowy landscape of her face. "It still hurts. I won't lie. But I missed you my whole life. How could I not forgive you now that I know you did it out of love and not neglect?"

Her smile was pure sunshine. "What about your father? You still seem pretty angry at him." It was true; I wasn't sure why, but it was harder for me to forgive my father. Was it because I had been close to him so many times before realizing we shared genes? Did I feel cheated because of that? "He loves you just as much as I do. It was his idea of bringing you into the safety of the convent when things turned to the dangerous."

"I was in danger many times, and he never bothered to step up." I stubbornly held on to my grudge. "Why didn't he do something when I was getting my head shoved into a toilet in DC? Or when someone spelled me into growing a rat's tail?"

She chuckled. "You were in no real danger, son. Life kicks you in the shins all the time but what doesn't kill you makes you stronger."

Come on, Mom. Platitudes, seriously? What doesn't kill you, makes you a very angry adult.

She laughed again. "I know it's an overused saying, but it's true. Everyone needs to suffer some hardships to learn how to navigate life efficiently." Maybe my telepathic skills were actually working after all. "You were never in any danger for your life. And when you were, your father and I took care of that without you knowing."

I had to smile. "That explains why that troll never found me." He would have pummeled me into a pulp if he had. I sighed. "I will work on that, Mother. I promise." As to underline my promise, I turned to my father, who was pretending not to be eavesdropping on our conversation. "Father, it will take some time, but I will get there. In the meantime, you're welcome into my life as long as you don't play the father card. I'm still too angry for that."

Brother John, aka my father, offered me his hand with a smile. I shook it and returned his smile. "It's a deal, Aiden. Thank you."

Maybe it was my imagination running rampant as it often did, but I could have sworn energy gathered where our hands met. Surprised, I shot a glance at him, but he only smiled as if he hadn't felt anything. What had he just given me? Or was it the opposite, and *I* had given him something? Why was magic so complicated? A matter for another time. I shook my head and rubbed my overheated hand on my pants, watching my father as he stashed his inside the wide sleeves of his habit.

Silva came over, patted me awkwardly in the shoulder, and said, "Happy birthday, man. Parabéns." I should be the one congratulating him, I guessed, but did he even know about Cristina's pregnancy? Had my friend known already when I worried about her digestive health? How could she not? Didn't women have like a sixth sense for that sort of thing? Not the kind that allows you to see dead people, but the kind that tells you when there's a little creature growing inside you. Then why didn't she tell me right away instead of letting me think she was sick? I scratched my head and then my day-old scruff; women were as complicated as magic.

With all those thoughts swimming around my head like fish in a tank—and just as smelly—I strolled over to my merman, who was now seated on the couch. As soon as he saw me approaching, he made room for me beside him. I sat next to him, our hips and thighs glued together, and dropped my head on his shoulder. He raised his hand to caress my face. "Are you having a good time, sweetheart?" he asked in a whisper.

I turned my head enough to plant a kiss on his shoulder. "I'm having a lovely time." I was slightly bewildered, maybe even a bit overwhelmed by the whole idea of a birthday party, something I had only heard of or seen others have. That confusion didn't prevent me, however, from feeling the warmth of long-yearned-for love swell in my heart. Just a year ago, I'd only one friend, Cristina, and even she had been a recent acquisition. I'd lived over thirty-five years of my life alone and friendless. Loveless.

Tears burned in my eyes. Damn it! I tried to surreptitiously brush them away with the back of my hand, but Naël closed his hand around my wrist to stop me. He placed a finger under my chin and tilted my face toward him to look me in the eyes. Everything was blurry through the watery curtain of my tears, but the eyes of my lover, my mate, still soothed me. "What are you crying about, Aiden?" I tried to dismiss it all with a smile, but he didn't let me go. "Are those happy or sad tears, sweetheart?"

I studied the face of the man I loved, dark amber skin, full lips set in a straight line, a sparse scruff, and the most beautiful brown eyes I had ever had the privilege of drowning in. I sighed. "Happy, Naël; these are very happy tears. I can't believe I have a family now. I have friends. Fuck, I even have parents." I choked out a chuckle, and he finally smiled. "I love you, Naël. I can't wait to be your lawful husband." I burst out laughing. "I never thought I would ever want to be anything lawful, but here we are."

He cupped the back of my neck with his hand and drew me in for a kiss. He licked the tears that gathered around my mouth and then let me taste their saltiness in his tongue. "I'm going to make you the happiest man alive."

With my lips still touching his, I asked, "Promise?" He nodded and swallowed me once again. When he pulled a few inches apart, I was panting. "Promise we will always have amazing and frequent sex. You're not going to start the ubiquitous 'I have a headache' shit, are you?"

He laughed, his warm breath mixing with mine. "I promise. Merfolk don't get headaches, so I can't use that excuse even if I wanted to." I was about to protest, but he covered my mouth with his again. "And I know I will never want to." He brushed his thumb over my lips, and I smiled, fulfilled and happy.

In silence, we settled back on the couch, our hands laced over my upper thigh and my head on his shoulder. We watched our friends and family move about the room, talking and laughing, throwing us smiles ever so often. Gods, I loved these people. Even the warlock moron who'd impregnated my best friend. And what was even weirder was they loved me back. The world had gone crazy, and I couldn't be happier.

"Naël." He grunted gently in response. "If Cristina has a girl instead of a boy, will she be a warlock or a witch?" My mate raised his head to look at me and burst out laughing. I bristled. "Inquiring minds want to know."

Still laughing, he kissed my forehead. "You're an idiot." He kissed me again before I could protest. "An idiot I love more than life itself."

All was well in the world.

THANK YOU FOR READING, *OF FIRE & BONE*, THE conclusion of the Of Magic & Scales series. You are cordially invited to Aiden's and Naël's Christmas wedding in the novella, **Of Magic & Bells**. It promises to be quite an occasion. Vee might even sneak in a unicorn.

If you liked this series then maybe you'll also enjoy my other MM paranormal romances, **_Infinite Blue_** and **_Lavender Fields_**

ACKNOWLEDGMENTS

I always have so many people to thank, I often blank on what to say. So bear with me for a minute.

To my editors, who put up with my intense hate-relationship with English prepositions and my penchant to totally pick the wrong idiomatic expressions, I owe you guys a huge thank-you. I hope I have never caused you a stress-related stomach ulcer.

To my beta readers, both those picked by my publisher and those who so kindly offered to help me out such as Lisa Meyer and Lori Barrett, thank you so much. Your feedback is invaluable, and your comments and reactions make my author's heart soar.

My amazingly talented cover designer, Claire

from BookSmith Designs, came up with incredible covers for the series, capturing the spirit and mood of the story so well that I can't imagine any other covers for the books. Thank you so much. So jealous of your talent.

To everyone else in the Hot Tree Publishing team including Becky (AKA boss lady) and all proofreaders, formatters, and whoever I'm forgetting, I owe a great big thank-you and many (however virtual) hugs.

To my family, friends, and critique group, thank you for all your patience, support, and wisdom.

And to my tiny country, Portugal, a special thank-you for giving me such an amazing magical setting for this series.

Obrigado pátria mãe.

Thanks for reading *Of Scales and Fire*. I do hope you enjoyed this story. I appreciate your help in spreading the word, including telling a friend. Before you go, it would mean so much to me if you would take a few minutes to write a review and share how you feel about my story so others may find my work. Reviews really do help readers find books. Please leave a review on your favorite book site.

Don't miss out on New Releases, Exclusive Giveaways and much more!

Join my newsletter: http://bit.ly/reisnewsletter
Join my reader group: http://bit.ly/RebelsOutcasts

I'd love to hear from you directly, too. Please feel free to e-mail me at

catarinadeobidos1@gmail.com or check out my website http://bit.ly/WebNatalina for updates.

Natalina wrote her first romance in collaboration with her best friend at the age of 13. Since then she has ventured into other genres, but romance is first and foremost in almost everything she writes.

After earning a degree in tourism and foreign languages, she worked as a tourist guide in her native Portugal for a short time before moving to the United States. She lived in three continents and a few islands, and her knack for languages and linguistics led her to a master's degree in education. She lives in Virginia where she has taught English as a Second Language to elementary school children for more years than she cares to admit.

Natalina doesn't believe you can have too many books or too much coffee. Art and dance make her happy and she is pretty sure she could survive on lobster and bananas alone. When she is not writing or stressing over lesson plans, she shares her life with her husband and two adult sons.

 twitter.com/TichaB

 instagram.com/reisnatalina

 bookbub.com/authors/natalina-reis

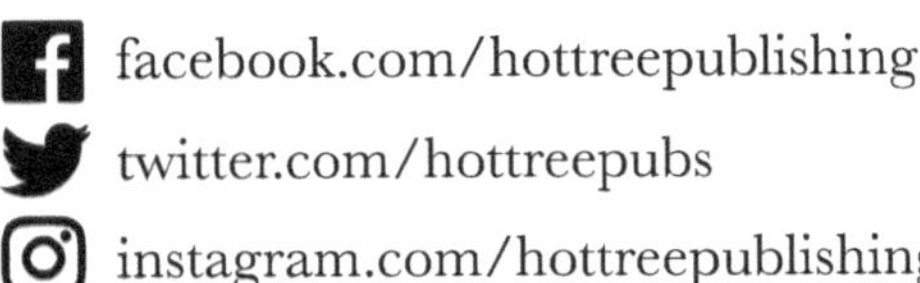 facebook.com/hottreepublishing

twitter.com/hottreepubs

instagram.com/hottreepublishing